BARRY GIFFORD

The Wild Life
of Sailor and Lula

Paladin
An Imprint of HarperCollins*Publishers*

Paladin
An Imprint of HarperCollins*Publishers*
77–85 Fulham Palace Road,
Hammersmith, London W6 8JB

Published simultaneously in hardcover
and paperback by Paladin 1992
9 8 7 6 5 4 3 2 1

Sailor's Holiday copyright © Barry Gifford 1991
Sultans of Africa copyright © Barry Gifford 1991
Consuelo's Kiss copyright © Barry Gifford 1991
Bad Day for the Leopard Man © Barry Gifford 1992

Sailor's Holiday, *Sultans of Africa* and *Consuelo's Kiss*
first published by Random House Inc. New York 1991
Bad Day for the Leopard Man
a Paladin Original 1992

The Author asserts the moral right to
be identified as the author of this work

A catalogue record for this book
is available from the British Library

ISBN 0 586 09190 4
       0 586 09191 2 (paperback)

Set in Baskerville

Printed in Great Britain by
HarperCollinsManufacturing Glasgow

Contents

This book is dedicated
to Monty Montgomery

Sailor's Holiday

A woman in a red dress came in the door unsteadily. 'Whoopee,' she said, 'so long, Red. He'll be in hell before I could even reach Little Rock.'

William Faulkner
Sanctuary

Lula Calls

'Mama, I do appreciate all you been doin' for me, you know that.'

'Listen, Lula, you can't go on workin' in a 7-Eleven like this. You're too smart to be wastin' your time sellin' Slurpees to high school kids and cans of King Cobra to drunks. I don't mind supplementin' your income, 'specially where Pace is concerned, long as I got it to give. But you can do somethin' better with your life.'

Marietta Fortune took a big sip of Martini & Rossi sweet vermouth and raised her eyebrows as she looked at her friend Dalceda Delahoussaye, who sat across from her at the patio table sipping the same. Marietta wanted Dal to know how exasperated she was by her daughter's seeming dearth of ambition.

'Well, Pace'll be out of school next week,' said Lula, 'and I gotta figure out what to do with him for the summer. I can't very well start on a new career with a ten year old trailin' after me.'

'*New?* You ain't never had one career yet, Lula, and here you are thirty years old.'

'Twenty-nine and a half, Mama. Keep it accurate.'

Marietta took another sip. 'You could get married.'

Dal frowned at Marietta and shook her head side to side in disapproval.

'OK, Mama, I can see where this conversation's headin', and I ain't goin' along with it. Far as that's concerned, you might be considerin' it yourself. Johnnie's still willin'.'

'Lula, we're not discussin' me. It's your life got to be lived.'

Lula laughed. 'Mama, you ain't fifty till tomorrow and you talk like you got one foot and four toes in the grave. Look, I gotta go pick up Pace. We'll be over around noon for your birthday. Say hi to Dal if she's still there. Bye.'

Marietta hung up and sighed.

'You and that girl don't never give each other a smidge of space,' said Dal. 'Why don't you just pretend to be the mature one and back off a spell, let Lula work her life out her own way.'

'Oh, she's done great this far, Dal, ain't she? Lula's approachin' middle-age and all she's got's an illegitimate child can't sit still for more'n two minutes 'cause he ain't never had no man around, and no prospects of any kind I can tell. I'm supposed to be comfortable with that?'

'Marietta, you're in a state for nothin'.'

The telephone rang and Marietta picked up the receiver.

'Yes?'

As soon as Marietta heard who it was she sat up straighter in her chair and her face lost most of its wrinkles.

'Why, Marcello, what a surprise. Uh huh, I think so. I certainly don't see why not. Around twelve-thirty would be fine. I'm already lookin' forward to it. Thank you for thinkin' of me. Oh, you're awful sweet. Bye, now.'

Marietta hung up.

'Don't tell me that old gangster Crazy Eyes Santos is comin' here?' said Dalceda.

Marietta nodded. 'Tomorrow afternoon, for my birthday. He remembered.'

'I just don't plain believe this!' Dal said, setting down her glass on the table. 'I thought he'd done a fade after Clyde died.'

'He did. I guess he's just sentimental now we're gettin' older.'

'Man's a killer, Marietta. He's been runnin' the rackets down here since we was girls together at Miss Cook's in Beaufort. He's married, too, of course. And besides, Johnnie Farragut's comin' tomorrow, ain't he?'

Marietta relaxed, sinking down in her chair and closing her eyes.

'Won't matter.'

'The hell it won't. I wouldn't miss this party for the world.'

'One thing about the rest of the world, Dal, they don't give a fig about us and they never have. That's why we got to stick together.'

Marietta's Party

Saturday morning it rained. By noon the rain had mostly stopped but the sky stayed grainy and the air was unseasonably cold. Marietta hated birthdays, especially her own. She'd learned, however, that there was no use denying them, so now she accepted the attention at these little gatherings if only for her grandson's sake. Like most children, Pace just loved birthday parties, and since Lula kept him and events under control, Marietta more or less sat back and endured the goings-on in relatively good humor.

As expected, Pace and Lula were the first to arrive.

'Happy birthday, Marietta!' Pace shouted, as soon as the door opened.

He gave her a hug and Marietta offered him her right cheek to kiss, which he did, and not ungladly, as he sincerely liked his grandmother, the only one he had.

'That's one of the nicest improvements about this boy, Lula, that he don't call me "Grandmama" any more.'

'Why's that, Mama? I thought you liked bein' considered old and put to pasture.'

Lula kissed Marietta on the other cheek and handed her a small package wrapped in red and green Christmas paper.

'Sorry about the inappropriate wrappin's,' she said, 'but it's all I had. Got ten rolls of it for a dollar at the 7-Eleven, left over from last year. Tell me, you want any.'

'Open it now, Marietta!' Pace said. 'Before anybody else gets here.'

'All right, Pace, I'll just do that.'

Marietta carefully unwrapped the gift, handing Lula the ribbon and paper to discard.

'Well, my goodness,' Marietta said, holding up a matching teacup and saucer. 'This is a lovely surprise.'

15

'It's real old, Grandmama – Marietta, I mean. Mama found it in a junk shop.'

'Lady said it's two hundred years old, Mama, but it's real pretty, I think.'

'Certainly it is. Just look at the gold edges. It's fine china, I can tell. I hope you didn't spend too much on this, Lula. I hear 7-Eleven wages ain't all that generous.'

'Enjoy it, Mama. I'll go see about the cake.'

The doorbell rang and Pace said, 'I'll get it!'

'Why, hello, honey,' Dal said, coming in. 'Don't you look handsome today.'

'Mama scrubbed me brand clean, Auntie Dal. She says it makes a difference.'

Dal laughed. 'It can indeed. Hello, Marietta,' she said, giving her a hug. 'I won't say happy birthday because of your complex.'

'What's a complex?' asked Pace.

'A foolishness that's recognized for what it is,' said Dal.

'Mama says I'm foolish lots of times.'

'That's different, dear,' Dal said, 'everyone is. You ain't old enough for the other thing yet.'

'I ain't old enough for much. When'll I be old enough for a complex?'

'For some it's all too soon and never too late.'

'Dal, hush,' said Marietta. 'Leave the boy be. Pace, you go on in the back, see you can help your mama with things.'

Pace walked toward the kitchen and the doorbell rang again. Dal opened the door.

'Afternoon, Dalceda. Am I early or late?'

It was Johnnie Farragut, the private investigator from Charlotte who'd been sweet on Marietta for thirty years.

'You're plumb on time, Johnnie,' said Dal. 'Marietta's right here.'

Johnnie gave Marietta a kiss on the cheek and handed her an envelope.

'Marietta, I ain't much of a shopper, as you know,' he said, 'but this is a certificate for a subscription to a ladies' magazine I thought you might like to look at while your hair's dryin' or somethin'.'

Marietta opened the envelope, took out the certificate and read it.

16

'*Spiffy*, "The Magazine for the New Woman."'

Dal giggled. 'See, Marietta, it ain't for *old* women.'

'Sounds like the name of a peanut butter,' said Lula, coming up to Johnnie and kissing him. 'That's so sweet of you, Johnnie. I'm sure Mama'll love readin' it.'

'Sure I will,' said Marietta, taking one of Johnnie's hands. 'It's real thoughtful.'

'Prob'ly be a few weeks before the first issue arrives,' Johnnie said.

'That won't bother Mama. You're familiar with her gift for patience.'

There was a knock on the door and Lula opened it. A short, wide, impeccably dressed man who looked to be about sixty, wearing a black toupee and yellow-framed sunglasses, stood in the doorway holding a large box with both hands. Lula noticed that his left thumb was missing.

'This is the home of Marietta Pace Fortune,' he said. It was not a question.

'Yes,' said Lula. 'Won't you come in?'

The man entered, saw Marietta and went to her.

'Marietta,' he said, balancing the box on one knee and bending forward to take in his own and kiss the hand she'd just held Johnnie's in, 'you're still a gorgeous woman. Your Clyde, *era nato colla camicia*. He was born lucky to have had you for a wife. But now, of course, he is dead and we are living.'

'Clyde been gone a whole lotta years, Marcello,' said Marietta. 'Why don't you set down that box?'

'Thank you,' he said, putting the box on the floor.

Pace came running up.

'Can I open it, Grand – Marietta?'

'In a moment, perhaps,' said Marietta. 'Marcello, this is my daughter's boy, Pace Roscoe Ripley. And this here's his mama, my precious Lula. This is my oldest and dearest friend, Dalceda Delahoussaye, whom you might remember. And here's Johnnie Farragut, who's in law enforcement over in Charlotte, an old pal of Clyde's. Everyone, this is Mr Santos.'

Santos nodded and smiled at all of them without removing his dark glasses.

'Mr Santos?' said Pace.

Santos turned to him, smiling.

17

'Yes, boy?'

'What happened to your thumb?'

Lula almost said something but held her tongue. She wanted to know what had happened to it, too. Marietta, she figured, already knew.

'You really want to know, hey, boy?' said Santos.

Pace looked up at Santos's large, flat red nose and blue lips and nodded.

'Marcello, you don't have to,' Marietta said.

He held up the four digits remaining on his left hand.

'When I was only a few years older than you are now,' Santos said to Pace, 'I worked in a slaughterhouse, where animals are killed and carved up and their body parts packaged to be sold in stores to be eaten. An older man attacked me because he did not like some things I had said about his work. I had said that he was lazy and a bad worker because he was drunk much of the time, and because of this the rest of us in the slaughterhouse had to work even harder at what already was hard work. The man became enraged and with a hatchet crusted with blood from the animals tried to chop off my left hand. Before he could do it I pulled my hand back and all he got was the thumb.'

'I bet you were real angry at him,' said Pace.

Santos nodded. 'Yes, I was. I was so angry, that even though this man was older and bigger and stronger than I was, I took the hatchet away from him with my other hand and hit him with it between his eyes.'

'With the blade part?' asked Pace.

'Yes, boy, with the blade.'

'Did you kill him?'

'He died,' said Santos. 'It was his own foolishness that killed him.'

'Oh, I know about that,' Pace said. 'He musta had a complex.'

Dal laughed and then quickly covered her mouth with her hands.

'Marietta,' Santos said, 'I regret that I am unable to stay longer, but there are people waiting for me. I will call you soon, if I may.'

'Please do, Marcello,' she said. 'And thanks so much for my present.'

18

Santos smiled. 'The present, yes. Well, it's a little something.' He turned to the others.

'It's been a pleasure,' he said, and went out.

All of the adults gathered in the doorway and watched Santos climb into the backseat of a black Mercedes-Benz limousine and be driven off.

'Look, Marietta, look!' Pace shouted.

Everyone turned from the door and looked at Pace. He had opened the box Santos had brought and was holding up a huge purple silk robe with black velvet lapels.

'There's writin' on it,' said Pace, showing them.

Across the back of the robe in bright gold capital letters were the words SANTOS BOXING CLUB, and underneath, in slightly smaller, silver letters, it said, BILOXI & NO.

'Can I put it on, Marietta? Can I?' Pace asked.

'Yes, child, put it on.'

'What a strange man,' said Lula.

'Everybody got their way,' said Marietta.

'Santos is someone used to gettin' *his* way most all the time, is my guess,' said Dal.

'So that was Crazy Eyes Santos himself,' said Johnnie.

'Well, come on now, Lula,' said Marietta, 'this is my birthday party. Let's get these folks some cake!'

The Theory of Relativity Revisited

All of the urinals were occupied, so Sailor Ripley used one of the stall toilets to relieve himself. As he did, he read the graffito someone had scrawled with a black felt-tipped pen on the wall container of Protecto toilet seat covers: *IRANIAN DINNER JACKETS*. Sailor snickered, zipped his jeans, picked up his suitcase and went back out into the Greyhound terminal. His bus to New Orleans was not scheduled to depart for another hour, so he bought a Jackson *Clarion-Ledger* from a vending box and sat down to read it on one of the hardwood benches.

ATLANTA'S BLACK MAYOR VISITS 'REDNECK BAR' caught his eye right away. The mayor of Atlanta, seeking white votes in his effort to become Georgia's first black governor, had gone to a Cobb County bar and defended the owner's right to put racist records on the jukebox. The candidate said, 'I'll go anywhere to talk to anybody about the future of Georgia,' and had brought with him a couple of records to give the owner, one by Ray Charles and one by Hank Williams, Jr. The bar owner told reporters that to avoid embarrassing the mayor he had removed two records from the jukebox: 'Alabama Nigger' and 'She Ran Off With A Nigger.' He intended to put them back, he said, after the visit.

'Life don't get no less stupefyin', that's certain,' Sailor whispered to himself, and turned the page.

Sailor had been working as a truck loader in a lumberyard out toward Petal, Mississippi, 'The Checkers Capital of America,' for six months, living alone in a crummy transient hotel in Hattiesburg, drinking too much, and thinking hard about Lula and their son, Pace. He hadn't known how awful it would be not to see them at all, especially Pace. During the almost ten years he'd spent in prison on the armed robbery conviction he'd kept alive the idea that when he got out they'd all be together and life could continue from there. Once he'd seen Pace and Lula, however, he'd panicked and run. The time since then had been hell for him. Sailor hated his life in Hattiesburg, where he'd gone for no reason other than he'd once heard a fellow inmate talk about how beautiful Hattiesburg was in the spring when the magnolias blossomed. The magnolias blossomed all right, but their beauty did not improve Sailor's mood. He needed a change, and New Orleans, where he and Lula had been happy for a few days a decade ago, was an easy target.

Sailor was thirty-two and a half years old, but he felt a lot older. The hard time in Huntsville had changed him, he knew that. Very little that he observed about the workings of the world made sense. Without the hope of ever again seeing the only two people he cared anything about, there didn't seem much point to life. *His* life, anyway. The hour passed and Sailor rose when he heard the passenger page for the bus to New Orleans.

He stowed his suitcase in the overhead rack and took a seat next to a window. Just as the bus turned down the street toward Interstate 59, Sailor saw a woman get out of a new blue BMW convertible, a cigarette stuck between her teeth, and toss her long black hair back over the collar of her suede jacket. Perdita Durango looked the same as she had ten years earlier, Sailor thought, when she'd dropped off him and her boyfriend Bobby Peru in front of the Ramos Feed Store in Iraaq, Texas. Five minutes later Bobby was dead, Sailor was caught red-handed and Perdita was to hell and gone in the getaway car. Suddenly life seemed a whole lot shorter to Sailor than it had the moment before.

Plan A

'You're goin' where?'

'New Orleans, Mama, to visit Beany. You remember, Beany Thorn? She wrote invitin' me and Pace, soon as school's out.'

'How could I ever forget that wild-ass child? She give away two, or was it three fatherless babies before she was seventeen?'

'One, Mama, and the boy woulda married her only Beany wouldn't. He was gonna be a dogcatcher like his daddy. Other two she had done away with early.'

'Cracked up Lord knows how many automobiles, too. And it was her lawyer daddy, Tapping Reeve Thorn, bribed a federal judge and got caught and both he and the judge did three years at some country club in Alabama. Then her mother, Darlette, drank herself brainless and had to be shipped out to a zombie camp up in the Smoky Mountains. After servin' his time, Tap threw himself away on a topless dancer in Charlotte and bought her a condominium. Last I heard he was racin' stock cars at the speedway and there was talk of him bein' indicted again for some junk bond scam. Them Thorns ain't exactly simple to forget, Lula. What's the trashy daughter up to in New Orleans? Hookin'?'

'She's married now, to a good man named Bob Lee Boyle, owns a alligator repellent manufacturin' company. They got a son, Lance, who's six years old; and a new baby girl, Madonna Kim. They live in a fabulous big house in Metairie, over in Jefferson Parish, and Beany says there's plenty of room for Pace and me to stay as long as we want. Plan A is to give my notice at the 7-Eleven.'

'Well, that's somethin'.'

'Mama, be honest. You got more than a little to be thankful for.'

'I'm late for the Daughters, Lula. Let's talk later.'

22

'I'm sure the memory of the Confederacy'd live on without you, Mama, but OK.'

'Bye, precious. Love you.'

'Love you, too.'

Plan B

'Most gators go for gars. Not often one tackles somethin' much larger, like a human.'

'Bob Lee knows more about alligators than anyone, almost,' said Beany. 'Least more about 'em than anyone I ever knew, not that I ever knew anybody before *cared*.'

Lula, Beany, and Bob Lee were sitting at the dining room table in the Boyle house in Metairie. Lula and Pace had flown in late in the afternoon, and they had just finished dinner. Pace and Lance were upstairs in Lance's room watching TV, and Madonna Kim, the baby, was asleep.

'It sounds fascinatin', Bob Lee,' Lula said, fiddling with the spoon next to her coffee cup. 'How'd you get started on gators?'

'Grew up around 'em in Chacahoula, where my daddy's folks're from. I spent considerable time there as a boy. We lived in Raceland, and my mama's people come from Crozier and Bayou Cane, near Houma. Later I worked for Wildlife Management at Barataria. Started workin' on my own mix after a biology professor from Texas A&M came by askin' questions. Told me a man could make a fortune if he figured out how to keep crocs from devourin' folks live on the Nile River in Africa, for instance, and in India and Malaysia. Crocs and gators react about the same to stimuli. Secret to it's in their secretions, called pheromones. They got glands near the tail, emit scents for matin' purposes. Other ones around their throat mark territory. Beasts use the sense of smell to communicate.'

'Lula and I've known a few pussy-sniffin' beasts ourselves,' said Beany, making them all laugh.

'If that's true, Lula,' said Bob Lee, 'then you know what I'm talkin' about. Same thing goes for these reptiles.'

'What do y'all call your product?'

'"Gator Gone." Got it trademarked for worldwide distribution now. Warehouse is in Algiers and the office is on Gentilly, near the Fair Grounds. Come around some time. Right now, though, I gotta go make some phone calls, you ladies don't mind.'

'We got lots to talk about,' Beany said. 'You go on.'

Bob Lee got up and went out of the room.

'He's a swell man, Beany. You're fortunate to have him.'

'Only man I ever met didn't mind my bony ass!'

They laughed.

'And he don't beg me to give him head all the time, neither. Not that I ever cared particularly one way or the other about it, but it's a change. Only thing is the name, Beany Boyle. Sounds like a hobo stew.'

'You look like you-all're doin' just fine.'

'Pace sure is a sharpie. Image of his daddy.'

'Ain't he? Breaks my heart, too.'

'You and Sailor ain't in touch, I take it.'

Lula shook her short black hair like a nervous filly in the starting gate.

'Haven't heard from him since he got out of prison over six months ago. We met that one time for about fifteen minutes at the Trailways, and then he just walked off in the night. Guess it was too much to expect we could work anything out. And I think seein' Pace scared Sailor, made those ten years I never went to visit him jump up in his face. I don't know, Beany, it's hard to figure out how I feel for real. And Mama don't make thinkin' for myself any easier.'

'Marietta's a vicious cunt, Lula, face it. She ain't got a life and she's afraid you'll get one. That's why she freaked when you and Sailor run off. I'm surprised she let you come here, knowin' how she hates me.'

'She don't hate you, Beany, and she ain't really vicious. Also I'm twenty-nine and a half years old now. She can't exactly tell me what I can or can't do.'

'Don't stop her from manipulatin' you every chance. So what's the plan?'

'Thought maybe you could work on one with me. I need help and I know it.'

Beany reached across the table and held Lula's hand.

'I'm with you, Lula, same as always. We'll figure out somethin'.'

25

The baby began to cry. Beany smiled, squeezed Lula's hand and stood up.

'There's my Madonna Kim,' she said. 'Another complainin' female. Let's go get her in on this.'

Poppy and Perdita

Carmine 'Poppy' Papavero put his lime green seersucker-jacketed right arm around Juju Taylor's DJ Jazzy Jeff and the Fresh Prince tee-shirted shoulders and smiled.

'You know, Juju, you keep doin' good like this, I'm gonna have to say somethin' nice about you to Mr Santos.'

'It definitely be a pleasure workin' for you, Mr Papavero. Tell Mr Santos can't nobody cover like Juju's Jungle Lovers. We handle however much shit you want. Got Lovers be in Alabama, too, you want to spread it out.'

'I'll keep it in mind. Meanwhile, you take care of Mississippi north of the Gulf and we'll see how it goes. What's this I hear about an LA gang moving in?'

'They show up here we be all over 'em like smoke on links.'

Poppy patted Juju on the back, then squeezed his thick neck.

'Be seeing you soon, Juju.'

Poppy walked out of the gang's safehouse and saw Perdita Durango leaning against the blue Beamer. He went over and kissed her forehead, which was on a level with his chin. Poppy went six-three and a hard two-forty. Perdita had never had a steady his size before. Poppy punished her during their love-making but never to the point where it became painful. She'd learned to enjoy the weight.

Perdita had met Poppy at Johnny Black's Black & Blue Club in Gulfport, where she'd gone with an acquaintance named Dio Bolivar, a local liquor salesman and small-time hoodlum with a pencil-thin mustache and flashy clothes. Poppy had come over to their table and asked what a beautiful lady like her was doing in a low-rent joint with an unsuccessful pimp. Dio heard this and jumped up like a jack-in-the-box, ready to duke until he saw who'd said it.

'Oh, good evenin', Mr Papavero,' Bolivar said, having recognized Crazy Eyes Santos's chief enforcer on the Gulf Coast. Poppy led her away, and that was the last Perdita ever saw of Dio Bolivar.

She had told Poppy about her childhood in Corpus Christi; how her sister, Juana, had been murdered by her husband, Tony, who had also murdered both of his and Juana's daughters before shooting himself, but not much else. She didn't want him to know about the jams she'd been in in Texas and Mexico and California. It was a good idea, Perdita thought, to start fresh, keep her mouth shut and let this big man pay the bills. He didn't seem to mind so long as she kept herself pretty and available. It wasn't hard work and Papavero wasn't nearly as moody as most of the other guys she'd known. Besides, Perdita felt grown up with Poppy, respectable, like a regular woman rather than a piece of Tex-Mex trash. She decided that this was a gig worth holding on to.

'These Jungle guys are turning out better than I thought,' Poppy said to Perdita as he drove them away. 'They force people to buy shit even if they're not users, just to stay healthy. Not even Santos thought of that!'

Perdita sat in the passenger seat with her body turned toward Poppy, making sure that her tight black skirt rode halfway up her thighs. Poppy looked over at her and stroked her legs with his hairy right hand.

'You really do please me, Perdita,' he said. 'I never told you, but I was married once. It didn't last too long, about five years. It ended, let's see now, when I was thirty, fifteen years ago. Her name was Dolores, but everybody called her Dolly. She worked in the Maison Blanche on Canal Street when I met her, in the women's apparel department. I went there to buy a birthday present for another girl. I saw Dolly and forgot all about the girl. She had big tits, a big nose and a flat ass. There was something about her, though, that got me, aside from her tits. Dolly had a way of looking at you that made you think she knew all about you, who you really were deep inside. It sounds dumb, I know, but if you'd met her you'd understand.'

'It don't sound dumb. I've known people like that. One guy, especially, who was a kind of strange, religious person. He's dead now.'

'Yeah? You have? Well, Dolly's the only one I've ever known

had that look, like she knew every rotten or good thing you'd ever done in your entire life. It was spooky.'

'So what happened to her and you?'

'I married her, like I said. It was going along good enough, I guess, but she didn't like not knowing what I did every day, where I went, and that sometimes I was out until five or six in the morning or took off without telling her for a few days.'

Poppy shook his head, remembering.

'No, she didn't like what I was doing. Dolly knew I was moving up in the organization, bringing home more money, which was OK because I'd made her quit her job at the Maison Blanche. But then she wanted a child and no matter what we did, she couldn't get pregnant. We went to a couple of doctors and they both said it was because of some defect she had in her system, and there was no way to correct it. They suggested we adopt, which Dolly didn't want to do. I wouldn't have minded. There's plenty of orphans need homes and that way she could have a kid, but for some reason she didn't want one unless it was her own. Her parents and grandparents were all dead, she didn't have any family but me.'

'What color hair did she have?' asked Perdita, lighting up a Marlboro.

'Kind of reddish-blond. Her mother was Polish, she told me, and her father was Czech. She kept pictures of them on the bedroom dresser. I came home one night late, about four A.M., from the Egyptian Sho-Bar on Napoleon Avenue that I was running then, and Dolly wasn't there. At first I thought maybe she'd gone down to the all-night pharmacy on Esplanade for something, but when she wasn't back by five I knew that wasn't it. I looked at the dresser, and the pictures of her parents were gone. Dolly walked out on me. No note, no phone call, nothing. I was upset at first, of course, but after a week I didn't care. I just hoped she was happier wherever she was, and I went on with my life.'

Perdita didn't say anything as Poppy sped them south on 59 toward New Orleans. They passed a Greyhound and Perdita thought how much better it was to be traveling in a new BMW than on a bus. She lowered the tinted window a crack and tossed out her cigarette butt. Sailor Ripley saw the blue car zoom by and a cigarette fly out and bounce off the side of the bus just below where he was sitting.

'What do you think, Perdita?' asked Poppy. 'Is that a sad story or not?'

'Heard lots sadder,' she said.

Poppy Papavero laughed and grabbed her left thigh.

'So have I, pussycat. So have I.'

'She left when?'

'Yesterday. I tell you, Dal, this is just another way for Lula to avoid facin' the future, if she's ever gonna have one's worth a thing.'

'Marietta, it don't matter how much or how little you fuss. Lula's gonna find herself or not and you can't do nothin' about it.'

'OK, Dal, I believe you, but that still don't make me feel any better. And why is it in the back of my mind I got this sneakin' notion Sailor Ripley ain't out of the picture?'

'He is the boy's father, after all. And it's plain Lula ain't yet resolved her feelin's about him.'

'But, Dal, it's been more'n ten years she's had to figure it out.'

'That ain't nothin' where love's concerned, Marietta, you know that. And Lula feels guilty as get-out over not havin' gone to see Sailor all that time he was shut away from society. You didn't have no little to do with that, either.'

'Dal, I swear on my grandmama Eudora Pace's grave I never told Lula not to visit Sailor. She was just busy bringin' up her son by herself and couldn't never get away.'

'This ain't worth our arguin' now, is it? You and I know well enough how much influence you keep over that girl.'

'I got to. Look at the fix Lula got herself in the last time she ran off. Mixed up with a bunch of deranged criminals in a West Texas desert, people gettin' shot and killed all around, and her pregnant besides. If Johnnie and I hadn't tracked Lula down in that Big Tuna hellhole who knows where she'd be today? Prob'ly'd have two or three more illegitimate children and be lost out in some godforsaken place like California, surrounded by a hundred kinds of drug-crazed devil worshipers.'

'Marietta, how you can carry on. Lula's just in New Orleans

visitin' an old friend. It'll be good for her, gettin' away for a bit. By the way, you heard any more from Santos?'

'Two dozen red roses arrived this mornin', with a card.'

'I'll be. What'd it say?'

'Oh, somethin' like, "To Marietta, who always deserves the best, from Marcello."'

'Natalie Suarez knows someone in NO knows Mona Costatroppo, the woman your playmate Crazy Eyes been keepin' down there the last few years.'

'So?'

'Natalie says this friend of hers heard from Mona Costatroppo that Santos cut her off flat about a month back, threatened to kill her if she made a fuss.'

'Now, Dal, do you believe that? People're always tryin' to find somethin' ugly to talk about. Here you are, always settin' yourself up as the voice of reason far as me and Lula's concerned, and you fall for this silly third-hand gossip out the mouth of a woman we both know don't have the brain of a peacock on mood pills.'

'I ain't fell for nothin'. I'm just tellin' you what I hear concerns Santos, is all. It may or may not be true, but it's out there in the air and I thought you deserved to know. Apparently the Costatroppo woman sold some of the jewelry and furniture Santos had given her and moved to New York or Chicago, afraid for her life.'

'I'd be more afraid for my life in one of those places than I would down here anywhere. And anyway, how do we know what this Troppo person done to Marcello riled him in the first place, if in fact there's any truth to the story at all?'

'Natalie Suarez claims he just got tired of her after she got a little fat and sloppy. Her friend said she'd developed a drinkin' problem.'

'There you are, then! Who wants to be around a drunk?'

'And of course there's his wife, Lina, who pretends ain't a thing wrong.'

'Maybe there ain't, Dal, you ever consider that? Marcello's a man knows his own mind, always has. Clyde didn't never have a bad word to say about him when he was alive, and I don't either. I vote we end this part of the conversation right now.'

'Fine with me, Marietta. Sorry I couldn't get to Tuesday's meetin' of the Daughters. Louis made me go with him to visit his mama in the nursin' home in Asheville. Don't make no sense draggin' me, I told him, she's so gaga. But I guess it helps him, me bein' there. What'd I miss?'

'Oh, Dal, you won't believe what Esther Pickens heard about Ruby Werlhi and Denise Sue Hilton's son-in-law. You know, Walker French-Jones, the tennis pro?'

Bright Lights, Big City

As soon as Sailor got off the bus he headed toward the Hotel Brazil. He didn't know if it was still there but he didn't bother to check a city directory, figuring he'd find something similar in the neighborhood if necessary. From Elysian Fields he cut across the park, surprised to see so many homeless people camped out and sleeping on benches. He turned left on Frenchmen Street and there it was, the Brazil, looking as dilapidated as it had ten or more years before, but still standing. He entered, asked the elderly white male desk clerk for a room overlooking the street, paid thirty dollars for two days in advance, took his key and hiked up the stairs to the third floor. Sailor could not remember which room he and Lula had stayed in, but this one was pretty close. He opened the window, leaned out and looked east. There was the river, huge and green, with a gray Yugoslav freighter, flanked by black tugs, pushing past the Bienville Wharf.

He lay down on the bed and lit up an unfiltered Camel. The hint of a breeze blew into the room, startling Sailor for a moment. It was unexpected and caused him to shiver, despite the intense heat and high humidity. The Hotel Brazil did not provide room-cooling except during winter, when there was no heat. A strange sensation came over him, as if an invisible, gauzy-feeling substance had intruded on the finger of fresh air and draped itself around his body. Sailor's cigarette burned down steadily between the index and second fingers of his right hand, its ash building but remaining attached due to his immobility.

'Lula's here,' Sailor said. He trembled and the ash fell off the cigarette on to the floor.

Sailor swung his legs off the bed, stood up and went back over to the window. He took a swift drag on the Camel and flicked it out into the street. Directly below, two old men, one black the other white, were struggling over a half-pint bottle of Old Crow.

'That's mine!' the black man shouted.

'Hell it is!' said the white man.

'I bought it, I'mo drink it!'

'Bullshit! Half's my money! Give it!'

'I knock yo teef out, ugly mufuck, you had 'ny.'

The white man lurched toward the black man, fell to his knees and wrapped his arms around the black man's legs.

'Let go, fo I smack yo bleach head!'

'Mine, mine!' screeched the white man, who was crying now.

The black man raised the bottle to his mouth and took a long swig. People walking along the sidewalk avoided them. The black man staggered to the curb, dragging the white man, who clung stubbornly to his legs. The black man stopped and took another long drink, killing the bottle.

'Here go, mufuck,' he said, bringing the dark brown bottle down hard on the white man's head.

The glass shattered, cutting into the bald, freckled skull of the genuflecting man, the pieces scattering over the sidewalk. The white man did not release his hold on the black man's legs. He remained attached, sobbing loudly, his body heaving, the top of his head a puddle of blood and broken glass. The black man balanced himself with his hands on the hood of a dirty beige '81 Cutlass parked by the curb and kicked loose his legs, leaving the white man slumped on the ground as he stumbled away.

Sailor looked down at the crying, bleeding man whom passersby continued to ignore. A New Orleans police car pulled up in front of the hotel and two cops got out. They lifted the injured man, holding him under each arm, deposited him in the backseat and drove off. The black man, Sailor noticed, was sitting on the ground, leaning against a shabby white building on the opposite side of the street. Above the man's head, in faded black paint, were the words JESUS DIED FOR THE UNGODLY. The man's eyes were closed and there were splotches of bright red, undoubtedly the other man's blood, on the front of his short-sleeved white shirt.

Sailor went back to the bed and lay down on his back. He had no idea where to begin looking for Lula, and he did not want to contact Marietta. A picture of Perdita Durango standing on the street in Hattiesburg flashed in his brain. Lula used to say the world was weird on top, he thought. She sure was right there. Sailor rolled over into a fetal position and closed his eyes.

Saving Grace

Elmer Désespéré put his railroad engineer's cap over his stringy yellow-white hair and went out. At the foot of the stairs of his rooming house he stopped and took a packet of Red Man chewing tobacco from the back pocket of his Ben Davis overalls, scooped a wad with the thumb and index finger of his right hand and planted it between his teeth and cheek in the left side of his mouth. Elmer replaced the packet in his pocket and strolled down Claiborne toward Canal Street. The night air felt thick and greasy, and the sidewalk was crawling with people sweating, laughing, fighting, drinking. Police cars, their revolving red and blue lights flashing, prowled up and down both sides of the road. Trucks rumbled like stampeding dinosaurs on the overhead highway, expelling a nauseating stream of diesel mist.

Elmer loved it all. He loved being in the city of New Orleans, away from the farm forever, away from his daddy, Hershel Burt, and his older brother, Emile; though they'd never bother a soul again, since Elmer had destroyed the both of them as surely as they had destroyed his mama, Alma Ann. He had chopped his daddy and brother into a total of exactly one hundred pieces and buried one piece per acre on the land Hershel Burt owned in Evangeline Parish by the Bayou Nezpique. After doing what he had to, Elmer had walked clear to Mamou and visited Alma Ann's grave, told her she could rest easy, then hitchhiked into NO.

Alma Ann had died ten years ago, when Elmer was nine, on November 22d, the birthday of her favorite singer, Hoagy Carmichael. Alma Ann's greatest pleasure in life, she had told Elmer, was listening to the collection of Hoagy Carmichael 78s her daddy, Bugle Lugubre, had left her. Her favorite tunes had been 'Old Man Harlem,' 'Ole Buttermilk Sky,' and Bugle's own favorite, 'Memphis in June.' But after Alma Ann was worked to death by Hershel Burt and Emile, Hershel Burt had busted

36

up all the records and dumped the pieces in the Crooked Creek Reservoir. Now Elmer had buried Hershel Burt just like he'd buried Bugle Lugubre's Hoagy Carmichael records. It made Elmer happy to think that the records could be replaced and that Hoagy Carmichael would live on forever through them. Alma Ann would live on as well, by virtue of Hoagy's music and Elmer's memory, but Hershel Burt and Emile were wiped away clean as bugs off a windshield in a downpour.

The only thing Elmer needed now was a friend. He'd taken the two-thousand-four-hundred-eighty-eight dollars his daddy had kept in Alma Ann's cloisonné button box, so Elmer figured he had enough money for quite a little while to come. Walking along Claiborne, watching the people carry on, Elmer felt as if he were a visitor to an insane asylum, the only one with a pass to the outside. When he reached Canal, Elmer turned down toward the river. He was looking for a tattoo parlor to have his mama's name written over his heart. A friend would know immediately what kind of person Elmer was, he thought, as soon as he saw ALMA ANN burned into Elmer's left breast. The friend would understand the depth of Elmer's loyalty and sincerity and never betray or leave him, this Elmer knew.

The pain was gone, too. The constant headache Elmer had suffered for so many years had vanished as he'd knelt next to Alma Ann's grave in Mamou. She soothed her truest son in death as she had in life. Jesus was bunk, Elmer had decided. He'd prayed to Jesus after Alma Ann had gone, but he had not been delivered. There had been no saving grace for Elmer until he'd destroyed the two marauding angels and pacified himself in the name of Alma Ann. It was he who shone, not Jesus. Jesus was dead and he, Elmer, was alive. He would carry Alma Ann's name on his body and his friend would understand and love him for it.

'Say, ma'am,' Elmer said to a middle-aged woman headed in the opposite direction, 'there a place near here a sober man can buy himself a expert tattoo?'

'I suppose there must be,' she said, 'farther along closer to the port.'

'Alma Ann blesses you, ma'am,' said Elmer, walking on, spitting tobacco juice on the sidewalk.

The woman stared after him and was surprised to see that he was barefoot.

Heart Talk

'Speakin' of abuse?' said Beany, as she fed Madonna Kim her bottle of formula. 'I didn't know that's what Elmo was doin' until I saw them women on Oprah's show talkin' about how their husbands, mostly ex now, 'course, like Elmo and me, used to take all kinds of advantages. Worst is the ones beat 'em up, which Elmo only done once to me, when he was stewed and I threw a pet rock at him after I'd found out from Mimsy Bavard the baby Etta Foy was havin' was his.'

It was nine A.M. and Beany and Lula were sitting on the front porch swing of the house in Metairie, discussing men. Pace and Lance were on the lawn shooting rubber-tipped arrows at a target, trading off turns with the only bow.

'Bob Lee wouldn't never hit me, even if he thought he had a reason to. He takes off, he's angry enough. Comes back about two hours later and raids the refrigerator.'

'Where's he go?'

'Oh, mostly he'll drive around, or maybe go to a movie at the mall. One time he come home with this really strange look on his face. I asked him, "You still mad at me, Bob Lee?" I don't recall now what it was set him off in the first place. I think somethin' to do with my lettin' Lance cry too long. Bob Lee's a real softie it comes to babies cryin', he'll just run and pick 'em up. I told him you got to let 'em settle down on their own or they just get so damned spoiled they're always fussin'. Anyway, he come in lookin' like a wild dog just bit the head off his favorite cat. And Lord knows, Bob Lee loves cats.'

'How come you ain't got any then?'

''Lergic. Me and Lance both. Bugs Bob Lee, but nothin' we can do about it. I tell him he's got his gators to pet.'

'So what weirded him out?'

'I'm tellin' you, this movie he seen, called *Blue Velvet*. You seen it?'

'No. Ain't heard of it.'

'After he seen it, Bob Lee couldn't even eat. He wouldn't let me go see it, though I wanted to. I woulda gone anyway, of course, but with Lance bein' a baby then I didn't get a chance. Bob Lee told me he coulda never imagined the awful behavior went on in that movie. He did say there was a couple pretty women in it.'

'Was it a porno?'

'Don't think so. Bob Lee don't care for 'em, though I don't mind 'em once in awhile if there's some laughs in it. Sorta horrifies Bob Lee I can take sex less than serious sometimes. This *Blue Velvet*, though, must be somethin' else entirely. He said it made his brain shut down, like all the fuses blew.'

'We oughta rent it for the VCR.'

'Good idea. Watch it while Bob Lee's at work.'

Pace came up on the porch and sat on the top step. Lance was still busy shooting arrows.

'What we gonna do today, Mama?' Pace asked.

'Thought maybe we'd go swimmin'. You like that idea?'

'I suppose.'

'C'mon, Pace!' Lance shouted. 'It's your turn!'

'Comin'!' Pace shouted back. He looked at Beany and said, 'Lance ain't a bad kid, but he goes bugshit you leave him alone a minute. You notice that, Aunt Beany?'

Pace got up and resumed playing with Lance.

'That boy is a natural, Lula,' said Beany. 'Don't know where you got him.'

'Got him from Sailor is where.'

'He ever hit you?'

'Sail? You jokin'? Sailor Ripley wouldn't raise a hand to me or nobody.'

'Hold it, Lula. He killed a man. Bob Ray Lemon. Remember?'

'That was different. He thought Bob Ray was tryin' to harm me. Imagine it still's eatin' at him, what he done.'

'Bet he misses seein' his boy.'

Lula watched Pace pull back the bowstring and send an arrow into the very heart of the target. Tears burst from her eyes and Beany handed her one of Madonna Kim's spit-up towels.

'He's just so beautiful and precious to me, Beany,' Lula said, wiping her face, 'just like Lance and Madonna Kim are to you. But he's really all I got in the world. If anything bad happened to Pace, I don't know what I'd do. Shoot myself, prob'ly.'

Madonna Kim coughed and knocked the bottle away. Beany put her over her shoulder and patted the baby's back.

'Stop talkin' foolish, Lula. Ain't nothin' but good gonna ride that boy.'

Madonna Kim let out a burp so loud that it startled Beany and Lula, and they laughed.

'Oh, Beany, I'm so glad I come to see you. It really means a lot to me, your takin' us in this way.'

'Hush. Means a lot to me, too.'

They looked at their boys playing on the grass in the morning sun, wrestling now, rolling around and laughing, Pace allowing the weaker, smaller Lance to pin him. They jumped up and ran over to the porch.

'Mama?' said Lance. 'Pace says we're goin' swimmin'. Is it time yet?'

Ill Wind

'Carmine, *come va?*'

'I am fine, Marcello. I know you are, too.'

'And how is that?'

'The other night I ran into the Calabrese, Jimmie Hunchback, at Broussard's. I asked him about you, and he said, "*Il vecchio porta bene gli anni*."'

Papavero heard Santos chuckle at the other end of the line.

'Old man, he calls me,' said Santos. 'I should call him up and tell him this old man still knows how *tenere il coltello dalla parte del manico*.'

Poppy laughed. 'Nobody will ever doubt that you know how to hold the knife, Marcello, or that you would use it if you had to. *Non ho notizie di te da molto tempo*. What can I do for you?'

'I wanted you to know that I'm coming in two days. The thing with Mona has caused some trouble there I must take care of myself.'

'*La Signora Costatroppo ha fatto parlare di sé*. The lady has caused much talk.'

Santos sighed. 'She knows too much, Carmine. *Il passato non si distrugge*. The past cannot be undone, but *non si sa mai quando può succedere una disgrazia*. One never knows when an accident might happen.'

'One would think that after all you've done for her, given her, she would be more respectful.'

'My friend, *a chi tutto, a chi niente*. Who can say what is enough or not enough for anyone? *Non fa niente*, it doesn't matter. I know where she hides and soon I can tell you, *mi sono liberato di un incomodo*.'

'Your life is long, Marcello. There is much to look forward to.'

'Mona was once a morsel to be savored, Carmine, but *un pranzo*

41

comprende molte pietanze. A meal consists of many dishes. Already *la ferita si sta cicatrizzando*. The wound heals as we speak. I have sent *un colpo di vento*, a gust of wind, to blow away the problem.'

'I will be glad to see you, Marcello. I'll be here.'

'*Bene*. I may need your help on a couple of matters. The business goes well with the *tutsuns*?'

'*Molto bene*, better than I expected.'

'You are a smart man, Carmine. You earn my respect. *Ciao*.'

'*Ciao*, Marcello. *Buon viaggio*.'

A Walk in the Park

The air seemed cooler in Audubon Park. Lula and Beany, who was carrying Madonna Kim in a pouch strapped to her chest, strolled slowly beneath the magnolia trees as Pace and Lance ran ahead, playing tag. Lula and the boys had swum most of the morning, and then they had all gone to the Camellia Grill and eaten a large, wonderful lunch which they were now walking – in the boys' case, running – off.

'I can't believe how safe and fine I feel,' said Lula, 'just bein' here. It ain't nearly so hot as I thought it'd be.'

'Wish you lived nearby, Lula. It'd be great to be able to hang out together like this whenever we wanted to. And the kids are gettin' along so good.'

Lula watched the boys circle a tree and take off at breakneck speed toward the lake, Lance chasing the fleeter Pace.

'Pace!' she shouted. 'You take care Lance don't fall in!'

'I will, Mama!' Pace yelled, just before he and his pursuer disappeared behind a boathouse.

'I gotta admit, Beany, Sailor been on my mind a whole lot lately, more than I'm comfortable about. I mean, he ain't never been off it entire since we met when I was sixteen. It's amazin', but that's almost half my life.'

'No point in fightin' it either, sweetie. Some things just meant to be. Guess it was destiny you and him'd be matched. But you don't even know where he might be, huh?'

Lula shook her head no, reached back with her right hand and wiped the sweat off the back of her neck.

'Don't know that I even want to see Sailor, really,' she said. 'Truth is, though, no guy I been out with before or since ever thrilled me like Sailor. I mean, really *thrilled* me, Beany, you know?'

'Not sure I do, Lula.'

'Like I would always, *always*, get excited that Sailor was comin' to get me, or I was goin' to meet him. Even when things between us wasn't so smooth. Didn't ever seem to matter what kinda problems we were havin', or what else was goin' on, I'd get a actual *thrill* thinkin' about him. That never's happened with another man, Beany, not like that. There's been moments I been happy, of course, and thought I was doin' all right. But I made love enough with other boys to know there can't never be anyone but him makes a difference in my soul.'

Lula stopped walking and Beany stopped, too. Lula put her forehead against the back of Beany's right shoulder and let the tears come. She was shaking, and Beany started to turn around, but Lula held her still.

'Wait, Beany, just let me rest my head on you like this. I'll be fine in a minute and I don't want you to look at me until I am.'

Beany didn't move.

'There,' Lula said, raising her head and smiling, giving her hair a shake, wiping her eyes with the backs of her hands, 'I'm better. Guess that's what they mean, havin' a shoulder to cry on,' she laughed. 'Never took it for real quite the same way before.'

Beany looked into her friend's red, watery, large gray eyes.

'You always got me to cry on, Lula,' she said, 'just like I hope I always got you.'

Lula hugged Beany, being careful not to squeeze too tightly and crush Madonna Kim between them.

'You got me, Miss Beany, forever.'

They disengaged and began walking again. Madonna Kim snoozed peacefully.

'Hey, where'd them boys go?' said Lula.

'Prob'ly runnin' around the lake. We'll find 'em. Lance been here lots of times. They won't get lost.'

Just then Lance appeared from behind the opposite side of the boathouse and ran over to Beany and Lula.

'I can't find Pace,' he said. 'He must be hidin' on me.'

Lula shivered. 'Where'd you see him last?' she asked.

'I tagged him and run on ahead, and when he didn't catch up I turned around and Pace wasn't nowhere. Mama, can I get a ice cream?'

Lula took off running toward the lake. She followed the path around the water but did not see Pace. She stopped to rest and think, and Lance came running up behind her.

'Aunt Lula, Mama says come quick. A lady saw Pace go off with some man.'

'Oh, shit. Oh, shit,' Lula kept saying, as she and Lance ran back toward Beany.

Beany and a thin, gray-haired woman of about fifty, wearing yellow shorts, a red tank top and green Nike running shoes, with a Sony Walkman headset radio hanging around her neck, were standing next to the boathouse.

'Lula, listen,' said Beany. 'This woman says she saw a boy looked like Pace walk away with a man.'

'The boy was about ten or eleven, with black hair,' the woman said. 'He was wearin' blue jeans and a blue tee shirt said "Tarheels" on it in white block letters.'

'Oh, shit,' said Lula. 'That's him, that's Pace!'

'Well, when I saw him I was joggin' into the park on the north path there, and this boy was holdin' hands with a young man not much more than a boy himself, maybe eighteen, nineteen. Was an odd-lookin' young man, too. Real slight build, wearin' overalls and a kind of railroad engineer's cap, with long, dirty-blond-lookin' curly hair hangin' down under it.'

'Pace wouldn't just go off with some stranger!' Lula said.

'Are you sure this guy in the overalls wasn't pullin' Pace along with him?' Beany asked the woman.

'He mighta been, I don't know. I just ran past 'em, goin' kinda slow, of course, so I got a good look at 'em both.'

Lula ran to the north path and followed it out of the park to the street. She stood there, breathing hard, looking each way, but there was nobody else around. Lula ran down the street to where it intersected a main thoroughfare. Cars whizzed by in both directions.

Lula grabbed a young black woman who was walking by and yelled at her, 'Did you see my son? He's ten years old and has black hair and he's wearin' a Carolina Tarheels tee shirt. A white man wearin' overalls just kidnapped him!'

'No, lady,' said the young woman, 'I ain't seen him.'

Lula let go and fell to her knees.

'Oh, shit! Oh, shit! Oh, shit!' she cried. 'Sailor, Sailor, I need you now!'

45

One Never Knows

Mona Costatroppo looked out the window of her room in the Drake Hotel in Chicago. Lake Michigan, she thought, staring at it, was as big as an ocean.

'What's the name again, this beach here?' she asked Federal Agents Sandy Sandusky and Morton Martin, both of whom were seated on the couch under a hideous oil painting of a tropical sunset.

'Oak Street,' Sandusky said. 'That's Oak Street beach.'

'About a billion bodies on it,' said Mona, 'look like flies on dogshit.'

She turned away from the window.

'So, you'll guarantee if I tell you all I know about Santos's organization you'll set me up someplace with a new identity?'

'Federal Witness Protection Program,' said Martin. 'Even Europe, you want to go there.'

Mona nodded. 'OK, you bums get outta here now, let me think this over.'

The agents rose together and Sandusky said, 'We'll be here tomorrow morning at ten o'clock, Ms Costatroppo.'

'Never figured anybody'd be callin' me Miz, 'less slavery got legal again. You be here what time you want. But now, get out.'

The agents left and Mona poured a healthy dose of Bombay Sapphire into a glass and drank it fast. She poured some more into the glass, emptying the fifth she'd bought that morning, and was about to swallow it when there was a knock at the door.

'Who's there?' she asked.

'Valet. I have your laundry.'

Mona walked over, the glass in her left hand, and turned the doorknob with her right.

'Put it on the bed,' she said, walking toward the window, not bothering to see who it was coming through the door.

As Mona lifted the glass to her lips and opened her mouth, she heard a loud pop. She dropped the glass and started to turn around, but before she could there was another loud pop, which she did not hear. Mona sat down suddenly on the floor, her head banging hard against the window that overlooked Oak Street beach and Lake Michigan, but she didn't feel a thing.

Night and Fog

Sailor was awakened in his room at the Hotel Brazil by a series of shrieks coming from the hallway. He jumped out of bed and stubbed the big toe on his left foot on the leg of the table next to the door, opened the door and limped into the hall. Two women of indeterminate age, one blond, one red-haired, were rolling on the carpet in front of the staircase attempting to mutilate each other in any way possible. They were screaming and cursing at the top of their voices. Sailor stood by the door to his room rubbing his sore toe and watching the women wrestle. He looked at his watch: it was a couple of ticks shy of six A.M. The more heavyset of the women, the blond, stood and grabbed the redhead and dragged her to her feet, then ran her into the wall, knocking the red-haired wrestler stupid and busting her nose. Blood spurted on the wall, the floor and the blond bruiser, further infuriating her. She yelled, 'You cunt!' and practically picked up the bleeder and threw her down the stairs. The blond stood in the hallway panting hard, wiped her face with her meaty right forearm, and spotted Sailor standing there in his underwear with his left leg resting on his right knee, holding his toe.

'What the fuck you lookin' at, buster?' she said.

Sailor lowered his leg and looked behind him. He was the only spectator. He turned back to the woman.

'Thanks for the wake-up,' he said, and went back inside his room.

The screaming ceased and Sailor limped over to the washbasin, where he rinsed his face, brushed his teeth and combed his hair. He pulled on his clothes and went out. There was no sign of the battling women, only a neck-high smear of blood on the wall.

The morning air was warm and foggy. Sailor headed for Rod's, a 24-hour cafe on Ursulines Street just off Decatur in the Quarter. He bought an early edition of the *Times-Picayune* from a machine, thinking he'd check out the job opportunities. Sitting at the counter in Rod's, Sailor ordered chicory coffee and a Spanish omelette. He lit up his first Camel of the day and opened the paper. There on the lower right of the front page was the heading, BOY VISITING CITY IS KIDNAPPED. Sailor read the article that followed.

A ten-year-old boy, Pace Roscoe Ripley, visiting the city with his mother, Lula Pace Fortune, of Bay St Clement, NC, was kidnapped in broad daylight yesterday afternoon while on an outing with friends in Audubon Park. A woman who apparently witnessed the abduction while she was jogging in the park described the kidnapper as being approximately eighteen or nineteen years old, with long blond hair, wearing striped overalls and a railroad engineer's cap. Pace Ripley was described by his mother's friend, Mrs Beany Thorn Boyle, of Metairie, as under five feet tall, black hair, wearing blue jeans, a blue and white tee shirt with the word 'Tarheels' on it, and white sneakers. Anyone with relevant information should contact the New Orleans Police Department. Tel. 555-0099.

'You got a directory here?' Sailor asked the fry cook.

'On the floor behind you,' he said, without turning around. 'Under the phone.'

Sailor flipped to the section listing residents of Metairie, and found BOYLE BOB LEE AND BEANY ... 833 CHARITY ... 555-4956. He put in a coin and dialed.

'Hello?' said Bob Lee.

'This is Sailor Ripley, Pace's daddy. Is Lula there?'

'Hold the phone.'

Sailor dropped his cigarette and stepped on it.

'Sailor?! Is it really you?'

'Oh, peanut, yes! It's me! I'm in NO. I just read about Pace in the paper.'

'Please come here now, Sail. I don't know what to do.'

'Don't do nothin', honey. I'm comin', your Sailor's comin'!'

Sailor hung up and ran out of the cafe. The fry cook heard the screen door slam, scooped up the half-done omelette from the grill and tossed it in the trash.

Marietta's Trial

'Mrs Fortune?'

'Speakin'.'

'This is Beany Boyle, in New Orleans? Lula's friend. Used to be I was Beany Thorn?'

'I remember you. Why are you callin' me? Has somethin' happened to Lula?'

'No, ma'am, not to Lula, but I got some terrible news.'

'Go on.'

'Pace been kidnapped, Mrs Fortune. We was all takin' a walk in the park and the boys, Pace and my son, Lance, took off outta Lula's and my sight – I was carryin' my baby, Madonna Kim? – and someone snatched Pace.'

'I knew somethin' awful'd happen if Lula left home! Put her on the line!'

'She's kinda out of it right now, Mrs Fortune. She asked me to call you.'

'You put Lula on the line right now, dammit!'

'I really can't, she's too broke up to talk to you. The police are handlin' it and Sailor's here.'

'*He's* there?! Satan takes a holiday!'

Marietta hung up.

'Mrs Fortune? Mrs Fortune, are you there?'

Beany hung up.

As soon as she'd cut Beany off, Marietta dialed Santos's private number. A man answered on the third ring.

'Bayou Enterprises.'

'This is Marietta Pace Fortune, Clyde Fortune's widow. I got to speak to Marcello Santos right away! It's urgent!'

'Wait,' the man said.

Two minutes later, Santos came on the line.

'Yes, Marietta. How pleasant to hear from you.'

'Marcello, somethin' real *un*pleasant's happened. My grandboy, Pace – you met him at my birthday party. Remember, he asked you about your thumb?'

'I do.'

'He's been kidnapped, in New Orleans!'

'When did this happen?'

'Yesterday, I believe. I just got the call. You gotta help find him! Lula's there and that horrible Sailor Ripley's with her. I'm gonna be about flat outta my mind in a New York minute!'

'Calm yourself, Marietta. I will do everything I can, of course. As it happens, I am about to leave very shortly for New Orleans. Before I go, I will contact people there who may be able to help. I will call you from Louisiana as soon as I have any information.'

'He's my only grandchild, Marcello! Lula knew how to raise him, this wouldn'ta happened.'

'Do you know how the kidnap occurred?'

'Someone stole Pace out of a park is all I know.'

'The police have been notified?'

'I suppose, yes. But you gotta get him back for me, Marcello, please!'

'I will make a call right away. Do you want me to send someone to stay with you?'

'No, no, I'll get Dal. You need the number where Lula's at?'

'It won't be necessary. Goodbye, Marietta. We will talk again very soon.'

'I appreciate this, Marcello. I wouldn't ask if it wasn't so important.'

'I know, Marietta, I understand. Goodbye.'

Marietta called Dal next.

'Dal? Pace been kidnapped in New Orleans by God knows who and Sailor's there reattachin' himself to Lula! Can you believe my life?! Who'd I kill, Dal? I ask you! What'd I do to deserve this?'

'Slow down a sec, peach. You're sayin' Pace been kidnapped and Sailor'n Lula're back together in NO?'

'That's it! That's the package.'

'What's bein' done?'

'I just now got off the phone with Santos. He's goin' there himself today. That slut friend of Lula's, Tap Thorn's daughter, called me, said they got the police workin' on it.'

'What'd Lula say?'

51

'She didn't. The Thorn girl wouldn't let her come to the phone. Said Lula was in a faint, or somethin'.'

'Wouldn't doubt it. I'll be over in a minute, Marietta. Is the back door unlocked?'

'Good, Dal, yes. Bye!'

Marietta dialed the number of Johnnie Farragut's office in Charlotte.

'JF Investigations. Farragut talkin'.'

'Crazed animal stole Pace in NO and Lula's back with Sailor!'

'Marietta? What?'

'Pace been kidnapped! Lula and him went to NO to visit Tap Thorn's most irresponsible child, the one married a alligator wrestler, and now Sailor's there, too!'

'Have they called the police?'

''Course they have. I called Santos soon as I heard, and he's sendin' in the troops. Johnnie, I tell you, it's another trial! Clyde burned to death, Lula run off with a robber and killer, now my precious grandbaby been taken!'

'I'm comin', Marietta. Take me two and a half hours. You call Dal yet?'

'She's on her way.'

'Good. I'm leavin' now.'

Marietta hung up, staggered into the front room, where only a few days before Pace had unwrapped her birthday presents, and collapsed into Clyde's worn old leather armchair. She heard the back door open and close.

'Marietta? Where are you?'

'In here, Dal.'

Dalceda Delahoussaye came in, dropped to the floor, and hugged Marietta's knees.

'Oh, Marietta, I'm so sorry. This is a nightmare.'

'I ain't certain there's a God, Dal, I never been convinced. But one thing I do know, there's a Devil, and he don't never quit.'

Brothers

Elmer's room was ten feet by ten feet. There were two windows, both of which were half-boarded over and nailed shut; a sink; a single bed; one cane armchair; a small dresser with a mirror attached; and a writing table with a green-shaded eagle-shaped lamp on it. The one closet was empty because Elmer had no clothes other than the ones he wore. He had been meaning to buy some new pants and shirts, but he kept forgetting. Elmer forswore shoes; they interfered with the electrical power he absorbed from the earth through his feet. In one corner was a pile about two feet high of canned food, mostly Campbell's Pork and Beans and Denison's Chili. On the dresser were two half-gallon plastic containers of spring water and a Swiss Army knife that contained all of the necessary eating untensils plus a can opener. There was no garbage in the room, no empty cans or bottles. Elmer disliked refuse; as soon as he had finished with something, he got rid of it, depositing it in a container on the street.

Pace slept on the bed. Elmer sat in the cane armchair, twirling his hat on the toes of his left foot and looking at the illustrations in his favorite book, *The Five Chinese Brothers*. His mother, Alma Ann, had read this story to him countless times and Elmer knew every word of it by heart. This was fortunate, because Elmer could not read. He'd tried, both in the two years he'd attended school and with Alma Ann, but for some reason he found it impossible to recognize the letters of the alphabet in combination with each other. Elmer had no difficulty identifying them individually, but set up together the way they were in books and newspapers and on signs and other things confused him. He had taken *The Five Chinese Brothers* with him from the farm and he looked at the pictures in it while reciting the story to himself several times a day. Elmer was anxious to show the book to his friend, but he would wait until he was certain Pace was really his friend. Alma Ann had told Elmer that sharing something, even a book, was the greatest gift one human being could bestow upon another. It was very important, she said, to have complete and utter faith in the sharer, to know that he or she would share in return. Elmer was not yet sure of this friend, since he had never had one other than Alma Ann, though he hoped that he and Pace would become perfect companions.

The five Chinese brothers were identical to one another, and they lived with their mother. They had no father. One brother could swallow the sea; another had an iron neck; another could stretch his legs an unlimited distance; another could not be burned; and another could hold his breath forever. Elmer recited the story softly to himself as he looked at the pictures, twirling his engineer's cap for a few minutes on one foot, then switching it to the other. The Chinese brother who could swallow the sea went fishing one morning with a little boy who had begged to accompany him. The Chinese brother allowed the boy to come along on the condition that he obey the brother's orders promptly. The boy promised to do so. At the shore, the Chinese brother swallowed the sea and gathered some fish while holding the water in his mouth. The boy ran out and picked up as many interesting objects that had been buried under the sea as he could. The Chinese brother signaled for his companion to return but the boy did not pay attention to him, continuing to hunt for treasures. The Chinese brother motioned frantically for him to come back, but his little friend did not respond. Finally the Chinese brother knew he would burst unless he released the sea, so he let it go and the boy disappeared. At this point in the story, Alma Ann had always stopped to tell Elmer that this boy had proven not to be the Chinese brother's perfect friend.

The Chinese brother was arrested and condemned to have his head severed. On the day of the execution he asked the judge if he could be allowed to go home briefly and say goodbye to his mother. The judge said, 'It is only fair,' and the Chinese brother who could swallow the sea went home. The brother who returned was the brother with an iron neck. All of the people in the town gathered in the square to see the sentence carried out, but when the executioner brought down his sword, it bent, and the Chinese brother's head remained on his shoulders. The crowd became angry and decided that he should be drowned. On the day of his execution the Chinese brother asked the judge if he could go home and bid his mother farewell, which the judge allowed. The brother who returned was the one who was capable of stretching his legs. When he was thrown overboard in the middle of the ocean, he rested his feet on the bottom and kept his head above water. The people again became angry and decided that he should be burned.

On the day of the execution, the Chinese brother asked the judge for permission to go home to say goodbye to his mother. The judge said, 'It is only fair.' The brother who returned was the one who could not catch on fire. He was tied to a stake and surrounded by stacks of wood that caught fire when lit, but the Chinese brother remained unscathed. The people became so infuriated that they decided he should be smothered to death. On the day of his execution, the Chinese brother requested that he be allowed to go home to see his mother. The judge said, 'It is only fair,' and of course the brother who returned was the one who could hold his breath indefinitely. He was shoveled into a brick oven filled with whipped cream and the door was locked tight until the next morning. When the door was opened and the Chinese brother emerged unharmed, the judge declared that since they had attempted to execute him four different ways, all to no avail, then he must be innocent, and ordered the Chinese brother released, a decision supported by the people. He then went home to his mother with whom he and his brothers lived happily ever after.

Elmer knew that he and Alma Ann could have lived happily ever after had she not been worked to death by Hershel Burt and Emile, who would have also worked him to death had Elmer not executed them. He hoped with all of his might that this boy Pace would be worthy of his friendship and not be like the boy who accompanied the Chinese brother to the sea. Elmer put down *The Five Chinese Brothers* and looked at Pace. The boy's eyes were open. Elmer stopped twirling his foot.

'You gonna let me go home to my mama?' Pace asked.

Elmer remembered what the judge had said to the Chinese brothers.

'It's only fair,' he said.

Pace sat up. 'Can I go right now?'

'Problem is,' said Elmer, 'I don't know I can trust you yet.'

'Trust me how?'

'To come back.'

Pace stared at Elmer's pale blue eyes.

'You're crazy, mister,' he said.

'Alma Ann said I weren't, and she knows better'n you.'

Pace looked around the room.

'Guess the door's locked, huh?'

Elmer nodded. 'I don't guess.'

'So I'm a prisoner.'

Elmer started twirling his cap on his right foot.

'You'n me is gonna be perfect friends.'

'Holy Jesus,' said Pace.

Elmer shook his head. 'Jesus is bunk.'

Full Circle

'I just couldn't handle it, peanut, seein' you and Pace so sudden after all them years livin' on nothin' 'cept hope. Reality's a killer, Lula, you know? That's why I run from you like I done. Been six months now, though, and I'm gettin' used to bein' outside the walls. Might be I'm more ready to deal with things the way they are, includin' you'n Pace.'

'If we ever find him.'

'We'll find him sweetheart. Ain't no kidnapper gonna keep our fam'ly apart. After all, we're together again, even though the circumstances is rotten.'

It was nine A.M. and Sailor and Lula were sitting at the kitchen table in Beany and Bob Lee's house having coffee. They'd been awake most of the night, not talking very much, mostly just holding and looking at one another and crying. They'd finally fallen asleep in each other's arms, fully clothed, emotionally exhausted, on the living-room floor. Lance had awakened them about an hour ago, shaking Lula, saying, 'Y'all can use my bed, Aunt Lula. I'm up.' The telephone rang and Beany came into the kitchen from the laundry room and answered it.

'Boyle home.'

She listened for a few seconds, then handed the phone to Lula.

'Police, for you.'

'This is Lula Fortune. Yes, Detective Fange, of course we can. My boy's daddy's here now, he'll be comin' with us. Soon as possible, I understand. Bye.'

She handed the phone back to Beany, who hung it up.

'Detective Fange wants us to come down to the police station, Beany, see if we can recognize any faces in their suspect books we mighta noticed in the park.'

'I'll go next door right now, make sure Tandy Flowers can watch the kids.'

A half hour later Sailor, Lula, and Beany were on their way to New Orleans police headquarters in Beany's red 1988 Toyota Cressida station wagon. Sailor and Lula sat in the backseat, holding hands and not talking, while Beany drove. She took Bonnabel Boulevard to Metairie Road, turned left and followed it west into Orleans Parish until they hit the Interstate, which she seldom used, preferring to drive on surface streets; but today was different, they were in a hurry, so Beany braved the truck traffic and headed downtown on Highway 10.

'You don't have to come in, Sailor, you don't want to,' Lula said, after Beany had parked the wagon and they were walking across the street to the station. 'No need for you to be uncomfortable.'

'It's OK, Lula. These kinda cops ain't much compared to them old boys at Huntsville. In there you blink more'n twice a hour and the man figures that's one too many, he'll lay your head open quicker'n grain goes through a pigeon. I'll be fine, honey, thanks for thinkin' of it.'

Detective Fange gave Beany and Lula several large books of mug shots to look through. Sailor sat next to them at the table, thinking that he might recognize one or two men he'd known in North Carolina or Texas prisons. Fange was a short, stout, dark-haired man in his mid-forties. He had a deep triangular crease in the center of his forehead that twitched every few seconds, and he had a habit of smiling briefly after he spoke a sentence.

'You even think you seen one of these fellas in Audubon Park, you holler, right?' said Fange, punctuating this order by exposing his tobacco-stained teeth for a half-second.

The two women nodded.

'I'll be in my office, two doors down, you need me.'

After Fange had gone, Beany said, 'That triangle on his forehead? That's right where the third eye is.'

'Third eye?' said Lula. 'What are you talkin' about?'

'It's the mystical one allows a person to see into the soul. Read about it when I was pregnant with Madonna Kim.'

'Beany, I just ain't up for that strange shit right now. Let's go over these faces.'

Beany and Lula looked carefully at each photo, full-face and profile of every man and a few women, but recognized none of them. Sailor didn't see anyone he knew until they were halfway through the final book.

'I know him,' he said, pointing to a particularly ugly white man who looked a lot like former President of the United States Lyndon Baines Johnson. 'He bunked in Walls Unit at Huntsville, same as me. Afton Abercrombie, that's him. Everybody called him LBJ, 'cause of the resemblance. He hated bein' called that since he was convinced it was LBJ allowed the Mafia to assassinate John F. Kennedy in Texas. Claimed Johnson was in cahoots with the Dallas organized crime people who done it. Abercrombie's kind of a nut about the subject, reads all the books come out concernin' the case. Says Crazy Eyes Santos had a lot to do with it, too.'

'What was he in for?' Beany asked, pointing to Abercrombie's picture.

'Multiple rape and attempted murder, I believe. Liked to screw old ladies, *real* old ladies, like in their eighties. He'd get jobs as a janitor or nurse's aide in nursin' homes and attack old women couldn't defend theirselves. Said most of 'em didn't complain, half of 'em bein' senile and not knowin' what was goin' on, and the other half thankful for the attention. What done Abercrombie in was rapin' a dyin' woman hooked up to some breathin' device. Tubes come loose durin' the assault that set off a signal and the nurses caught him in the act.'

'One real sick puppy,' said Beany.

'No doubt about it,' Sailor said. 'Abercrombie jacked off a dozen times a day, dreamin' about old ladies. Good poker player, though.'

After they'd finished looking through the books, Beany and Lula stopped into Detective Fange's office. He looked up from his desk and the triangle on his forehead twitched.

'No luck, hey, ladies?' he said.

Lula shook her head no.

'What now?' she asked.

'We got bulletins out about the boy, and officers showin' copies of the photo of him you give us. Any information turns up, I'll let you know.'

'We're gonna keep searchin' ourselves,' said Sailor.

'Expect you would,' said Fange. 'Let's hope Pace just walks in the door tonight askin' what's for supper. Happens sometimes.'

Detective Fange gave a quick smile and returned his attention to the papers on his desk. Sailor took Lula and Beany by the arm and led them to the elevator.

Perdita Durango was sitting in Poppy Papavero's blue BMW in front of the building when Sailor and the two women came out. She was waiting for Poppy, who had told her he had to drop into the police station for a minute in order to renew his hunting license. Poppy had laughed after he said this, and told her to leave the motor running. Perdita dipped her head as soon as she spotted Sailor, hoping he wouldn't look in her direction. He guided his female companions across the street without turning toward Perdita, and she relaxed as she watched him climb into the backseat of a red station wagon and drive away. She wanted to follow Sailor and find out where he was staying. He was the only person alive who could link her to the robbery attempt more than ten years before in Texas. Perdita thought about this while she waited for Poppy. There was only one thing to do, she decided, and that was to kill Sailor.

'Thanks for waiting, sugar,' said Poppy, as he got into the car. 'Eddie Fange's one serious coonass, but he's dependable as trouble. He sure is upset about this kidnapping case, though, I can tell.'

Poppy steered the BMW into traffic.

'What case is that?'

'A ten-year-old boy was kidnapped out of Audubon Park. Here, Eddie gave me a photograph.'

Poppy took the picture out of the left breast pocket of his jacket and handed it to Perdita.

'Boy's name and address are on the back,' he said. 'Some Short Eyes got him, I bet. Those are the scum of the planet. They ought to be shot on the spot and their bodies fed to the gators.'

Perdita read the name, Pace Roscoe Ripley, and the address, 833 Charity Street, Metairie, Louisiana. She memorized the address and handed the photo back to Poppy.

'Yes,' she said, 'that's terrible.'

The Cuban Emerald

'You partial at all to hummin'birds?' asked Elmer.

'What you mean, "partial"?' said Pace.

Elmer Désespéré sat in the cane chair twirling his engineer's cap on the toes of his city-dirt-blackened right foot.

'Mean, do you like 'em.'

Pace rested on his elbows, dangling his legs over the edge of the narrow bed.

'Ain't seen many, but I suppose. They just birds.'

Elmer bared his mossy teeth. 'One time Alma Ann and me spotted a Cuban Emerald,' he said, and shifted the cap to his equally soiled left foot. 'Alma Ann had her a bird book said that kinda hummin'bird don't naturally get no further north'n South Florida. But we seen it hoverin' over a red lily at Solange Creek. Alma Ann said it musta been brought up by someone to Louisiana 'cause it was too far for it to've strayed.'

'What color was it?'

'Green, mostly, like a emerald, and gold.'

'You ever seen a emerald?'

'No, but they's green, I guess, which is why the bird's called that.'

'What's Cuban about it?'

Elmer frowned and let the hat fall off his foot.

'This'n's special, Alma Ann said. Ain't no other bird like it over the world.'

'My mama and me had us a bird, but it died.'

Elmer's eyes opened wide. 'What kind?'

'Parakeet. It was blue with a white patch on the head. His name was Pablo.'

'How'd he die?'

Pace shrugged. 'We just found him one mornin' lyin' on his side on the floor of his cage. I took him out and looked in his mouth.'

61

'Why'd you do that?'

'What the doctor always does to me when I'm sick, so I done it to Pablo.'

'See anythin'?'

'Not real much. Pulled out his tongue with my mama's eyebrow tweezer. It was pink.'

'You bury him?'

'Uh-uh. Mama wrapped Pablo in a ripped-up dishtowel and put him in the freezer.'

'Why'd she do that?'

'We was gonna burn him later, but we forgot. Mama says throwin' a body on a fire's the only way to purify it and set free the soul. The kind of Indians they got in India do it, Mama says. But we just forgot Pablo was in the freezer till a bunch of time later when Mama was cleanin' it out and found the dishtowel all iced up. She run hot water over it and unrolled it and there was Pablo, blue as always.'

'What'd she do?'

'Stuffed him down the disposal and ground him up.'

Elmer whistled through his green teeth. 'Don't guess that done heck for his soul.'

Pace lay back on the bed and crossed his arms over his chest.

'I reckon his soul had pretty well froze solid by then,' he said.

'If I ever had a Cuban Emerald died on me, I wouldn't burn it, or stuff it in no disposal, neither. I'd eat it.'

Pace closed his eyes. 'The beak, too? Bird beaks is awful sharp.'

'Yes, I believe I would. I'd swallow it beak and all, so my insides'd glow emerald green.'

'Don't know how I ever coulda thought you was crazy, Elmer. I apologize.'

Elmer nodded. ''Preciate it.'

Keeping the Faith

Santos looked in the mirror over the washbasin in the restroom of his office on the top floor of the Bayou Enterprises building on Airline Highway in Kenner and adjusted his hairpiece. He used a wet tissue to scrub off the excess mucilage that had trickled down and dried on his forehead. Santos took off his yellow-framed dark glasses and stared at himself. He hated the nickname Crazy Eyes, but he had to agree with the old Don, Pietro Pericolo, who had given it to him when he was the Don's driver, that his eyes were indeed very strange. The red pupils spun and danced inside the green irises, which were surrounded by yellow sparks. Santos put his sunglasses back on. The old Don had been dead for many years now, and Marcello still missed him. Don Pericolo had kept his word and made certain that Santos was in position to take over the organization when the stomach cancer claimed him. On his deathbed, the old Don had motioned for Santos to come closer, and whispered in his ear, '*Che cosa viene appresso*, Marcello?' Then Don Pericolo had died, his last taste of life softly settling on Santos's face.

'What comes next, Don Pericolo?' Santos said to his own reflection.

He went into his office and sat down behind the gigantic oak desk that had been built in Palermo more than one hundred years before for Lupo Sanguefreddo, Don Pericolo's predecessor. Santos pressed a button that was on the underside of the right top drawer and the door to an outer room opened, admitting Carmine Papavero.

'Marcello, you look *meraviglioso!*' said Carmine.

'Sit,' Santos said, motioning with his right hand to a chair on the opposite side of the desk. 'There is a serious matter that I would appreciate your trying to do something about. A young boy has been kidnapped here in New Orleans, the grandson of an old friend of mine. I want you to find him, if possible.'

'Marcello, I know of this situation already. I have a photograph of the boy.'

Carmine took the photo out of his pocket and put it on Santos's desk.

'Is this the grandson of your friend?' he asked.

'It is. How did you get this?'

'From Eddie Fange, the detective who takes care of the Orleans Parish payoffs. It's his case.'

'Very good, Carmine. My friend is very worried about the boy, as you can imagine.'

'Of course, Marcello. It's a horrible thing, the theft of a child.'

'*Tutto ciò mi preoccupa*. The way the world is today worries me. With all these *pazzi* running loose, nobody is safe, not even a small boy.'

Carmine nodded. 'I have a description of the kidnapper. He was *scalzo*, barefoot. An insane person.'

Santos sighed deeply. 'I must call the child's grandmother now and comfort her. Go and find out what you can.'

Carmine stood, picked up the photo and replaced it in his coat pocket.

'Please convey to her my sympathies,' he said, and left the room.

Santos nodded and began dialing Marietta's number. She answered before the second ring had ended.

'Lula?' Marietta shouted.

'It is I, Marietta, Marcello.'

'Oh, Marcello, I'm frantic. There ain't been no word yet.'

'I just wanted to inform you that my people are doing everything they can.'

'Dal and Johnnie are helpin' me get through this. They're lambs.'

'Marietta, you know I think a great deal of you. Had it not been for my respect for Clyde, things could have been different.'

'Let's not talk about that kind of thing now. I'm way too upset to consider mighta-beens. I appreciate your efforts on behalf of my family. I'm in your debt.'

'No, Marietta, where we are concerned there is no debt, only friendship.'

'Marcello, if some maniacal creature's harmed my beautiful grandboy I'll just die!'

'It is at such moments that my old friend Don Pericolo would say, *non bisogna abbattersi così facilmente*. One should not get discouraged so easily. You must remain strong.'

'Yes, Marcello, you're right, of course.'

'We will speak soon, Marietta. Goodbye.'

'Bye.'

Marietta hung up and wiped the tears from her eyes with a vermilion silk handkerchief that had belonged to her grandmother, Eudora Pace.

'The gangster got a line on the case yet?' Johnnie asked.

Marietta stared hard at him, then said, 'Who ain't a gangster these days, Johnnie Farragut? The whole world's nothin' but a big racket, with one murderin', thievin' bunch tryin' to horn in on another. Least Santos is on our side, and I'm glad we got him.'

'Amen,' said Dalceda. 'Anybody ready for another cocktail?'

Night in the City

'My daddy murdered a man once,' Pace said. 'I heard my grandmama talkin' about it with her friend Johnnie, who's a private investigator and carries a gun. Mama thinks I don't know Sailor really killed Bob Ray Lemon, but I do. He'll get you, too, soon as he finds out what's happened and where I am, which'll be any minute. Him or Crazy Eyes Santos, Grandmama's other man friend, who's a big gangster and kills people all the time. Won't bother him a bit to twist your puny chicken head clean off the neck. You'd best just let me go and run for it, or you'll be fish scum, you'll see.'

Elmer Désespéré was beginning to realize his mistake. He had grabbed an unworthy boy, someone not suited to be his perfect friend, and he was in a fix over what to do about it.

'I done murdered two men,' said Elmer, who was sitting in the cane armchair across from where Pace sat on the floor next to the bed. Elmer had tied Pace's hands together behind his back after the boy had attempted to put out Elmer's eyes with the fork part of the Swiss Army knife. 'And prob'ly I'll have to murder a mess more before I'm through, includin' you, it looks like.'

'Let me go and you won't have to kill me. I won't tell anyone where you live. You don't let me go, they'll find us and kill you sure. Least right now you got a choice.'

Elmer stood up. 'I got to go out, get some fresh water. I'll figure out later what I'm gonna do, when I talk to Alma Ann. She'll guide my hand.'

Elmer took hold of Pace, dragged him into the empty closet and shut the door.

'I wouldn't be surprised she instructs me to twist *your* puny chicken head,' Elmer shouted. 'Clean off the neck!'

He went out into the street and headed for the Circle K convenience store. This child was a puzzlement, Elmer thought.

He would have to be more careful of who he snatched next. Follow him for a while, maybe, see if he acted right. This one weren't no good at all and likely never would be. Can't trust a pretty face, ain't *that* the truth!

Elmer had been thinking so hard about Pace that he did not realize he'd turned the wrong way off Claiborne. Somehow he had wandered on to a street called St Claude and he was lost. It was very late at night and Elmer missed Alma Ann. He wished she were here and he was tucked into bed with her reading to him. He saw some men gathered up ahead at the corner and he walked toward them. Before Elmer had gone halfway, he noticed that three men were walking toward him, so he stopped where he was and waited, figuring if the direction he needed to go in was behind him then he wouldn't need to cover the same ground. The three men, all of whom were black and no older, perhaps even younger, than Elmer, surrounded and stared at him.

'Come you ain't got no shoes on?' asked one.

'Don't make no connection otherwise,' said Elmer.

'Feet's black as us,' said another of the men.

'You heard of the Jungle Lovers?' the third man asked.

Elmer shook his head no.

'We them,' said the first man. 'And this our street.'

'You a farm boy?' asked the second.

Elmer nodded. 'From by Mamou,' he said. 'Road forks close the sign say, "If It Swim I Got It."'

'Where that?'

'Evangeline Parish.'

The three men, each of whom was wearing at least one gold rope around his neck, began moving around Elmer, circling him, glancing at one another. Elmer stood absolutely still, unsure of what to do.

'You got any money, hog caller?' said one of the men.

'No,' said Elmer.

The man behind Elmer pulled out a Buck knife with a six-inch blade, reached his right arm around Elmer and slit his throat completely across, making certain the cut was deep enough to sever the jugular. Elmer dropped to his knees and stuck all four fingers of his left hand into the wound. He sat there, resting back on his heels, blood cascading down the front of his overalls and on the sidewalk, for what seemed to him like a very long time.

Elmer looked up into the dark eyes of one of the men and tried to speak. He was asking the man to tell Alma Ann he was sorry to have failed her, but the man did not try to listen. Instead, he took out a small handgun, stuck its snub nose all the way into Elmer's mouth and pulled the trigger.

The Edge of Life

'Don't worry about it, Sailor,' said Bob Lee, 'I can afford to take the day off. This ain't no small matter, after all, and the police can't be expected to exercise a whole lot of manpower over one more stole child.'

'Want you to know I 'preciate it, Bob Lee,' Sailor said, 'extra much. What you and Beany's doin' for me and Lula's special. I mean, you got your own two kids and a new business to worry about. I ain't about to forget it.'

Sailor and Bob Lee were preparing to hit the streets together and search for Pace.

'Just let me kiss Beany goodbye and we can get movin'.'

Sailor waited for Bob Lee in the living room. Lula was still asleep, having taken a medication Beany's doctor had prescribed to help her relax. How he, Sailor, could have been so selfish, so stupid, so cowardly, astounded him. Had he acted like a man six months ago, Sailor thought, this wouldn't have happened. It had been his opportunity, after wasting the dime, to take care of Pace and try to make things up to Lula. They were his responsibility and he'd failed them and himself as well. Sailor prayed now for another chance. Ten years in the joint had proven to him that it wasn't every man who had a choice in life. The fact that he'd blown it twice before with Lula ate at Sailor. It was his fault, he'd decided, that their precious son was in this unholy circumstance. If anything terrible happened to Pace, Sailor knew he would be unable to go on living.

In Huntsville, Sailor had come in contact with the most hard-luck boys he ever could have imagined. Most of them were murderers or had been involved, as he'd been, in the commission of crimes during which one or more persons had died. One fellow, Spook Strickland, a tough nut from Anniston, Alabama, where he'd been a Grand Dragon or Imperial Wizard

69

in the Ku Klux Klan, had told Sailor his belief that God's message was that nobody *deserved* to live. The gospel according to Spook Strickland maintained that staying alive was an option not available to everyone, and that's why people like him existed, to destroy the least worthy among them. Sailor had asked him why God had created billions of people in the first place, and why He continued to produce more, a question that gave Spook Strickland a good, long laugh. After he'd settled down, Spook had told Sailor that most human beings were provided for target practice. Those people were slaves, Spook said, disposable and without redeeming value. Organizations such as the Klan and the Great Whites, the prison gang Spook led at Huntsville, were placed on earth as reminders of the true nature of homo sapiens, and to maintain a necessary order. Each member of the Great Whites had on the underside of their upper right arm a tattoo of a shark with the words ORDER AT THE BORDER OF HELL etched around it. Spook Strickland had tried to get Sailor to join but Sailor resisted, even though things might have gone easier for him while he was inside, since Spook's gang controlled many of the more worthwhile and profitable functions in the prison, including drugs, cigarettes, and the machine shop. Sailor had hung out with the Great Whites, though, more for protection from the Mexican Mafia and Uhuru Black Nation than out of subscription to their ideas. He had needed to stay alive, that's all. He had, and now it was up to him to act right.

'Ready to roll, fella,' said Bob Lee, putting a hand on Sailor's right shoulder. 'Beany'll make sure Lula's all right while we're gone. Told her we'd call in a couple of hours or so.'

Perdita Durango had parked a few houses away behind a silver Plymouth Voyager. She watched Sailor get into the passenger side of Bob Lee's black and tan Lincoln Town Car, and started the engine of Poppy's BMW as Bob Lee backed down the driveway into the street. She followed the Lincoln on to Veterans Memorial Boulevard and headed east two cars behind, turning right on Pontchartrain, then going east again on 610. Bob Lee got off the Interstate at Gentilly Boulevard and backtracked to St Bernard Avenue, where he pulled into a shopping center and parked in front of a storefront office that had the words GATOR GONE, INC. stenciled on the tinted window glass. Perdita brought the BMW over near the shopping center entrance and kept the engine idling.

Bob Lee got out of the Town Car and went into the office of Gator Gone, Inc. Sailor stayed in the car.

Perdita picked up the Smith & Wesson .357 Magnum from the floor between her feet, shifted the BMW out of neutral into first gear and glided toward the black and tan Lincoln. She pulled into the parking space to the right of Bob Lee's car, shifted the BMW into reverse, keeping the clutch and brake depressed, and lowered her window. Sailor was staring straight ahead as Perdita raised the gun with both hands and aimed at his right ear. The instant she pulled the trigger Sailor leaned forward to pull his left pantsleg over his boot. The bullet went behind Sailor's head through the Lincoln's windows into the roof of a pink Acura parked on the other side, ricocheted off the Acura and to the right into the yellow wood facing of the building. Sailor hit the deck and kept his head covered with his arms while Perdita peeled the BMW backward out of the parking space, spun a one-eighty, braked hard, shifted furiously into first and floored the gem of Bavarian engineering, fishtailing her way out of the shopping center. Sailor opened his door, rolled on the pavement and looked up in time to see its blue butt with the words PAPA UNO on the license plate streak away.

Bob Lee came running out of Gator Gone, Inc., saw Sailor stretched out on the ground, and yelled, 'Ripley! You all right?'

Sailor rolled over on his back, saw the frightened look in Bob Lee Boyle's big brown eyes, and closed his own.

'I'm fine, Bob Lee,' he said, and grinned, feeling the sun on his face. 'Just never know what part of your life's liable to open up again at any particular time.'

Sailor opened his eyes and saw the crowd of people gathering around him. He scrambled to his feet and brushed himself off.

'Come on, Bob Lee,' he said, 'let's go find my boy.'

Out of this World

Guadalupe DelParaiso had lived at the same address all of her life, which was seven months more than eighty-six years. She had never married, and had outlived each of her sixteen siblings – nine brothers, seven sisters – as well as many of her nephews and nieces, and even several of their children. Guadalupe lived alone in the downstairs portion of the house her father, Nuncio DelParaiso, and his brother, Negruzco, had built on Claiborne Avenue across the street from Our Lady of the Holy Phantoms church in New Orleans. The neighborhood had undergone numerous vicissitudes since Nuncio and Negruzco had settled there. At one time the area had been home to some of the Crescent City's most prominent citizens, but now Our Lady of the Holy Phantoms, where the DelParaiso family had worshiped for forty years, and where Guadalupe and her sisters and brothers had attended school, was closed down, and the street was littered with transient hotels, beer and shot bars, pool halls, and the drunks, junkies and whores who populated and patronized these establishments.

Guadalupe rented the upstairs rooms in her house by the week. She made sure to get the money in advance and kept a chart on the wall in her kitchen listing the dates the rent was due for each room. Guadalupe would rent to singles only, and not to women or blacks under the age of fifty. She had not left the house in four years, depending on her bachelor nephew, Fortunato Rivera, her sister Romana's youngest son, who was now fifty-two years old, to bring her groceries and other supplies twice a week. She paid Fortunato for what he brought her on Wednesdays and Sundays, and gave him a shopping list for the next delivery. Guadalupe had not been sick since the scarlet fever epidemic of 1906. The doctor who attended her at that time told her mother, Blanca, and Nuncio, that Guadalupe's heart had been severely damaged by the fever and that he did not expect her to live beyond thirty. It was

Guadalupe's oldest sister, Parsimonia, however, who succumbed to a weak heart at the age of twenty-nine. As the years passed, Guadalupe only became stronger in both body and mind.

Guadalupe was making up her list for Fortunato, who would be coming the next day, Wednesday, when she heard a pounding noise, like the stamping of feet, coming from the room above the kitchen. She had rented the room almost a week before to a soft-spoken, polite but bedraggled-looking young man whom, she believed, worked for the railroad. The young man had seen the ROOM FOR RENT sign in the front window and had taken what had once been her brothers Rubio, Martin, and Danilo's room immediately. He paid Guadalupe a month's advance because, he told her, it looked like the kind of a place his mama, Alma Ann, would have been pleased to occupy. Guadalupe had not seen the young man since the day he'd rented it.

This pounding disturbed Guadalupe; she could not concentrate on her grocery list. She went into the pantry, picked up her broom, brought it back with her to the kitchen and bumped the end of the handle several times against the ceiling.

'You stop!' she shouted. 'No noise in Nuncio's house or you get out!'

The pounding did not stop, so Guadalupe put down the broom, left her part of the house and walked slowly up the stairs. She stopped at the door to the young railroad worker's room and listened. She could not hear the pounding as distinctly from the hallway as she could in her kitchen, but she heard it and knocked as hard as she could on the door with her left fist.

'You stop! You stop or leave Nuncio and Blanca's house!'

The pounding continued and Guadalupe removed her keychain from the right front pocket of her faded rose-colored chenille robe and unlocked the door. The single overhead sixty-watt bulb was burning, but there was nobody in the room. The noise was coming from the closet, so she opened it. A body hurtled past Guadalupe so fast she did not see who or what it was, and by the time she turned around, it was gone. Guadalupe had been tremendously startled; suddenly she felt faint, and staggered to the cane armchair. She sat down and attempted to calm herself, but she was frightened, thinking that the shadow that had rushed out of the room had been the ghost of her severely disturbed brother Morboso, the one who had hanged himself in that closet. It had been Parsimonia who discovered Morboso swinging there, and it was this incident, Nuncio and Blanca believed, that had damaged Parsimonia's heart and led to her premature death. The ghost of Morboso DelParaiso was loose, Guadalupe thought. Perhaps he had driven away the young railroad man, or even murdered him as he had the pretty young nun, Sister Panacea, whose body Nuncio and Negruzco and Father Vito had secretly buried after midnight on October 21, 1928, in the garden of Our Lady of the Phantoms. Guadalupe rested and remembered, seeing again what she could not prevent herself from seeing.

Pace ran down the stairs and managed to turn the big gold knob on the front door by holding it between the bottom of his chin and his neck. He ran a block down the street before he stopped in front of an old Indian-looking guy who was leaning against the side of a building sipping from a short dog in a brown paper bag.

'Untie me, mister!' Pace shouted at him. 'Get my hands loose, please!'

The Indian's eyes were blurry and he seemed confused.

'A crazy man kidnapped me and tied me up!' Pace yelled. 'I just ran away! Help me out, willya?'

The Indian held out his half-pint of wine, as if he didn't know what to do with it if he assisted Pace.

'Put your bottle down on the ground and undo this here knot,' said Pace, turning around and showing the Indian his hands.

The old guy bent over and carefully deposited his sack on the sidewalk, then straightened up and tugged on Pace's hands until they were freed.

'Thanks a lot, mister,' said Pace, tossing away the strip of bedsheet Elmer had used to bind him. He reached down and picked up the Indian's short dog and handed it to him. 'Don't know if God loves ya,' Pace shouted, 'but I do!'

Pace ran along Claiborne until he saw a police car parked at the curb. He went over to the car and stuck his head in the open window on the passenger side.

'Evenin', officer,' Pace said to the policeman sitting behind the steering wheel. 'I'm Pace Roscoe Ripley, the boy got kidnapped in the park the other day? Are you lookin' for me?'

The Overcoat

Federal Bureau of Investigation agents Sandy Sandusky and Morton Martin stopped into the Lakeshore Tap, a tavern on Lincoln Avenue about a mile from Wrigley Field. In another hour or so, when the Cubs game ended, the place would be packed; at the moment, the two agents were the only customers. They sat on adjoining stools, ordered drafts of Old Style, and drained half of their beers before Sandusky said, 'Is there a field office in North Dakota?'

'Where in North Dakota?' asked Martin.

'Anywhere.'

'Why do you ask?'

'Because that's where we're going to be transferred to unless we can nail whoever ordered the hit on Mona Costatroppo, that's why.'

Both men took another swig of beer.

'We know it was Santos,' Martin said.

'The man hasn't had a rap pinned on him once. Never done time, Morty, never had a speeding ticket.'

'If we can locate the shooter, we got a chance.'

'He's in the sports book at Caesar's Palace right now, a hooker on each arm, betting trifectas at Santa Anita with the fee.'

'So what do we do, Sandy?'

'Buy bigger overcoats.'

Sandusky swallowed the last of his draft and climbed down from his stool.

'Order me one more, Morty. I'll call the office.'

Sandusky came back five minutes later, a big grin on his ruddy face, and slapped Morton Martin on the back.

'Give us a couple shots of Chivas,' Sandusky said to the bartender.

'What's up?' asked Martin. 'Santos turn himself in?'

'Not quite, but Detroit picked up the hammer.'

'No kiddin'. I thought you told me he was in Vegas juggling bimbos.'

'Where I'd be.'

The bartender brought two Scotches and Sandusky slapped down a ten.

'Keep the change,' he said. 'Looks like I won't need a new overcoat, after all.'

Sandusky handed a glass to Morton Martin, tapped it with his own, and said, 'To Tyrone Hardaway, aka Master Slick, resident of Chandler Heights, Detroit, Michigan, product of the Detroit public school system, who just couldn't keep his mouth shut or the blood money in his pocket for more than twenty-five minutes.'

Sandusky and Martin knocked down the Chivas.

'Apparently, this Hardaway was letting all of his homeboys know what a big man he was, working for the guineas. He was buying gold chains, leather jackets and primo drugs for everyone in the neighborhood while bragging about the fresh job he'd done in Chicago for the famous Mr Crazy Eyes. Somebody snitched on him, of course, and the Bureau brought him in no more than an hour ago. They say he told them that Santos's people forced him to whack the broad; otherwise, Tyrone said, the organization was going to move him off his turf and let another gang handle the crack trade.'

'I know J. Edgar Hoover always said there was no such thing as organized crime in this country, but I'd bet Tyrone is telling the truth.'

Sandusky laughed, and motioned to the bartender. After both men had refills, Sandusky held up his glass and admired its amber contents.

'To the truth!' he said.

'Yes, Mama, he's here with us now, and he's doin' fine.'

'Put the boy on the line, Lula.'

Lula handed the phone to Pace.

'Hi, Grandmama. Marietta, I mean. How you?'

'Pace, darlin', you call me Grandmama all you want. We been so worried! Your Auntie Dal and Uncle Johnnie been with me the whole time, waitin' for news. Your mama says you ain't got a hair out of place. Tell me what happened.'

'I escaped, is all. The man left me tied up in a closet and when someone opened the door I ran out of there fast as I could. Bo Jackson couldn'ta caught me. I was flyin'!'

'Who was this man? Did he harm you?'

'Crazy kid, not too much older'n me, really. Name was Elmer Désper-somethin'. He was searchin' for a friend, he told me. His mama died on their farm and after he didn't get along with his daddy and brother, so Elmer killed 'em. Least that's what Sailor said. Elmer's dead, too. Found him this mornin' with his head blowed off. He didn't really hurt me none, only tied up my hands when he put me in the closet. I got a wino to undo me after I escaped.'

'What a terrible time for you! Is Sailor intendin' to stay with y'all for a while?'

'I hope so, Grandmama. He's my daddy.'

'I'm just so pleased you're safe, sweetie pie. I'll see you real soon. Let me have your mama again. Love you.'

'Love you, Grandmama.'

Lula took the phone.

'Mama, I want you to know Sailor and I've decided to try to stay together. We got a lot of talkin' to do and things to work out, we know, but we both think it'd be best for us and Pace if we can be a fam'ly.'

'Lula, you know I only want what's best for you and my grandboy, so I hope you know what you're doin'. This ain't the proper moment for us to get into this, what with Pace just bein' found and all, but I got a strong opinion on the matter, as you could imagine.'

'Yes, Mama, I can. We're all gonna stay here with Beany and Bob Lee while Sailor and I figure out what to do. Bob Lee's offered Sail a job at the alligator repellent factory, and Beany'd like me to take care of Madonna Kim and Lance when she enrolls in the St John the Baptist College of Cosmetology in Arabi. There's plenty of room here, and if things work out between me'n Sailor, we'll find our own place.'

'Well, Lula, I've promised Dal I'd hold my tongue until we're all calmed down from the kidnappin', so I will.'

'Mama, it *is my* life.'

'Johnnie got some business to attend in NO next week and he's asked me to come with him. You can't believe what a rock Johnnie's been for me these last few days.'

'You oughta marry him, Mama, before you get too old to enjoy yourself.'

'Lula, hush. I expect we'll be stayin' at the Sonesta.'

'Separate rooms?'

''Course, separate rooms. Listen, Lula, I'm thinkin' I'll attend the Daughters meetin' this afternoon, now we got Pace safe, so I'll say bye. I'll let you know when Johnnie and I'll be in.'

'OK, Mama.'

'Keep a eye on my grandboy, now. Love you, Lula.'

'Love you.'

Marietta was hanging up when Dalceda Delahoussaye came in through the back door like a fireball.

'Marietta! I been dialin' you like mad!'

'I was talkin' to Lula, honey, and Pace. He ain't hurt and he sounds fine. Man who took him's dead.'

'Lula told us he was fine last night!' Dal shouted as she raced through the kitchen into the front room.

'Needed to hear his precious voice. Dal, what are you doin'?'

Dal had switched on Marietta's nineteen-inch Sony Trinitron and was flipping the dial.

'What I was callin' you about was Santos. What number's that all news channel?'

78

'Eleven, I believe. What about Santos?'

'He's been arrested! Look, here it is.'

'Arrested? What are you ravin' about?'

'Hush and listen!'

'In New Orleans this morning,' said the television news reader, 'federal agents took into custody reputed organized crime king Marcello Santos on charges of conspiracy to commit murder and murder of his alleged mistress, Mona Costatroppo, in Chicago last week.'

Videotape came onscreen showing Santos, his hands cuffed in front of him, being taken out of the backseat of a black car and led by FBI men up the steps of a courthouse. His sunglasses were askew, as was his toupee. He was obviously shouting something at the reporters following him, but it was impossible to hear what he said. The news reader continued:

'Santos, known as "Crazy Eyes" because of an unusual congenital ophthalmic condition that causes his eyes to frequently change color and appear unstable, became the head of the Pericolo crime family following the death of Pietro "The Sicilian Salmon" Pericolo in 1962. According to noted organized crime authority Hieronymous Bernstein, author of the best-selling book, *From Fear to Uncertainty: Behind the Breakdown of the Mafia*, the Pericolo family, which controls rackets across the southern United States, especially along the Gulf Coast, had its foundation in Palermo under the leadership of the legendary gangster Lupo Sanguefreddo, who was assassinated while having a shave in the barbershop of the Egyptian Gardens Hotel in Miami Beach in 1939. Sanguefreddo was fighting a deportation order at the time of his death.'

Marietta turned off the set.

'Don't know how they can get away with sayin' all that stuff about a man never been convicted of a thing!' she said. 'Do you believe he done it, Dal?'

'You mean had Mona Costatroppo killed?'

Marietta nodded.

'Hard to say. That kind of woman digs her own grave.'

The telephone rang and Dal picked it up.

'Hello, Johnnie. Yes, we just watched it on the news. She's all right. Yes, I will. She talked to Pace and he's fine. Yes, OK. Bye.'

Dal hung up and said, 'Johnnie wanted to know if you'd heard about Santos. Says he'll be back around six. I'm goin' to the Daughters at two. You comin'?'

'Might as well. They'll all want to know about Pace.'

'Don't be worryin' too much about your old buddy Marcello. He'll find a way out, like always.'

'Ain't it somethin', though, Dal, how it's just one weird thing happens after another?'

'Stay tuned,' said Dal, opening the front door. 'I got a powerful hunch there ain't never gonna be a end to it.'

A Well-Respected Man

'It's the terrible truth, Jimmie. They are transferring Santos to Chicago tomorrow for the arraignment. No bail is being allowed until after the charges are brought. And even then, who knows? Our attorney here in New Orleans, Irving Bocca, says there is no guarantee the Chicago judge will grant bail, no matter what amount. The government wants him bad, and they figure this is their best shot. I don't blame them, either, for thinking that. You know Marcello wanted to take care of this business himself, and I believe he acted too hastily, though I know nothing of the details.'

'Who is handling the case in Chicago for him?'

'Louis Trifoglio. The father, not the son.'

'Good. So, you know how to proceed?'

'*Conte pure su di me*. Jimmie, you can count on me.'

'You have my blessing, Carmine. Have you settled things yet with Tiger Johnny?'

'Yes. *Ci comprendiamo*. I am certain we understand each other.'

'You know, as far as I am concerned, *è un buon' a nulla*. He is good for nothing, like all of the Ragusas.'

'*C'è voluto del bello e del buono per convincerlo*. It took some convincing, but things will be all right.'

'If you say it, it must be so. *Ciao*, then, Carmine. You will keep me informed of Marcello's circumstances.'

'Of course, Jimmie. I will. I am grateful for your blessing. *Ciao*.'

Both Jimmie Hunchback, in New York, and Poppy Papavero, who was sitting in Santos's chair in the office of Bayou Enterprises, hung up. Poppy had been entrusted to run the organization in Marcello's absence, regardless of how long that might be, and he was pleased with the knowledge that Santos's associates had agreed without debate about his capability. He picked up the receiver again and dialed Perdita's number.

'Yes?'

'Perdita, my pet, things are good, under control. While Marcello is away, I am in charge. Now listen, I've been thinking about us, what we should do.'

'Do about what?'

'I think we should get married. What do you think of that idea?'

'Heard worse.'

Poppy laughed. 'Does that mean you say yes?'

'Sure, it's what you want.'

'It is. I know of a good house to buy, in a good place; a modest yet spacious house in a convenient location. It belongs now to Irving Bocca, who is willing to sell.'

'Where's this house?'

'Metairie. It will be perfect, Perdita. We won't know anybody there, and nobody will know us.'

Evidence

After an unusually late supper, Bob Lee excused himself and said he had to go back to the office to take care of the paperwork he'd ignored during the excitement of the last few days, and Beany took Lance and Madonna Kim upstairs to put them to bed, leaving Lula, Pace, and Sailor at the dining-room table. Lula had told Beany not to worry about the dirty dishes, she'd heated up more of the Community coffee Sailor had taken such a liking to, and poured them each another cup. During the time Lula had gone into the kitchen for the coffee and come back, Pace had put his head down on the table and dozed off. Lula sat next to Sailor and together they watched their son sleep.

'Well, peanut, I'd like to believe we got us a fightin' chance.'

'You'd best believe it, Sail. Look at that little boy breathin' there. If he ain't worth the effort won't never nothin' will be. Pace and us both just come through the worst scare we've ever had, and I guess to hell we've had a few in our short lives. It's one thing your gettin' yourself in deep shit with bad actors like Bob Ray Lemon in North Carolina and Bobby Peru in Texas, but now you got a fast-growin' son needs you. Reverend Willie Thursday back home in Bay St Clement says a boy without a father's a lost soul sailin' on a ghost ship through the sea of life.'

'It ain't my intention to let you and Pace down, and I won't be playin' no chump's game again, neither. Speakin' of the past, though, I seen Perdita Durango.'

'Here in New Orleans?'

Sailor nodded. 'Didn't figure on tellin' you this, but someone took a potshot at me in the shoppin' center by the Gator Gone office the other day. I'm pretty sure it was Perdita. I made Bob Lee swear he wouldn't say nothin' about it.'

'But, Sail, why would she want to shoot you?'

'Maybe she thinks I'm out to get her for runnin' out on me and

83

Peru. I'm the only one could ID her for the caper. I also spotted her on the street last week when I was leavin' Hattiesburg. She was with the same blue BMW squealed away from the shootin' in the shoppin' center.'

'Sweet Jesus, honey. What're we gonna do about this?'

'Don't panic, peanut. I'll just have to keep the eyes in the back of my head open. Prob'ly Perdita was aimin' to warn, not kill, makin' sure I knew it was her had the drop on me. I wouldn't say nothin' to the cops, anyway.'

'Sail, this unpredictable scary behavior don't almost improve my peace of mind.'

'I know it, but you're my baby Lula, and at least we're in it together again. You, me, and Pace, that is. Reverend Willie Thursday won't be preachin' no ghost ship sermon concernin' our son.'

Lula leaned over and kissed Sailor below his left ear.

'I love you, Sailor Ripley. I always figured we'd find our way.'

Sailor grinned and put his left arm around Lula, pulling her closer to him.

'Peanut, it was just inevitable.'

Sultans of Africa

'Piero Aldobrandi, unhelmeted, was wearing the black cuirass and the red commander's scarf and carrying the baton which linked him forever to this scene of carnage. But the figure, turning its back to the spectacle, relegated it to the mere status of landscape, and the face, strained by a secret vision, was the emblem of a supernatural detachment.'

Julien Gracq,
Le Rivage des Syrtes

'The best thing you can hope for in this life is that the rest of the world'll forget all about ya.'

Coot Veal shifted his shotgun from right to left and checked the fake Rolex on his right wrist. Buford Dufour had bought the watch for forty bucks in Bangkok when he was in the air force and sold it later to Coot for fifty.

'Half past four,' he said. ''Bout time to give it up, I'd say.'

Pace Ripley pulled a brown leather-coated flask from the left hip pocket of his army surplus field jacket, unscrewed and flipped open the top and took a swift swig of Black Bush that he'd filched from his daddy's bottle.

'Want 'ny?' he asked Coot, holding out the flask.

'Naw. I'll get mine shortly.'

Pace recapped the flask and put it back in his pocket.

'What you mean, Coot, hopin' you get forgot?'

Coot Veal, who was fifty-eight years old and had never been farther away from South Louisiana than Houston, Texas, to the west; Mobile, Alabama, to the east; and Monroe, Louisiana, to the north; who never had married or lived with a woman other than his mother, Culebra Suazo Veal, who had died when Coot was forty-nine; grinned at the fifteen-year-old boy, his friend Sailor Ripley's son, and then laughed.

'Mean it's not in a man's interest to let anyone interfere with or interrupt what's there for him to do.'

Coot pulled out a pistol from his hip holster and held it up.

'This here's a single-shot Thompson Contender loaded with .223 rounds. Not the biggest gun in the world, not the best, either, but it suits me. Read about a Seminole brought down a panther with one in the Everglades.'

Coot replaced the pistol in its holster.

'Zanzibar slavers over a century ago called the gun the Sultan of Africa. The world's still ruled by weapons, Pace. They're what separates the operators from the pretenders.'

Pace looked out over the marsh. He and Coot hadn't had a fair crack at a duck all day. Water had somehow leaked into his high rubber boots and soaked his woollen socks.

'OK, Coot,' he said, 'let's hit it. Gettin' skunked like this is insultin'.'

Backfire

Pace and Coot were riding in Coot's 1982 Dodge Ram pickup, headed home to New Orleans.

'You think I should go to a hooker, Coot? I mean, before I start in on regular girls. To have me some experience.'

Coot laughed and spit out his open window. Pace uncorked the flask and swallowed some Bush.

'Tough call, kid,' said Coot. 'Only time I used one I was about your age, maybe a year older. My daddy, Duke Veal, had fashioned me a shoulder holster to wear when I was playin' Chicago gangster. I had a old Chinese target pistol was missin' the firin' pin and stuck it in the shoulder holster. Put on my Sunday suit coat over it and marched down to Rampart Street. Wanted to take off the coat in front of a woman, impress her, so she'd think I was a real racket boy.

'I found me a big, tall red-headed gal and followed her upstairs to her crib. Price was three dollars, plus one or two for the room. Four or five dollars altogether. It was about all the dough I had at the time, but I was convinced this was my best idea to date and I was goin' through with it, hell or high water. Made damn sure she saw me take off my jacket, but she was a seasoned whore. Didn't bat an eye or laugh at me, neither one. Just laid there on the bed with no kind of look at all on her face. I left the holster on, only took off my pants. Did the deed, stood up, put my pants and coat back on and got out of there. Woman never said a word about the gun or nothin' after I give her my money. Haw! How's that for a backfire?'

'You ever tell your daddy 'bout it?'

'Duke? Hell, no. I had, he woulda kicked my sorry ass to Memphis. Duke Veal didn't take kindly to throwin' away good money on bad women.'

'Guess you're sayin' I oughta save mine.'

Coot nodded and turned on the headlights.

'Might be best,' he said. 'But I think I still got that old shoulder holster around someplace, you decide you need it.'

The Middle Years

'That you, Sail?' Lula shouted.

Sailor Ripley let the screen door slam shut behind him.

'No,' he said. 'It's Manuel Noriega.'

Lula came into the front room from the kitchen and saw Sailor slump down into the oversized, foam-filled purple chair that Beany and Bob Lee Boyle had given them last Christmas.

'Who'd you say? Barry Manilow?'

'No. Manuel Noriega, the deposed president of Panama.'

'Uh-uh, you ain't him. You got too good a complexion.'

Lula went over and kissed Sailor on the top of his head.

'Long day, huh, Sail?'

'You know it, peanut. Gator Gone's goin' great guns since the envir'mentalists got that new reptile protection law passed. Ever' fisherman in the state of Louisiana needs it now. You up to fetchin' me a cold Dixie?'

'*No hay problema, esposo*,' Lula said, heading toward the kitchen. 'Bet even Bob Lee never figured his gator repellent'd go this good.'

'Yep. That one ol' formula 'bout to make him a rich man. He's talkin' about settin' up a Gator Gone Foundation that'll make funds available to poor folks been victims of gator and croc attacks who're in need of ongoin' medical treatment.'

Lula returned with the beer and handed it to Sailor, who drank half of it right away.

'Thanks, honey,' he said. 'Sure build up a thirst overseein' that shippin' department. You know we're gonna build us our own warehouse in Gretna?'

Lula sat down on the zebra-striped hideaway.

'First I heard. Beany ain't said nothin' about it.'

'Yeah, the Algiers location can't hold us, and besides, makes more sense to own than rent.'

'Best thing we coulda done is settle here, Sail. New Orleans give us a whole bunch more opportunity than we ever coulda got back in North Carolina.'

Sailor took another swig of Dixie.

'Not the least of which is bein' a thousand miles away from your mama. We never woulda had a chance in Bay St Clement, peanut. Not with Marietta on my case.'

'She's calmed down now, darlin', since she seen how swell a daddy you been to Pace. Also your workin' so hard for Bob Lee and everythin'.'

'Wouldn'ta made it this far is all I know.'

The telephone on the front hall table rang. Lula got up and answered it.

'Ripley home. Hi, Beany. Uh huh, Sail too. God don't make men the way He used to, like Mama says. Madonna Kim got over her cold yet? Uh huh. Suppose I might could. Lemme ask God's almost-best piece of work.'

Lula tucked the receiver into her breast and turned toward Sailor.

'Honey? Beany'd like me to 'comp'ny her to Raquel Lou Dinkins's house for about a hour? See her brand new baby, Farrah Sue. You-all be able to survive without me that long?'

Sailor tipped the bottle and drained the last bit of beer, then nodded.

'Hell, yes. Me'n Pace'll get us a pizza or somethin'. Where is that boy, anyway?'

'Went huntin' this mornin' with Coot Veal, your buddy married his mama.'

Lula put the phone back to her mouth and left ear.

'Want me to drive?' she asked Beany. 'Uh huh. See ya in a minute.'

Lula hung up, picked up her purse and car keys from the table, went over to Sailor and kissed him again on the top of his head.

'Sweetheart, you know what?' she said.

'What's that?'

'You losin' some hair right about there.'

'Where?'

'Kinda in the middle toward the back.'

Sailor felt around on his head with the fingers of his right hand.

'I can't feel nothin' missin', Lula. Anyway, it can't be. Nobody in my fam'ly went bald. Not my daddy or his daddy or my mama's daddy.'

'None of 'em lived long enough to go bald, darlin'. Don't worry about it, just a small patch is all. I gotta go.'

Sailor jumped up and dropped the beer bottle on the floor.

'Goddammit, Lula! You just gonna run out and leave me after tellin' me I'm goin' bald?'

'Bye! Back soon!'

Sailor watched Lula go out the front door, heard her open and close the door of her new Toyota Cressida station wagon and start the engine. He went over to the hall mirror and leaned his head forward while attempting to look up into the glass, but he couldn't see the top of his head. He turned sideways, tilted his head toward the mirror and rolled his eyes all the way over, but that didn't work, either. The front door slammed and Pace came in.

'What you doin', Daddy?' he said. 'And where's Mama goin'? What're you all twisted around for?'

Sailor bent forward toward the mirror again, angling off slightly to the right.

'Take a look, son. Am I losin' my hair?'

Pace stared at Sailor, then shook his head slowly.

'More likely you're losin' your mind, Daddy. We gettin' a pizza for supper?'

Rattlers

The Rattler brothers, Smokey Joe and Lefty Grove, non-identical sixteen year old twins who were named by their daddy, Tyrus Raymond Rattler, after the two men his daddy, Pie Traynor Rattler, considered to have been the two best pitchers in major league history, tooled through Gulfport along Old Pass Christian Road in their Jimmy, trading swigs off a fifth of J.W. Dant. They were headed back to New Orleans from Biloxi, where they had gone to pay their respects to the memory of Jefferson Davis on his birthday. Smokey Joe and Lefty Grove had taken advantage of the school holiday to visit Beauvoir, the last home of the Confederate president. The federal holiday officially honored the birth of the Reverend Martin Luther King, Jr, who happened to have been born on the same day as Jeff Davis, a convenience appreciated by the Rattlers.

Their mother, Mary Full-of-Grace, had been institutionalized for the past six years in Miss Napoleon's Paradise for the Lord's Disturbed Daughters in Oktibbeha County, Mississippi, and the Rattler boys had considered visiting her but decided the drive was too far for the short time they had. Besides, Lefty Grove reasoned, she wouldn't recognize them for who they were. The last time they'd gone up with their daddy, six months before, she'd called them the apostles James and John, sons of Zebedee. Sometime during the twins' seventh year, Mary Full-of-Grace became convinced that she was in fact the Holy Virgin, mother of Jesus. She'd insisted that the people about her were not who they pretended to be and that every man she encountered desired to sleep with her. Tyrus Raymond took her to several doctors during the following two years, but her condition worsened, resulting finally in the diagnosis of a breakdown of a schizoid personality, with the recommendation that she be institutionalized as a hopeless case.

'What you think about Mama?' Lefty Grove asked Smokey Joe, who was behind the wheel.

'What you mean, what I think?' said Smokey Joe, reaching out his right hand for the bottle.

'Mean, you got a notion she ever gonna recover her mind?'

'Ain't 'xactly likely, how Daddy claims.'

Smokey Joe took a quick swallow of Dant and handed the fifth back to his brother.

'You finish it, Lef'. I be dam see the road.'

'Want me to drive? I feel good.'

'Feelin' good and drivin' good ain't the same. I'll handle her home.'

Lefty Grove put his red and yellow LA Gear high tops up on the dashboard and sucked on the bottle.

''Bout Ripley?' said Smokey Joe. 'Figure to trust him?'

'You mean on the deal, or just keep his mouth shut?'

'Either.'

'Need a third, Smoke, you know? Pace a good boy.'

'Mama's boy, you mean.'

'Least he got him a almost sane one.'

Smokey Joe snorted. 'What you mean, almost sane?'

'Like Daddy said when he come home after deliverin' Mama to Miss Napoleon's, "Ain't one of the Lord's daughters got a firm grip on life." He put a extra pint of fear in their blood, makes 'em more uneasy than men.'

'Daddy ain't naturally wrong.'

'Uh-uh,' said Lefty Grove. 'He's a Rattler, by God.'

In Bed with the Rattlers

Pace stared out the window of his room at the maple tree in the backyard. A blue shape flashed from branch to branch. Pace raised his right hand, formed his fingers into a gun and pointed the barrel at the flitting patch of blue.

'Bam!' he said, bouncing the tip of his index finger off the glass. 'You done bought the farm, Mister Jay.'

Pace lowered his hand and relaxed his fingers. He heard the downstairs telephone ring.

'Son!' Sailor shouted. 'Phone for you!'

'Comin', Daddy!'

Pace stood up, pushed his feet into a pair of thongs, walked downstairs and picked up the telephone receiver from the hall table.

'Pace Ripley speakin'.'

'Hey, boy, how you?' said Lefty Grove Rattler. 'What you been up to?'

'Oh, hi, Lefty. Nothin' special. Went duck huntin'.'

'Got you a few birds, huh?'

'Naw. Weren't a good day.'

'Been thinkin' 'bout what we discussed?'

'Haven't had time, tell the truth.'

'You still like the idea, though, don't ya? Better'n workin' at Popeye's.'

'Know that, Lefty Grove. I like it, sure. Mean I'm in, I suppose.'

'Knew we could count on you, Pace. Smokey Joe'll be glad to hear it.'

'Thought he don't like me.'

Lefty Grove laughed. 'He don't like nobody much, even me. Ain't to worry.'

'I guess I won't, then.'

'There you go. Meet us at Nestor's Sandwich City on Magazine, tomorrow evenin' at six.'

''Cross from Jim Russell's Record Shop?'

'Got it right and tight tonight, Pace Roscoe.'

'How you know my middle name's Roscoe?'

'Us Rattlers is straight from the gate to the plate, boy. Got to know who you're dealin' to, well as with. Abyssinia.'

Lefty Grove hung up and Pace stood in the hallway holding the phone to his left ear.

'You still on the line, son?' Sailor shouted from the kitchen.

Pace put the receiver back in the cradle.

'All through, Daddy.'

'Come on in, then,' said Sailor, 'have a piece of your mama's pecan pie. You been lookin' skinny.'

Pace massaged the back of his neck with his right hand. His head ached and he needed a drink.

'Back in a minute, Daddy,' he said, and went out the front door.

Pace sat down on the bottom step and rested his head and arms on his knees. The Rattlers were dangerous, sly boys, all right, and now he was about to climb into bed with them. At first Pace had thought they were joking when they proposed that he join them in knocking off the shakedown drop in the Quarter. Lefty Grove explained to him how each Thursday afternoon at three o'clock the weekly protection money from the businesses in the French Quarter was delivered to an idle caboose on a sidetrack near the Bienville Wharf. The collection remained there, cared for by two men, until approximately three forty-five, when a private armored car came to fetch it. Pace was both scared and excited by the idea of committing a crime. Something inside him wouldn't allow Pace to resist the promise of the thrill.

A cousin of the Rattlers, Junior Broussard, had worked for Carmine 'Poppy' Papavero, the Gulf Coast rackets boss, for four years until Junior's death a couple of months back. Junior's wife, Manuela, had shot him, Lefty Grove said, during an argument about Junior's friendship with a woman named Jaloux Marron, a hostess at one of Papavero's nightclubs. Until then Junior had been in charge of the protection haul. Lefty Grove and Smokey Joe had overheard their cousin talking about the setup with their daddy, Tyrus Raymond, and decided to snatch the cash if they could. Junior being out of the way made things easier, Lefty Grove explained, because they wouldn't have to kill their own cousin if they were forced to. Three guns were better than two, the Rattler brothers figured, and Lefty Grove had tapped Pace to complete the trio. The deal was set to go down next Thursday. Today was Sunday. Pace had four days to make up his mind.

'What you doin' sittin' out here?' Sailor asked from behind the screen door.

Pace lifted his head. 'Just thinkin', Daddy.' He stood up. 'Guess I'm a little tired. Me and Coot got out early this mornin'.'

'Well, come have some pie. Your mama'll be insulted we don't make a major dent in it.'

Down Time

'Daddy?'

'Yes, son?'

'You never have talked much about the time you done in prison.'

Sailor sliced into his wedge of pecan pie with one side of his fork, scooped up the piece, delivered it his mouth, chewed and swallowed. Pace sat across the table from him, holding a fork in his right hand, ignoring his own piece of pie.

'Not much to say, I guess, Pace. Jail time is down time far's I'm concerned. You don't come out any different thàn how you went in, 'cept older. That's if you come out at all.'

'How many times you been in, Daddy?'

'Twice.'

'Once for manslaughter and the other for armed robbery, that right?'

'Correct. Didn't mean for the first to happen. Just a bar fight with a slime-bucket named Bob Ray Lemon was botherin' your mama. I was nineteen years old and didn't know no better'n to knock the sorry son of a bitch cold. He didn't get up and they stuck me in a work camp up on the Pee Dee River for two years. I'd had me any kind of lawyer I wouldn'ta done a minute.'

'What happened the other time?'

Sailor put down his fork and shook his head.

'That was my mistake. Lucky I'm even here to talk about it. Your mama and me was tryin' to get to California from North Carolina, runnin' from your grandmama, Marietta, and her detective friend, Johnnie Farragut, who she'd signed on to track us down. Marietta didn't like the idea of her fine and only daughter takin' up with a ex-con such as myself. Lula met me at the gate the day I got my walkin' papers from Pee Dee, and we took off in her old white Bonneville convertible. Made it as far as West Texas when we about run out of funds. That's where I went over the line.'

Sailor stood up and walked over to the refrigerator, opened it, took out two bottles of Dixie beer, shut the door, came back over to the table, handed one to Pace and sat back down. He popped his open and took a long swallow.

'How you mean "over the line," Daddy?'

'Your mama was pregnant with you and we was stuck like bugs in a bottle, stranded in a podunk town called Big Tuna. Met a mean fella there named Bobby Peru. Lula said he was a black angel and told me I should stay away from him, but of course I didn't pay no attention and got hooked in on a plan to rob a feed store over to the county seat, Iraaq. We went ahead and done it and Bobby got his head blowed off. I got caught, of course, and Peru's girlfriend, a strange Tex-Mex gal named Perdita Durango, who was drivin' the getaway car, escaped. They sent me to Huntsville, where I put in ten years down to the hour.'

'Whatever happened to Perdita Durango?'

Sailor smiled, lifted the brown bottle to his lips and took a sip.

'Oh, she's around somewhere, I suspect. A Grade-A piece of work like her don't just fade away.'

'What was it like inside the walls, Daddy? How'd you get by?'

'Remindin' myself every minute of every day how stupid I was to end up there in the first place. Knew if I was still alive when I got out I'd do anything, any kind of straight job, not to go back again. And I thought about your mama and you, how you-all were gettin' along. Figured you both were better off without me, the way I'd been goin', but knew if I had the chance to change, I would. Until I could prove it to myself, though, it wouldn't do to make you and your mama suffer my ignorance. That's why it took a little while after I got sprung for us to get back together. I had me some serious readjustin' to do.'

'Bet there's some lost souls behind them bars.'

'The lostest, son. Now eat your pie and drink that beer and we'll get us some rest. Tomorrow's already feelin' like it's gonna be longer'n today.'

After Hours

Sailor flopped down into the Niagara, levered the footrest chest high, fingered the space command and flipped on the new RCA 24-inch he'd bought at Shongaloo's Entertainment Center right after his recent raise from Gator Gone. He dotted the i across cable country until it hit channel 62, when the sound of CCR's 'Bad Moon Risin'' stopped him. It was past one o'clock in the morning. Pace was asleep upstairs and Lula was at Beany's, baking cakes for the Church of Reason, Redemption and Resistance to God's Detractors fundraiser. Sailor ticked the volume up a couple of notches. Suddenly the music faded out and a man's face in close-up came on the screen. The man was about forty years old, he had blond, crew-cut hair, a big nose that looked like it had been sloppily puttied on, and a dark brown goatee.

'Howdy, folks!' said the man, his duckegg-blue eyes blazing out of the set like laser beams. 'I'm Sparky!'

The camera pulled back to reveal Sparky standing in front of an old-fashioned drugstore display case. Behind the counter and just to the side of Sparky's left shoulder was another man of the same approximate age but four inches taller. This man had thick, bushy black hair with a severe widow's peak and a discernibly penciled-in mustache under a long, sharply pointed nose.

'This asparagus-shaped fella behind me's my partner, Buddy,' Sparky said, and Buddy nodded. 'We'd like to welcome you-all to Sparky and Buddy's House of Santería, the store that has everything can make that special ceremony just right.'

The words SPARKY & BUDDY'S HOUSE OF SANTERIA 1617 EARL LONG CAUSEWAY WAGGAMAN, LOUISIANA flashed on the screen in giant red letters superimposed over the two men. The letters stopped flashing and Sailor sat up and took a closer look. Blood root suspended from the ceiling and dozens of jars filled with herbs, votive candles in a variety of colors, and various unidentifiable objects lined the rows of shelves behind Sparky and Buddy. Sparky raised his arms like Richard Nixon used to, the fingers of each hand formed in a V.

'We've got the needs for the deeds, ladies and gentlemen. We've got the voodoo for you! Oh, yes! We've got the voodoo, hoodoo, Bonpo tonic, Druid fluid, Satan-ratin', Rosicrucian solution, Upper Nile stylin', Lower Nile bile'n Amon-Ra hexes, Tao of all sexes, White Goddess juice'll kick Kundalini loose, the Chung-Wa potion'n ev'ry santería notion!'

Sparky lowered his arms, walked forward past the camera eye, then returned carrying two twisting snakes in each hand.

'Get a load of the size of these rattles, Pentecostals!' he shouted, raising his right arm, the one draped with a pair of diamondbacks. 'And ladies, check out these elegant coachwhips!' Sparky raised his left arm to show them off. 'Hey, Buddy! Tell the good folks what else we got!'

Sparky walked off-camera again and Buddy leaned forward over the counter, pointing to the floor with his right hand.

'Take a good look here, people,' he said, and the camera eye dipped down, closing in on a one-hundred-ten-pound brindled pit bull stretched out on the floor, his head resting between his front paws, a seeing-eye harness strapped to his barrel chest. Next to his enormous head was a black water bowl with the name ELVIS stenciled on it in raised white letters. 'We got a good selection of man's best friends, too.'

Sparky's legs came back into view and the camera panned back up.

'Mullahs, mullahs, mullahs!' Sparky intoned. 'You got trouble with the Christian Militia? Come on down! And hey, troops! Them mullahs makin' you a cardiac case? Those Ayatollah rollers got you grittin' your bicuspids? You-all come on down, too! We are a hundred and five per cent bona fide non-sectarian here at Sparky and Buddy's!'

Again the giant red letters spelling out SPARKY & BUDDY'S HOUSE OF SANTERIA 1617 EARL LONG CAUSEWAY WAGGAMAN, LOUISIANA flashed on the screen.

'Right, Buddy?' Sparky said, and the flashing letters blinked off.

'Affirmative, Sparky!'

'And, Buddy, we got a special I ain't even told my mama about!

106

This week only we discountin' mojos. Mojos for luck, love, recedin' hairlines, bald spots, money honey and – my own favorite, works like a charm – irregularity. This one's guaranteed to get you goin' and flowin'!'

Sailor watched as from behind the counter Buddy lifted up two wine glasses filled to the brim with amber liquid. He handed one to Sparky and together they raised the glasses high.

'Well, Buddy, as our old pal Manuel used to say in Tampa many years ago, *salud* and happy days! This is the four-hundred-sixty-sixth appearance we've made for Sparky and Buddy's House of Santería. Remember, we're at 1617 Earl Long Causeway, in the community of Waggaman, servicin' all of south Louisiana. Y'all come on down!'

'Bad Moon Risin'' started up again and the giant red letters reappeared for several seconds before the station segued into the video of L.L. Cool J's 'Big Ole Butt.' Sailor pressed the OFF button on his space command. He sat still for a minute, then lifted his left arm and with his fingers explored the crown area of his head where Lula had told him his hair was thinning. He got up and went over to the hall table, picked up the pencil and pad next to the telephone and wrote down Sparky and Buddy's address.

'They do it different now, Lula. Ain't hardly no cuttin' to speak of. Drop a line in through the navel and reel the creature out. Stick a Band-Aid on it. Make two tiny incisions on the sides, is all.'

'But, Mama, you gotta stay in the hospital least one night. The doctor told you that.'

'Don't know why. I might could take off right out of there, I feel good enough.'

'Doctor says if there's a stone they gonna have to cut it out the regular way. That happens, you'll be in there three, four days.'

'There ain't no stone and I ain't lettin' 'em run no tubes through me.'

'You'll let 'em do what's necessary, Mama. This is your gall bladder we're discussin' now, not no perm job. I'll be into Charlotte tomorrow at noon, so I'll see you about one-thirty, all goes well. Dal's pickin' me up.'

'You already talked to her?'

'Of course, Mama. We got it worked out how to take care of you.'

'You're still the one needs takin' care of, Lula. How's my grandboy doin', anyway?'

'Pace is just fine, and so's Sailor. He got him a raise a couple weeks back. Bob Lee's Gator Gone repellent's sellin' better'n ever.'

'Sailor throw the new money away on a TV or a truck?'

'Oh, Mama, you ain't never gonna give him a chance to redeem himself, are you?'

'Guess you're still attendin' that crackpot church, else you wouldn't be usin' that word.'

'The Church of Reason, Redemption and Resistance to God's Detractors ain't no kinda crackpot outfit, Mama, and you know it.'

'Know nothin' of the kind. Saw where that preacher of yours

got arrested for havin' a video camera hid in the ladies' restroom at the church buildin'.'

'It wasn't Reverend Plenty put it there, Mama. There's always snakes in the forest.'

'With that type of weird individual leadin' the flock, Lula, you can't expect no better. Reverend Willie Thursday spoke here in Bay St Clement last Sunday about false prophets like Goodin Plenty, sayin' how the world depends on them to save it. That's stupid talk, Lula. No way the world's welfare revolves around any one person. You'd best get shut of that nut case soon as now.'

'The Three R's is right thinkin', Mama. Goodin Plenty just got a different way of gettin' his point across.'

'Such as when he run off to Barbados with his twelve-and-a-half-year-old stepdaughter and she said after how he made her do them disgustin' things with chicken parts!'

'Mama, Rima Dot Duguid done long since been committed. And you tellin' me now you believe what you read in the *National Enquirer*?'

'If she's in the bin, it's no thanks to that perverted sinner.'

'Mama, let's stop this. You gotta get your mind right for the comin' ordeal. I'll see you tomorrow.'

'Just as well. Here's Dalceda now, comin' in the back door.'

'Bye, Mama. Love you.'

'Love you, Lula. Dal says for me to assure you she'll be at the airport on time. That is if Monty, her new Lhasa apso, don't play sick again.'

'I'm sure everything'll be fine, Mama. Bye.'

Good Enough

Pace got up late. He didn't want to go to school. He lay in his bed, listening for noises in the house. Lula had delivered her cakes to the church and then had Beany drive her to the airport. Sailor was at the Gator Gone warehouse. Pace opened the drawer of his bedside table, took out a pack of Camels and shook one loose. He reached back into the drawer and found a book of matches that had the words WHATEVER HAPPENED TO SEAN FLYNN? printed on it, struck one and lit up the cigarette.

He thought about this deal with the Rattler brothers, and the more he thought about it the less he liked it. Now that he knew the score, however, there would be no easy way to back out. The Rattlers, Smokey Joe in particular, would not take kindly to the idea of Pace's walking around with this information in his head. Either they'd have to alter their plans and choose another target, or do something about Pace, and Pace figured the Rattlers didn't take full possession of more than one idea at a time.

The other night Pace had watched a movie on TV with Sailor called *Bring Me the Head of Alfredo Garcia*. It was about an out-of-luck American piano player in Mexico who searches for the body of a guy who'd impregnated the daughter of a wealthy *patrón*. The American must cut off the corpse's head and bring it to the *patrón* in order to earn a reward. The movie, Pace remembered, got progressively weirder and wackier, with the American doublecrossing and being doublecrossed by everyone he meets. There was a lot of killing, so much killing that the movie became kind of a comedy, with mutilation upon mutilation. The last part was the best, he thought, when the American has the head in a sack covered with flies as he drives his battered old convertible through the sun-baked, scabrous Mexican countryside, swatting away the flies that threaten to engulf him. Pace wondered why the American didn't just put the head in the trunk of the car.

110

The Rattlers weren't about to let him beg off. Better to tough it out, Pace decided. Lefty Grove and Smokey Joe didn't fool around, and *Bring Me the Head of Pace Roscoe Ripley* was one movie Marietta Fortune's only grandboy was insufficiently prepared to appreciate. Pace lolled around the house most of the day, reading around in one schoolbook and another without retaining much of anything. He didn't so much dislike school as he disliked having to show up there every weekday. If attendance were voluntary, he thought, then school wouldn't be so bad. He could quit in another year, when he turned sixteen, but he knew that his parents wouldn't like it. Sailor hadn't finished grammar school, so of course he expected Pace to go to college and go on to become president of the United States or something. Pace wondered how many presidents had been the son of a twice-convicted felon.

At four o'clock the telephone rang and Pace answered it.

'Pace, honey, that you?'

'Yes, Mama. You at Grandmama's?'

'I am. Just wanted you and Daddy to know I made it safe and sound. Auntie Dal picked me up at the Charlotte airport and we drove through a absolute terror of a rainstorm all the way to Bay St Clement. Started pourin' the instant our plane landed and it's still comin' down like a shower of Pygmy darts on a safari. Lightnin', too. Sky's blood red. How's it there?'

Pace looked out a window.

'Nothin' special. Sorta gray.'

'How was school today?'

'Same as ever.'

'OK, sweetie pie. You need somethin' and Daddy ain't around, go to Beany, you hear?'

'I'll be fine, Mama. Tell Grandmama hello and hope she comes through.'

'Hush, 'course she will. Take care now, Pace. Love you.'

'Love you, Mama.'

'Be home soon's I can.'

'Bye, Mama.'

'Bye.'

Pace hung up and checked his pockets to make sure he had some money, then left the house and headed for Nestor's Sandwich City to meet the Rattlers. He took a bus to the corner of Canal and St Charles, got off, walked one block down Canal to Magazine, turned right and continued walking. At the northeast corner of Felicity and Magazine, an obese black woman with the largest bosom Pace had ever seen was sitting on the curb with her legs in the street, singing 'Give Me That Old-Time Religion.'

'It was good for the Baby Jesus,' she sang, 'it was good for the Baby Jesus. It was good for the Baby Jesus and it's good enough for me!'

Pace kept walking, wondering how in the world a woman's breasts could grow that large, and he picked up the tune. He began singing, half to himself, half out loud, inventing verses as he headed to the rendezvous.

'It was good for Elvis Presley,' Pace sang, 'it was good for Elvis Presley. It was good enough for Elvis Presley but it weren't good enough for me.'

Pace used Stonewall Jackson, Jimmy Swaggart, Paula Abdul, Magic Johnson, Jimmie Rodgers, and the Ninja Turtles in his altered version of the hymn before he reached Nestor's. He entered Sandwich City and stopped singing when he saw Lefty Grove and Smokey Joe sitting on stools at the counter eating fried oyster po'boys.

'Isn't that Pace goin' into Nestor's?' Beany Boyle asked her son, Lance, as she turned right off Napoleon Avenue into Magazine.

Lance leaned forward over the front passenger seat of his mother's Taurus station wagon and took a look.

'Yeah, that's Pace,' he said, and flopped down on the backseat next to his sister, Madonna Kim.

'That Nestor's supposed to be some kinda drug den, ain't it?' said Beany.

'I guess,' Lance said. 'The Rattlers hang out there, I know.'

'The who?'

'Rattlers, Mama. They're brothers.'

'Them the ones their daddy set fire to the high school in Cut Off after they quit teachin' Creationism? And the mama's stuck away in some Mississippi home for the depraved?'

'Think so. They're mean ol' boys.'

'Wonder if Sailor and Lula know where their boy's spendin' his time.'

On his way home from Nestor's, Pace stopped to read a handbill posted on a telephone pole in front of Panther Burn Items.

A CHALLENGE TO WHITE PEOPLE

ARE YOU TIRED OF . . .

Affirmative action quotas that discriminate against Whites in hiring, promotion, and admission to colleges?

A non-enforced immigration policy that has flooded our country with millions of scab-laborers and welfare parasites?

The brain-washing, by the schools and the media, of White Youth with racial self-hatred and genocidal race-mixing propaganda?

A non-White crime wave which makes our cities unsafe for our families?

Sham elections that allow only the lying toadies of the criminal ruling class to enter the halls of government?

The turning of this once-great White Nation into an impoverished banana republic ruled by traitors and criminals, owned by foreign corporations and populated by mongreloids?

If so, why not join with the thousands of your White kinsmen and kinswomen of the Third Position who are fighting for White survival?

JOIN THE WHITE ARMED RESISTANCE! IF YOU ARE INTERESTED IN OUR IDEAS PLEASE WRITE OR CALL . . .

WAR, PO Box 2222, New Orleans, LA 70115

Recorded Message (555) MAKE-WAR

When he'd finished reading and turned to go, Pace was startled to see a tall, thin, red-faced man in his mid-thirties wearing a yellow straw cowboy hat, plain long-sleeved white shirt with the cuffs and collar buttoned, and sharply creased black slacks standing directly behind him reading the same handbill over his right shoulder.

'Knew a fella worked derrick with told me his wife started complainin' once, ridin' in the car,' said the man. '"Life with you's just terrible," she said to him, and threatened to throw herself right out of the car on to the road. "Hold on just a minute," this fella told her, "let me see I can get up some speed." He guns it up toward eighty, then cuts the wheel hard into a hundred-eighty degree spin, car rolls over four times and somehow they both survive without even one broken bone between 'em. Fella said after that whenever they was drivin' and he started goin' a little too fast, she just quit talkin' and clamped on her seat belt.'

Pace slid away from between the pole and the man, nodded at him and walked off without feeling compelled to reply.

Killers

'It's awful what's goin' on in the world, Lula, and it ain't about to stop until the worst. Am I right, Dal?'

Marietta was lying in her hospital bed, reading the Charlotte *Observer*, and talking to Lula and Dalceda Delahoussaye, each of whom were seated on chairs on opposite sides of the bed. They were waiting for the doctor to stop by before having Marietta taken to the operating room.

'Looks it,' said Dal. She and Marietta had been friends since their days together at Miss Cook's in Beaufort, more than forty years before. Since that time they had never lived farther apart than a ten-minute walk.

'Whole planet's come unhinged,' said Marietta. 'Look at this: "Uniformed Gunmen Kill 8 at Cockfight." That's the headline. "Men in military uniforms sprayed gunfire at a group of people attending a cockfight in central Colombia late Saturday, killing eight people, local news accounts said yesterday. The private Radio Cadena Nacional and the domestic news agency Colprensa said the gunmen killed eight people and wounded four in Yacopi in Cundinamarca state, 60 miles north of the capital of Bogota." Dal, ain't that where Louis used to do business, Bogota?'

'No, Marietta, it was La Paz, Bolivia, but it weren't no better there. Had them a brewery Louis sold 'em parts for. The company needed their own army to protect it and the workers. Louis stayed down there three months once, settin' it up and makin' sure it run right. You remember, Marietta, that's the time I took advantage of his absence to redecorate the livin' and dinin' rooms? He come back and didn't even notice.'

'Some husbands is like that, Dal.'

'*Some* husband is right.'

'Mama, did you take that yella pill the nurse give you?'

'Yes, Lula, dear, I took the yella pill.'

115

'Suppose to calm you.'

'I'm calm.'

The doctor came in, followed by a nurse.

'How we doin', Mrs Fortune?' he said. 'You ready?'

Marietta folded the newspaper and handed it to Lula.

'Been ready for two hours, Dr Bonney. Been borin' Mrs Delahoussaye here and my daughter to death. Don't think you know Lula, do you? Lula, this is Dr Bonney, a descendant of Billy the Kid. Don't he have the most beautiful wavy black hair and blue eyes? Doctor, this is my favorite daughter, Lula Pace Fortune.'

'Lula Ripley, now,' Lula said, extending her right hand to the doctor. 'How do you do?'

They shook hands.

'You live in New Orleans, your mother's told me.'

'Yes, with my husband and son. He's fifteen.'

'It's my grandboy's fifteen,' Marietta said. 'And his daddy that acts like it.'

'Mama, stop! Sailor's providin', and he ain't been in no trouble for years.'

'Mrs Fortune,' said Dr Bonney, 'I'm gonna let Nurse Conti here prepare you for surgery, if you don't mind. Ladies, I'm afraid you'll have to leave now.'

Dal stood up and kissed Marietta on the cheek.

'You be fine, love,' said Dal. 'I'll talk to you tonight.'

Lula leaned over and kissed her mother on the forehead.

'Be tough, Mama.'

'Ain't it strange how I always think of your daddy at moments like this?' said Marietta. 'Clyde's face slides right into focus whenever I have a serious situation to consider.'

'Don't worry, Mrs Fortune,' Dr Bonney said. 'You won't hardly be able to tell we touched you.'

'Didn't think Billy the Kid fathered any children,' said Lula.

'I'm not a direct descendant of his, Mrs Ripley, but we are of the same stock.'

'Every family's got its killers, Doctor,' said Marietta, staring straight at Lula. Then she turned and smiled at Dr Bonney. 'It ain't as if there's anything you could do about it.'

116

'Pace, buddy? Bob Lee mentioned to me today that Beany told him she saw you goin' into Nestor's Sandwich City yesterday down on Magazine. That right?'

Pace looked at Sailor, then away. They were in the kitchen and Pace was eating a bowl of cereal. The Wheaties box with a picture of Michael Jordan on it was on the table between them.

'I guess.'

'What you mean, you guess? Either it was you Beany seen or it wasn't. Which?'

'Mean I guess it was me, she says so.'

'So what's happenin' in Nestor's these days other'n dope deals?'

Pace scooped up a tablespoonful of Wheaties and crammed it into his mouth. He couldn't answer while he chewed. The telephone rang and Sailor picked it up.

'Ripley home, Sailor speakin'. Hi, peanut, how you? That's good. Told you she'd pull through. Your mama's like a big dog on a red ant. How long you figure? Uh huh. Well, do what's needed. I know. Oh yeah, we're fine. Pace is sittin' here wolfin' his Wheaties like any other All-American pup. We're busier'n blazes at the factory. OK, I will. Love you, too, peanut. Bye now. Uh huh. You bet. Bye.'

Sailor hung up.

'Mama says to tell you she loves you and that both Grandmama and Auntie Dal send their love. Mama's got to stay with your grandmama for several days, until the doctor says Marietta can get around on her own. Now, what's news at Nestor's?'

'Nothin', really, Daddy. Met up with some boys there, is all.'

'You in any kinda fix, son?'

'No, Daddy, I ain't.'

'You'd tell me, you was, wouldn't you?'

' 'Course.'

'Come to me anytime 'bout anything, you understand? Ain't nothin' can upset me 'less you're less'n straight about it.'

'I hear you, Daddy. Thanks.'

There was a knock on the back door and then it opened. Coot Veal came in.

'Hey, Sail!' Coot said. 'Hey, Pace!'

'Hello, Coot,' said Sailor. '*Que paso?*'

Coot had on a yellow and blue LSU baseball cap with a drawing of a tiger on it and a white tee shirt with the words BUBBA'S BILOXI PORK BAR printed on the front and WE MIGHT BE CLOSED BUT YOU'D NEVER KNOW IT on the back. He took a clean bowl and a spoon out of the dish tray, sat down at the table and poured himself some Wheaties.

'I was a kid,' Coot said, 'they had Bob Richards on the box. Bet you don't know who Bob Richards was,' he said to Pace.

'Right again,' said Pace.

'O-lympic pole vault champ, I believe. And a good Christian. Hollywood even made a movie about him. Or was that Bob Matthias? Maybe they made movies about both of 'em. Matthias was a O-lympic athlete, too. And prob'ly not a bad Christian, either, though I don't know for sure. What I do know for sure is I ain't partial to this new deer dog law they're tryin' to put through in Mississippi. The rich folks there get it in and next week the sonsabitches in Baton Rouge be hollerin', too.'

'What law's this?' asked Sailor.

'Seems the Miss'ippi Property Rights Association's lookin' to outlaw huntin' with dogs, only allow still-huntin'.'

'They can't do that,' Pace said.

'Hell, they can't!' said Coot. 'Look what they done about abortion and taxes. Ask your daddy, he knows. Landowners want the territory to themselves, and there ain't much open territory left. No more road huntin' at all, they say, from trucks or standin'. Wanna do away with dogs altogether. You 'magine not allowin' blue ticks or runnin' walkers in the woods? Only place you'll be able to see 'em is up in the Madison Square Garden prancin' around with a tube pushed up their asshole.'

'Why they doin' this?' Pace asked.

'What begun it was a old boy in Petal, I think it was, got shot

118

by a hunter after he chained up the hunter's dogs runnin' loose on his property.'

'I used to work over in Petal,' said Sailor.

'Didn't know that,' said Coot.

'For a short time, in a lumberyard. After I weren't required by the Texas state prison system to stay close to home no more.'

'Some bad apples, no question, could ruin the sport for ev'ryone. Let their hounds run wild, kill people's pet ducks, scare children. But it ain't most of us can't control our dogs. Hell, a man's dogs is part of his fam'ly. Problem is the landowners who do their huntin' in private clubs. They buy up all the land in the first place and don't leave nothin' for the common man. People should be let to hunt the way they like to hunt. Miss'ippi state legislature done already passed a bill bans huntin' from within one hundred feet of the center line of a road. Now they mean to regulate firearms, too.'

'It don't sound good,' said Sailor.

'Pretty quick this whole country'll be nothin' but a suburb of Tokyo, anyway. We're lucky, they'll let us out on Sunday to take a leak. Other six days we'll be too worried or busy bendin' over to risk it.'

Sailor laughed. 'Got a point there, Coot.'

Coot stood up. 'Gotta take a leak, too,' he said, 'while I still got the chance. How you doin', Pace? Stayin' out of trouble?'

'Mostly.'

'All a man can do,' said Coot.

Jaloux

Inez's Fais-Dodo Bar had been a fixture on Toulouse Street in the Quarter for more than thirty years. The original owner, Inez Engracia, had been shot to death by a jealous lover six months after the place opened. Inez's heir, her sister Lurma, sold out to Marcello 'Crazy Eyes' Santos, the organized crime king of the Deep South, who was now serving a life sentence in the Federal Correctional Institution at Texarkana for conspiracy to commit murder and the murder of his mistress, Mona Costatroppo. Mona had been killed in a hotel room in Chicago, where she was waiting to testify against Santos as part of her participation in the Federal Witness Protection Program. The Crazy Eyes Gang and its holdings, legitimized as Bayou Enterprises, were being overseen in Santos's absence by Carmine 'Poppy' Papavero. Papavero had invited Bob Lee Boyle to have a drink with him at Inez's to discuss the possibility of Bayou Enterprises becoming involved in the distribution of Bob Lee's Gator Gone repellent and related products. Bob Lee knew better than to reject outright Papavero's overture, so he accepted the meeting and asked Sailor to accompany him.

'You know more about this kind of thing than I do, Sail, that's why I wanted you to come along.'

Bob Lee and Sailor were walking along Toulouse toward Inez's at nine o'clock in the evening. They'd left Bob Lee's Grand Prix in the parking lot of Le Richelieu on Barracks Street, where Sailor knew the attendant, Fudge Clay. Fudge's brother, Black Henry, had been at Huntsville with Sailor for two years until another inmate had carved up Black Henry in the shower room, the result of miscommunication concerning a sexual question.

'What the hell I know, Bob Lee? Only thing is to listen to the man, hear what he has to say and take it or don't take it from there.'

The two Gator Gone representatives turned into the Fais-Dodo and Sailor immediately spotted Carmine Papavero. The Gulf Coast mob boss, wearing his signature burgundy blazer, was seated at a large corner table with three other men. Papavero's photograph had appeared often enough in the local newspapers and on television since he'd replaced Marcello Santos that even Bob Lee, who made no effort to keep up on current events, recognized him. As Sailor and Bob Lee approached his table, Papavero rose to greet them. He was a large man, his belly strained at the single-buttoned sports coat, and he wore a wide yellow tie decorated by a hand-painted pink flamingo.

'Mr Boyle, I believe,' said Carmine Papavero, reaching his thick right hand toward Bob Lee, who took it quickly into his own and participated in a solid shake.

'Yes, sir,' said Bob Lee. 'And this is my colleague, Mr Sailor Ripley.'

Papavero withdrew his right hand from Bob Lee's and thrust it at Sailor, who reciprocated.

'A pleasure, Mr Ripley. Please, sit down both of you.'

Two of the men who had been seated at Papavero's table got up and walked away, allowing Bob Lee and Sailor to take their chairs. Papavero did not bother to introduce the man who remained, an extremely thin, blue-skinned individual with a pinhead and creaseless ears the size and shape of dieffenbachia leaves. Bob Lee looked once at the man and did not look at him again. Sailor recognized the man instantly as the former inmate at Huntsville who had stabbed Black Henry Clay, Fudge Clay's brother, to death in the shower room. He was not certain if the man, whose name was Zero Diplopappus, recognized him.

'You fellas need drinks,' Papavero said, and signaled a waitress who stood near the table, her only duty while it was occupied by Carmine and his group.

'Dixie,' said Bob Lee.

'Two,' said Sailor.

'Two Dixies,' said the waitress. 'Anybody else need anything?'

Zero Diplopappus's ears waved once, as if a sudden breeze had sliced through the room, but he did not speak. Papavero did not reply and the waitress walked away.

'Mr Papavero, sir,' said Bob Lee.

'Please, call me Poppy. All of my friends do.'

'I just want you to know, sir, that I agreed to meet with you out of respect, not because I'm interested in changing my arrangements for product distribution.'

'That's fine, Mr Boyle – Bob Lee – I understand, and I appreciate your candor. But I am in a position to make you an offer, a generous offer, on behalf of Bayou Enterprises for fifty-one per cent of the Gator Gone Corporation. You would be retained, of course, as director of the company. Name your price.'

'Can't do it, Mr Papavero.'

'Poppy, please.'

'I just don't want to sell Gator Gone. It's all I have. I invented the repellent and started by manufacturing it and shipping it out of my garage. I worked real hard, along with Sailor here, to build up the business. We just now got it goin' good, and I ain't ready to give it up. Don't know that I'll ever be.'

The waitress brought the two beers, placed them on the table along with two glasses and left.

'Mr Ripley, is it?' Papavero said to Sailor.

'Yes, sir.'

'Why don't you take your beer over to the bar and drink it there. I'd like to discuss this business in more detail with Bob Lee here, a little more privately, if you don't mind.'

'I don't mind,' said Sailor. 'OK with you, Bob Lee?'

Bob Lee nodded and Sailor stood up, picked up his Dixie and went over to the bar. Zero stayed in his seat.

'You a friend of Poppy's?'

Sailor turned around and saw a young woman, no more than twenty-two, with short, white-blond hair, wearing long purple and pink parrot earrings. Her small cat's eyes were clear green.

'Just met him.'

'I'm Jaloux Marron. How about you?'

Sailor smiled. 'I'm nothin' of the kind. But my name's Sailor.'

Jaloux Marron smiled, showing uneven, very white teeth.

'Hey, Sailor, buy me a drink?'

'Buy you a beer's about it. I ain't rich.'

'Good enough.'

Jaloux gave the high sign to the bartender, caught his eye and pointed to Sailor's bottle, then at herself. The bartender nodded, cracked open a cold Dixie and set it in front of her.

'How you like NO?' she asked Sailor.

'Pretty much. I live here.'

'No kiddin'? You look too decent.'

'First time anybody accused me of that.'

'Guess there's more to you than meets the eye.'

'You meet my eye just fine, Miss Marron.'

'Just Jaloux'll do.'

'Everybody's damn informal around here.'

'It's that kinda place. You want to go someplace else, get some room service?'

Sailor laughed. 'Can't do it.'

'Guess you really are decent.'

'Really married, anyhow. You know Papavero?'

'Sorta. I work for him, just like everyone else.'

'I don't.'

'Yeah, you-all're too decent.'

Bob Lee came over and touched Sailor's arm.

'Let's go, Sail,' he said, and headed for the door.

Sailor took a long drink of Dixie, then said, 'Been swell meetin' ya, Jaloux. You're a good-lookin' lady, if you don't mind my sayin' so.'

'Don't never mind that kinda talk, Sailor. Be nice to see you again, especially when you ain't feelin' so decent.'

Jaloux took a card from a small sequined handbag and held it out to Sailor.

'Don't lose this, OK?' she said.

He took the card and read it. The words NIGHT TALK and a telephone number were printed on it. Sailor looked into her little green eyes.

'Try not to,' he said, and walked out of the bar.

'What d'ya think?' Sailor asked Bob Lee as they headed toward Barracks Street.

'Think it's time to go home, watch "Fishin' Hole" on ESPN.'

At the parking lot, Sailor decided not to say anything to Fudge Clay about seeing Black Henry's slayer in the Fais-Dodo, and he didn't exactly know why.

Down to Zero

'We ain't gonna need no masks,' said Smokey Joe, 'because they ain't gonna be nobody left over to identify us.'

'Don't mention that little fact to Ripley, brother. Might could weird him out.'

Lefty Grove and Smokey Joe Rattler were sitting in their Jimmy, which was parked on Decatur Street near the corner of Esplanade, waiting for Pace. Lefty Grove zipped open the green Tulane Wave athletic bag that was on the floor between his feet, removed a Black Magic sheath-sprung switchblade and put it into his pants pocket. He took out two Colt Pythons, stuck one in his belt and handed the other to Smokey Joe.

'Where'd ya find these nifty partners?' Smokey Joe asked.

'Skeeter McCovery brung 'em back from Mobile last month. Skeeter says there's more weapons per square mile in Alabama than there are wanted men in Florida, which is sayin' somethin'.'

'Well, he ain't no liar and he done a job or two. You figure on Ripley packin'?'

'Don't see a need for it. We got enough to put out all the lights.'

The Rattler brothers sat and smoked Marlboros. Lefty Grove was wearing a powder blue tank top with the words HAVE YOU HUGGED A COONASS TODAY? stenciled on the front, black Levi's with the bottoms rolled twice, and a pair of brand new Head tennis shoes without socks. Smokey Joe wore a black tee shirt emblazoned with a rubberized image of Michael Jordan executing a reverse dunk, the rubber part of Jordan's dangling tongue torn off, faded Lee Riders ripped at both knees, and green Converse high tops without socks. Both boys planned to wear red and white cotton handkerchiefs tied around their heads to cover their hair. Tyrus Raymond, their daddy, had told them that people are more easily identified by their hair, both color and style, and by whether or not they have any, than by any other common characteristic.

'How many years Daddy been considered dead now?' asked Smokey Joe.

''Bout twenty, I believe. Why?'

'Don't know. Just thinkin' how his name bein' engraved on that Vietnam Memorial in Washin'ton is kinda spooky.'

'Daddy don't mind. Far's the government knows he's long gone, so he don't have to pay no taxes or nothin' forever. Pay for ever'thin' with cash the way he does, use out-of-state driver's licenses and not registerin' nothin' in his name means he's about free as any man can be. Bein' declared legally dead has all the advantages of bein' really dead without none of the drawbacks, such as *bein'* dead. Long as you're alive, you ain't got nothin' to worry about.'

'Seems to me, only way a man got nothin' to worry about is if he is dead. Long as you're alive you got problems, Lef', even if all the governments of the world got your account cancelled. Devil got your name down's a differ'nt story.'

'How's that?'

'That ol' boy make you wish you was back on earth payin' your neighbor's taxes, I'm right convinced.'

'Ain't wise makin' reference to no devil around Daddy, you know. He'll think it's Mama's blood talkin'. There's Pace Ripley comin' now.'

Pace walked up to the passenger side and nodded.

'Nice afternoon for a armed robbery, Ripley, don't ya think?' said Lefty Grove.

'Cloudy day like any other.'

The Rattlers wrapped the red and white kerchiefs around their heads, knotted them at the back and got out of the truck. Pace had on a plain white tee shirt, an unzipped beige windbreaker, blue Wranglers and red Air Jordans with tube socks.

'You carry this,' said Smokey Joe, handing Pace a canvas mail sack. 'Just do what we talked over and one day we'll three be eatin' Big Macs on Mars.'

Lefty Grove slapped a black Baltimore Orioles baseball cap on Pace's head.

'Wear this,' Lefty Grove said, 'so they can't see your hair.'

The Rattlers carried the Pythons stuffed into the front of their pants with their shirts over them. Pace followed behind as they made their way across the railroad tracks by the wharf. It was three-twenty-five on a Thursday afternoon when they boarded the discarded brown caboose. Zero Diplopappus saw them first, but there was no conversation. Smokey Joe shot Zero in the head at point-blank range and didn't wait for him to go down before facing the other protector of the take and holding the Python in front of his eyes. The money was on a table in large, brown paper shopping bags. Pace shook the contents of each bag into the canvas mail sack while Lefty Grove guarded the door. Nobody spoke. When all of the money had been collected, Pace slung the sack over his right shoulder and exited the caboose with Lefty Grove. Smokey Joe grinned at the man he had covered.

'You're all dead,' croaked the man, whose name was Dewayne Culp. Dewayne Culp's skin was yellow and heavily wrinkled, and he had an enormous Adam's apple that ascended and descended inside his thin, withered neck like a rickety elevator in a decrepit hotel.

'Uh-uh,' said Smokey Joe, before he pulled the trigger again, 'you are.'

The three boys were in the Jimmy headed east on Chef Menteur Highway when the two armored car guards entered the caboose. One of them bent over Dewayne Culp, took one look and stood up. The other guard helped Zero Diplopappus to his feet and handed him a handkerchief, which Zero used to wipe away the blood on his face from where he'd been grazed by Smokey Joe's bullet.

'It was them two punk cousins of Junior's,' said Zero, 'the Rattlers, with another kid. They thought I was dead.'

Zero's massive ears flapped a couple of times, then he laughed.

'Third kid was the likeness of a fella I run into the other day,' he said, 'an ex-con I done time with in Texas, name of Sailor Ripley. Would be somethin' if it turned out to be his boy, wouldn't it?'

'Know why the Good Lord created women?'

'Why's that?'

'Sheep couldn't do the dishes.'

The Rattler brothers both laughed hard. They were sitting in the pickup cab. Pace was riding in the back of the truck, his black cap pulled down as far as it would go. The plan was to hide out in Mississippi for a spell, close to Miss Napoleon's Paradise, so Smokey Joe headed the Jimmy north on Interstate 59 toward Meridian, where they'd connect to Highway 45 and shoot straight into Lookout World. Nobody would figure on their being with the Lord's Disturbed Daughters, the Rattlers thought, and this way they could spend some time with Mary Full-of-Grace.

'We'll stash the money with Mama,' said Lefty Grove. 'It'll be safe there.'

'You sure, Lef?' said Smokey Joe. 'She finds out, she'll just give it away.'

'I'll make sure she don't know she even has it. Hide it when she ain't lookin' in that old trunk from Grammy Yerma ain't been taken out from under her bed since she come there.'

Pace watched the Sportsman's Paradise roll away from under him. He considered the situation, not quite comprehending the fact that he and his semi-moronic compañeros were now officially fugitives from Gulf Coast Criminal Central. Pace had gotten into the deal in the first place based on his notoriety as the son of Sailor Ripley, the Texas killer and bandit. That was a sure-enough hoot, seeing as how Sailor had been caught during his first attempted robbery and the only killing he'd done had been an accident in North Carolina. Pace's daddy had never gotten away with a thing, but his reputation as a hard case, false though it was, had tainted his boy and pressured Pace into acting stupid. Maybe that was it, Pace thought, us Ripleys is simply dumb as they come. No good reason I should be speedin' away with these backyard chicken fuckers. Ought to be life weren't always more ornery a animal.

Pace wished he'd taken along his flask. A healthy hit of Black Bush would drop him over the edge just now. WELCOME TO LOUISIANA flashed by and Pace knew they'd crossed into Mississippi. Suddenly the sun faded and Pace looked up. Black clouds formed like Mike Tyson's fists were about to batter the planet. He pulled his windbreaker up over his head and closed his eyes. Is this what it felt like to you, Daddy, Pace whispered, when you were in the deep shit?

Talk Turkey to Me

Poppy Papavero and Zero Diplopappus sat in the front seat of Poppy's powder blue BMW, which was parked next to the curb outside ARRIVALS at the New Orleans International Airport. Zero's head had a white bandage wrapped around it that pinned back his elephantine ears so that he looked like Chuck Connors as Geronimo in the movie based on the life of the Apache chief. Both Connors and the gangster had blue eyes, however, rendering any actual resemblance to Geronimo extremely dubious. Poppy puffed on a Monte Christo while they waited for his wife, Perdita, to arrive on a connecting flight from New York. She had been in Europe for three weeks, shopping and sight-seeing.

'Don't worry, Poppy,' said Zero, 'we'll find these guys and get the money back. I got a good idea where they are.'

'Yeah? Where's that?'

'Up by Starkville. The Rattler mother's a crazy, been locked up in some home there for years.'

'What makes you think that's where they've gone?'

'They're kids. If they ain't with the papa, which they ain't – 'cause we checked, and that guy's plenty crazy, too – then they're with the mama. My guess is they go see her before goin' anywhere else.'

'Ah, they could be in Memphis by now, or Chicago.'

'I'll get 'em, Poppy, believe me.'

Poppy looked at Zero, took the cigar out of his mouth and grinned.

'I do, Zero, I believe you.' He tossed what was left of the Monte Christo out the window.

Zero's eyes narrowed and half closed.

'I'm gonna fillet all three of 'em,' he said.

'Mm, mm,' said Poppy. 'I can smell that deep-fried boy cookin' right now.'

At his house in Metairie, Sailor put the card Jaloux Marron had given him on the table by the telephone and dialed the number printed on it. Someone picked up after three rings.

'Night Talk. This is Cindy speakin'. Call me Cin. And what do you want to talk about?'

'Hello,' Sailor said, 'I'd like to speak to Jaloux, please.'

'She's on another line at the moment. Would you like to talk to me, or would you prefer to wait? I'm sure I can tell you whatever it is you need to hear.'

'I'm sure you can, but I need to speak with her.'

'Hang on, then, honey.'

A radio station came over the line while Sailor was on hold.

'In other news, the state of Nevada has six hundred to seven hundred fifty new residents who are multiplying rapidly, but many of them may not live out the year. The Nevada Department of Wildlife has transplanted wild turkeys to western and southern parts of the state to establish the birds, which are not native to Nevada, in an effort to increase the population for hunting, a biologist involved with the project said today.

'"The population is growing so fast I expect we might have a hunt by next year," he said. "We'll probably set up isolated hunts. In the meantime, the birds are relatively visible and are tremendously spectacular to watch, especially during mating. When the male turkey struts, his tail feathers fan out with very colorful displays. And they're darn fast birds, too," he added, "able to run as fast as a horse and fly as rapidly as smaller ducks."

'According to this report, the transplanted turkeys are mostly of the Rio Grande variety, and they thrive on river bottom lands instead of the forests the birds usually enjoy. Most of these turkeys came from Amarillo, Texas.

'Nationwide, the turkey population has grown to four million after a low of thirty thousand at the turn of the century, when unregulated hunting, clearing and burning of native hardwood habitat and human encroachment threatened the species. By all accounts, the wild turkey has made quite a North American comeback.

'From New York City, where the only Wild Turkey you can find is in a bottle, comes another kind of news. A twenty-three-year-old woman, who was raped and robbed when she was trapped between a subway revolving-gate exit and a locked fence blocking the stairs to the street, won the right to sue the Transit Authority for negligence. The woman, a television makeup artist, was on her way home at ten P.M. last July nineteenth, when she left the station through a one-way revolving turnstile and found the stairs to the street barred and locked. A man she asked for help came through the turnstile, produced a knife, and robbed and raped her. It is not clear how he got out, but police believe he had a key or squeezed over the gate.'

'Hi, this is Jaloux. We can talk now.'

Sailor was startled by the sudden switch from the radio to reality.

'Uh, hello, Jaloux. This is Sailor Ripley. We met the other evenin' in Inez's Fais-Dodo Bar and you give me your card.'

'Uh huh. What you want to talk about, Sailor?'

'I need some information, Jaloux, about my son, and I thought you might could help me get it.'

'What's his name?'

'Pace. Pace Roscoe Ripley. He's fifteen and I found out from a note he left me that he was involved in a robbery of funds belongin' to your boss, Mr Papavero. I was hopin' to find out where Pace is now, if Papavero and his bunch got it figured out yet.'

'Honey, this is somethin' I *can't* talk about. I'm sure you understand.'

''Course. I was just hopin' we could make a date to meet somewhere – anywhere, anytime – long as it's soon.'

'Give me your number, Sailor. I'll ask around and call you back.'

'Fine. It's 555-8543. I was thinkin' about callin' you anyway, Jaloux, you know? I mean, I had you on my mind.'

'Talk to you later, Sailor Ripley. You can tell me what I had on when you had me on your mind. Bye.'

She hung up before he could say, 'Thanks, Jaloux.'

Scooba's

The boys stopped at Scooba's Cafe in Lookout World, population 444, to have something to eat after a long night on the road and before visiting Miss Napoleon's Paradise. Lookout World had been named by the daughter of Fractious Carter, Metamorphia, after his death in 1962 at the age of 101. Until then, the town was called Carter, having been owned, operated and maintained by him since its incorporation. Metamorphia was fifty-nine years old when her father died and she was his sole heir. She'd never married and had waited all of her life to get away. Before taking off, Metamorphia changed the town's name to what she shouted out at Fractious's funeral. 'Look out, world!' Metamorphia cried as she walked away from the grave. 'I ain't sixty yet!'

Nobody in Lookout World had heard from her for forty years, except for a picture postcard of the Halliday Hotel, Ohio and 2d streets, 'Grant Stayed Here,' postmarked Cairo, Illinois, and dated 2 October 1969, which was received by Leander Many, Fractious Carter's lawyer, who was at that time ninety-four and about to be a terminal victim of emphysema, brought on, Many believed, by his lifelong penchant for the practice of onanistic asphyxia. Metamorphia wrote: 'Bet you Bastards think I am Beyond Hope. Maybe your Right. Lester says I got a Head Start to Satan.' Neither Leander Many nor anyone else in Lookout World knew who Lester was.

Lefty Grove and Smokey Joe each automatically ordered hotcakes, grits with gravy, and chicory coffee, the same meal Tyrus Raymond Rattler ate every morning of his life since his sons could recall. Pace stared at the counter girl. She was about his age, under five feet tall, too skinny to lie on, with messy mud-red hair and bad acne. She looked like he felt.

'Come, boy,' she said, 'already sunup in Lowndes County.'

'Grits 'n' gravy, is all,' Pace said. 'And a Coke, you got one.'

132

'Got it.'

She went off to put in their order and Pace picked up a day old *Delta Democrat-Times* that was lying on the stool next to him. Sailor had told Pace how it had been his own daddy's practice to turn to the Obituaries page first thing; it had become Sailor's habit, too, and now Pace searched for the death column. It was always interesting to read about other people's lives, Sailor said. It took your mind off your own.

JOE SEWELL, 91, HALL OF FAMER TOUGHEST TO STRIKE OUT was the top line. 'Joseph Wheeler Sewell, the eagle-eyed batter who struck out only 14 times during a fourteen-year major league career, died on Tuesday at his home in Mobile, Alabama,' Pace read. 'He was elected to the Baseball Hall of Fame in 1977 and was ninety-one years old when he died. Over eleven seasons with the Cleveland Indians and three with the New York Yankees, from 1920 to 1933, Joe Sewell struck out only three times in two seasons and only four times in two others. Umpires deferred to his judgment to the point where if he chose not to swing at a pitch, they would virtually always call it a ball.

'Mr Sewell, who was born in the town of Titus on 9 October 1898, said that he developed his batting skills as a youngster in rural Alabama by repeatedly tossing rocks and lumps of coal into the air and belting them with a broomstick. No one in major league history who played as much struck out less, and Mr Sewell played a lot. He entered the American League as a twenty-one-year-old replacement for Ray Chapman, the Indian shortstop who became the only big-leaguer to die in a game when he was struck in the head by a pitch thrown by Carl Mays of the Yankees. From 7 September 1920 until 2 May 1930, when he was kept in bed with a brain fever, Mr Sewell played in 1,103 consecutive games.

'At five feet, six-and-a-half inches tall and 155 pounds, Joe Sewell compiled a career batting average of .312, including a high of .353 in 1923 and nine other .300 seasons. Most of his 2,226 hits were singles, but none was of the broken-bat variety. Aside from his record of 115 straight games without striking out in 1929, the most compelling evidence of Mr Sewell's uncanny ability to put wood solidly on to the ball was that *he used only one bat during his entire major league career*. It was a thirty-five-inch, forty-ounce Ty Cobb model Louisville Slugger he kept in condition by seasoning it with chewing tobacco and stroking it with a Coca-Cola bottle.

'Mr Sewell was a star football and baseball player for the University of Alabama, and led the school baseball team to four conference titles before joining the minor league New Orleans Pelicans in 1920. Before that summer ended, he was on a World Series championship team as Cleveland beat the Brooklyn Dodgers.

'After his career ended, Mr Sewell worked for a dairy and was a major league scout. In 1964, at the age of sixty-six, he became the Alabama baseball coach, winning 114 games and losing ninety-nine in seven seasons. His two younger brothers, Tommy and Luke, both of whom are dead, also played in the major leagues. Mr Sewell is survived by a son, Dr James W. Sewell of Mobile, a daughter, L.C. Parnell of Birmingham, ten grandchildren and fourteen great-grandchildren.'

The waitress brought the boys' breakfasts and set the plates down on the puce Formica counter.

'Need anythin' else, y'all holler,' she said.

'What's your name?' asked Smokey Joe.

'Hissy. Mama's Missy, sister's Sissy.'

'What's your daddy's?'

'Ever'body calls him Bird-Dog, but his real name's Buster. Buster Soso.'

Pace put down the newspaper and picked up the can of Coke Hissy Soso had brought him and studied it.

'What you eyeballin' that can for?' asked Lefty Grove.

'Wouldn't do to rub a old wood ball bat with this, would it?' said Pace.

Lula's Plans

'Hi, Sail, sweetie. How're my boys?'

'Oh, Lula, it's you.'

'Who were you expectin' to call? Ann-Margret, maybe?'

'No, honey, I thought it might be Pace. How's Marietta?'

'Mama's recoverin' faster'n they'd like, as if we couldn'ta guessed she would. Dal and I can't no more keep her down than Imelda Marcos could quit buyin' shoes. I'm thinkin' I might stay another couple days, though, just to make certain her heart don't start flutterin', like after she had that bad fall last summer.'

'Whatever's best, peanut.'

'Then, of course, Reverend Plenty's appearin' in Rock Hill on Monday? I'm also thinkin' it could be a excitin' deal to go hear him at the openin' sermon of the first South Carolina branch of the Church of the Three R's. I could stay over in Charlotte with Bunny Thorn, Beany's first cousin once or twice removed? The one lost her left arm, most of it anyway, in a car wreck at the beach in Swansboro when she was eighteen? You remember my tellin' you about her? I ain't seen Bunny in years. She owns a laundromat out by the Speedway. Wonder if Bunny'd go hear Goodin Plenty with me.'

'Sounds all right to me, Lula. Stay as long as you need.'

'How's Pace? He gettin' to school on time and eatin' proper?'

'He's been keepin' busy.'

'You got a eye on him, Sail, don't you?'

'Don't be worryin' about us Ripley males, honey. We're survivors.'

'Glad to hear it. Sailor?'

'Yes, ma'am?'

'You love your Lula?'

'I do, peanut. Always will, too.'

'*Hasta siempre*, darlin'.'

'*Hasta siempre*.'

135

The Shining Path

'Glad you could make it, Coot,' said Sailor. 'This'd be a tough one to face alone.'

'Got plenty of food, weapons and ammo and the Ram's gassed to the gills. Figure we can work the give-and-go, you'n me's all we got, like them Shinin' Path people in Peru. You heard of 'em, haven't ya? The Cocaine Commies? Good Chinese-style guerilla fighters, though. What's your idea on the procedure?'

Coot Veal was decked out in his best cammies, black lace-up Red Wings, green Semper Fi hat, and double-reflector wrap-arounds. He took a small black leather pouch containing an Urban Skinner out of a pocket of his field jacket, clipped it on to his belt and twisted it front to back. The telephone rang and Sailor lifted the receiver.

'Ripley.'

'Sailor, I got bad news.' It was Bob Lee Boyle.

'What now?'

'Bomb blew out the front door and some windows of the new warehouse.'

'When'd this happen?'

'About a half hour ago. Guess Papavero don't take no like a man.'

'Not many do.'

'I ain't changin' my mind, though, Sail. I mean, Gator Gone's *mine*.'

'I'll back you, Bob Lee, whatever you decide.'

''Preciate that, Sailor Ripley. Knew you would. I'm goin' over to assess the damage now. Comin'?'

'Can't, Bob Lee. Pace is in some trouble and I got to attend to it first. I'm sorry but it's priority.'

'Understand. Anything I can do?'

'Make sure you don't say nothin' to Beany or it'll likely get

136

back to Lula. Coot Veal's here. Think we can handle it, thanks the same.'

'OK, good buddy. Let's each check in later.'

'You got it, Bob Lee. *Cuidado*, hear?'

'I'll try.'

'And give me a holler you hear direct from them boys.'

'Sail?'

'Uh huh?'

'This what's called a hostile takeover bid?'

Sailor hung up and told Coot what had happened.

'This sad ol' life's becomin' a tougher proposition all the time,' Coot said. 'I had me a terminal disease no tellin' what I'd do. As it is my short list is gettin' longer all the time.'

'Figure it'll be any better in the next?'

'You turnin' Hindu?'

'Heard a piece on the news earlier about a sixteen-year-old boy, not much older'n Pace, escaped from Cuba on a surfboard.'

'A surfboard?'

'Yeah. Seems a East German tourist bought the kid a wind-surfin' board and he took off for Florida. Made it thirty miles before the boom broke, which he managed to re-rig somehow, well enough to go another thirty miles when the thing give out for good. Got picked up by a Bahamian freighter crewed by Koreans couldn't speak Spanish or English. They notified the US Coast Guard, who took the boy the last thirty-mile stretch into Key West. Kid said he was goin' to live with relatives in Miami. Didn't seem to think what he done was so remarkable. Just wanted to be free, is all.'

'Desperate people do all kinds of incredible things.'

Sailor nodded. 'Made me wonder about Pace. What made him so damn desperate that he'd do this fool thing with them worthless Rattlers?'

Coot shook his head and said nothing, just took off his shades, checked them for smudges and put them back on. The doorbell rang and Sailor answered it.

'Hi, Sailor man.'

'Thanks for comin' by, Jaloux. You find out anything?'

Sailor let her in.

'Poppy's wife – sometimes I go shoppin' with her? – she told me they figure the boys is headed north into Mississippi.'

137

'What's there?'

'Rattler brothers got a insane mama locked up in a place called Miss Napoleon's Paradise for the Lord's Disturbed Daughters. Perdita says Zero, Poppy's top gun, is goin' after 'em with some pistols. Zero was wounded durin' the takedown and he won't be lookin' to take no prisoners.'

'You say Perdita?'

'Yeah. Poppy's wife. Why?'

'She a Tex-Mex woman, last name of Durango?'

'Don't know that I ever heard her own last name, but yeah, she's from Texas and looks Mexican, all right. You know her?'

Sailor nodded. 'I did. Listen, Jaloux, you been a big help. Anything I can do for y'all, let me know.'

'There is, Sailor man. Definitely is somethin' you can help me with.'

'I got to get goin' now, Jaloux. My boy's in tough and I got to find him before this Zero does.'

'I'm goin' with you, then.'

'Really, Jaloux, you don't want to get mixed up in this, 'specially as how you're an employee of Mr Papavero's. Me and my pal Coot here can handle it, I hope.'

'I'm comin' along, Sailor. I know right where Miss Napoleon's is, 'count of I used to live nearby in Starkville for two years when my mama was married to her third husband, man named Dub Buck owned a Buick dealership. Had him a string of signs on old Highway 82 from Eupora to Mayhew said, "Buy Buck's Buicks." Dub had did some small piece of time before Mama met him, for exposin' his self in a public park up in Greenville. I liked him, though. Dub died of food poison in Nogales one weekend when I was fourteen. Least that's what Mama said when she come home without him. She and me moved to NO right after.'

'Coot, this here's Jaloux Marron,' said Sailor. 'She's gonna show us the way.'

'Semper Fi, Miss Marron,' said Coot, tipping his cap.

'Can't say the same, Mr Veal.'

Back to Buddhaland

Smokey Joe pulled the Jimmy up to the premium pump at the self-serve Conoco in Meridian and cut the engine.

'Be right back,' he said to Lefty Grove, as he got out and headed for the pay-in-advance window.

As he approached the pay window, Smokey Joe could see that there was a problem. A medium-sized black man in his thirties, with long, slanted, razor-shaped sideburns, wearing a camel hair sportcoat, was arguing with the Vietnamese kid behind the bulletproof pane.

'Pay for cigarettes!' said the Vietnamese kid, nodding his head quickly, causing his lank, black forelock of hair to flop forward almost to the tip of his nose.

'I paid you for 'em, motherfucker!' the black man shouted. 'You already got my money!'

'No, no! Pay now! You pay for cigarettes!'

Standing off to one side, about eight feet from the man, was a young black woman wearing a beige skirt that ended mid-thigh of her extraordinarily skinny legs, and a short brown jacket that she held tightly around her shivering body despite the intense heat.

'Pay him or let's go!' she shouted. 'I ain't wastin' street time on no cigarettes!'

'Keep the damn cigarettes, then, chump monkey!' the man yelled at the kid, throwing a pack of Winstons at the window. The pack bounced off and fell on the ground. 'And go back to Buddhaland! Leave America to us Americans!'

The man turned away from the window and saw Smokey Joe approaching.

'Hey, man,' he said, 'you familiar with this area?'

'Why?' asked Smokey Joe.

'My wife and me got a problem with our car, see, and we need –'

139

'Sorry,' Smokey Joe said, 'I don't have any money to give away today.'

'No, man, I don't want no money. All we need is a ride. We got to get our car towed.'

'Call a tow truck.'

'That's the problem, see, we don't know our way around here and we got to get the car fixed.'

There was a large sign next to the garage door in the station that said MECHANIC ON DUTY 24 HOURS. Smokey Joe pointed to it.

'There's a mechanic right here,' he told the man.

'Wouldn't let no chump monkey from Buddhaland touch it!'

'Come on!' shouted the woman, her thin naked knees shaking. 'Turn loose, Chester. It ain't happenin'!'

Smokey Joe saw the man's eyebrows twitch and his face contort, twisting up on the left side, his nostrils flaring. The man hesitated for a moment and Smokey Joe braced himself, thinking that the man might attack him. But the man turned his back to Smokey Joe and followed the woman into the coffee shop of a motel next door.

'Ten bucks premium,' Smokey Joe said to the kid, sliding a bill on the metal plate beneath the window.

As Smokey Joe pumped the gas, a well-dressed, overweight, middleaged black woman, who had just finished fueling her late-model Toyota sedan, said, 'Shouldn't be treatin' nobody like that. Ain't no way to be treatin' people here. This ain't no Asia.'

She got into her car and drove away. One of the Vietnamese attendants, dressed in a clean, crisp blue uniform, walked out of the garage and over to Smokey Joe.

'This is bad neighborhood,' he said, shaking his head. He took the fuel hose from Smokey Joe, who had drained his ten dollars' worth, and replaced it on the pump.

Smokey Joe slid behind the steering wheel of the Jimmy and started it up.

'You hear any of that?' he asked Lefty Grove.

Lefty Grove nodded and said, 'Even gettin' gas nowadays reminds me of what Ray L. Menninger, the veterinarian-taxidermist, who Daddy said was the most honest man in Iguana County, Texas, used to say: "With me, one way or the other, you get your dog back."'

140

The Paradise

Nell Blaine Napoleon had moved into The Paradise eighty-two years ago, when she was four and a half years old. Her father, Colonel St Jude Napoleon, a career army man, and her mother, Fanny Rose Bravo, had designed and had the twenty-six-room Paradise house built for them, and they had both lived and died there. Nell was their only child. By the age of twelve, Nell had decided to devote her life to the well-being of others. She was initially and forever inspired by a local black woman called Sister Domino, who spent each day administering to the sick and needy. Sister Domino allowed the young Nell to accompany her on her rounds of mercy, and taught her basic nursing skills, which Sister Domino had acquired at the Louise French Academy in Baltimore, where she had lived for eighteen years before returning to her Mississippi birthplace. Sister Domino's ambition had been to assist Dr Albert Schweitzer at Lambarene, in Africa, and she read everything she could about him and his work, constantly telling Nell what a great man Schweitzer was and how there could be no higher aspiration in life than to work to alleviate the suffering of those persons less fortunate than themselves. The 'Veritable Myriad' Sister Domino called the world's population.

Nell's parents never attempted to dissuade their daughter from her passion, or to turn her away from Sister Domino. Both St Jude Napoleon and Fanny Rose Bravo were great believers in self-determination, and if this was the path Nell chose to follow, it was her business and no one else's. Their feeling was that there were certainly worse directions a life could take, and they let her be. The only time Nell had unwillingly had to separate herself from Sister Domino was the period during which she was required by her parents to attend Madame Petunia's School for Young Women in Oriole, between the ages of fourteen and seventeen. During her holidays, however, Nell would be back at Sister Domino's side, going from home to home among the poorest residents of Oktibbhea, Lowndes, Choctaw, Webster, Clay, Chickasaw, and Monroe counties. Following graduation from Madame Petunia's, Nell never wavered, dedicating herself fully to Sister Domino's work, which became her vocation also.

After her parents were killed by a falling tree that had been struck by a double bolt of ground lightning during a late-August electrical storm, Nell, who was then twenty-four, inherited The Paradise and invited Sister Domino to live there with her, which offer Sister Domino accepted. Eventually, Sister Domino and Miss Napoleon, as Nell came to be called, succeeded in converting the house into a combination hospital and retreat for those individuals incapable of dealing on a mutually acceptable basis with the outside world. Sister Domino's mandate, however, held that those residents of The Paradise be *serious* Christians. No blasphemy was tolerated and no waffling of faith. This policy, though, extended only to The Paradise; those persons she and Nell treated outside the house were not required to adhere to Christian tenets, the Lord's beneficence being available to the Veritable Myriad.

Sister Domino never did get to the Congo to assist Dr Schweitzer, though Nell offered to pay her way. There was always too much work to be done at home, Sister Domino said, and when news of Dr Schweitzer's death reached her, Sister Domino merely knelt, recited a brief, silent prayer, arose and continued scraping the back of a woman whose skin was inflamed and encrusted by eczema. Sister Domino died three years later, leaving Nell to carry on alone. As the years passed, however, Nell limited her ministrations to women, preferring their company to that of men, whom, Nell concluded, tended toward selfishness in their philosophy, which displeased her. Once made, Nell's decision was irreversible, and her devotion was further refined by her increasing acceptance of nonviolent, mentally disturbed women. A decade after Sister Domino's death, Nell officially registered her home with the county as Miss Napoleon's Paradise for the Lord's Disturbed Daughters. A large oil portrait of Sister Domino, painted from memory by Nell, hung on the wall opposite the front door so that the first sight anyone had upon entering was that of Miss Napoleon's own patron saint.

Mary Full-of-Grace Crowley Rattler fit in perfectly at The Paradise. As the mother of Jesus Christ, it was simply a matter of being acknowledged as such that contented her. At no time during her stay had Mary Full-of-Grace caused Miss Napoleon the slightest difficulty, not even when another woman, Boadicea Booker, who also believed she was the mother of the Christ child, lived at The Paradise. Boadicea had died within three months of her coming, so it was possible, Miss Napoleon believed, that Mary Full-of-Grace had no knowledge of her existence. When Tyrus Raymond Rattler and his sons came to visit Mary Full-of-Grace, Miss Napoleon was pleased to welcome them, as they were unfailingly polite and well-behaved. Even when Lefty Grove and Smokey Joe were small children, Miss Napoleon noticed, they had minded their father precisely and comported themselves properly in the presence of their mother. Therefore, when Mary Full-of-Grace's sons and another boy appeared on the front porch of The Paradise one windy afternoon, Miss Napoleon welcomed them inside.

'Afternoon, L.G.,' she said. 'Afternoon, S.J. Your mother will be pleased to see you. And who is this young gentleman?'

'Hello, Miss Napoleon,' said Lefty Grove. 'This is our friend, Pace Ripley.'

Pace set down the sack he'd been carrying and nodded to the old woman, who was barely more than four feet tall. Pace figured her weight at about seventy-five pounds. His daddy could lift her off the ground with one hand, he figured, dangle her by her ankles with his arm stretched straight out.

'Hello, ma'am,' Pace said. 'Beautiful place you got here.'

'My parents, Colonel St Jude and Fanny Rose Bravo, built it and left it in my care so that I might care for others. You boys can go right up, if you like. Mary Full-of-Grace is in her room. She never leaves it until dark.'

'Thank you, Miss Napoleon,' said Smokey Joe. 'We 'preciate all you done for Mama.'

'The Lord prevails and I provide,' said Miss Napoleon, as the Rattler brothers, followed by Pace, who carried the sack, filed up the stairs.

Mary Full-of-Grace was sitting perfectly still in a high-backed wing chair next to the windows when the boys entered her room. Her long, silver-blue hair hung in two braids, one on either side of her V-shaped head. She wore a white, gauzy robe with a golden sash tied at the waist. Pace noticed that she had almost no nose,

143

only two air holes, and hugely dilated brown eyes. She kept her long, thin hands folded in her lap. Her fingers looked to Pace as if they were made of tissue paper.

'Hello, Mama,' said Lefty Grove, who kissed her forehead.

'Hello, Mama,' said Smokey Joe, who followed suit.

The brief, soft touch of their lips left dark marks on her skin.

'This boy here's our associate, Pace Ripley,' Lefty Grove said.

'Hello, Mrs Rattler,' said Pace, trying to smile.

Both brothers looked quickly and hard at Pace.

'This here's the mother of Baby Jesus,' said Smokey Joe.

Mary Full-of-Grace stared out the window to her left.

'My son is soon in Galilee,' she said. 'I keep the vigil.'

Smokey Joe motioned to Pace and Pace slid the sack containing most of the money from the robbery under the light maple four-poster bed.

'Well, Mama, we don't mean to disturb you none,' said Lefty Grove. 'We'll just come back by and by.'

Smokey Joe headed out the door and Pace followed.

'By and by,' said Mary Full-of-Grace. 'He will be by, by and by.' She continued to stare out the window.

'So long, Mama,' said Lefty Grove, closing the door behind him.

They did not see Miss Napoleon on their way out but Pace spotted the portrait of Sister Domino.

'Who's that?' he asked, walking over to take a closer look. 'And what does this mean?' he said, reading the words carved into the bottom of the frame. 'God's Gift to the Veritable Myriad.'

'Must be was Miss Napoleon's mammy,' said Smokey Joe. 'What the hell you think?'

Pace trailed the Rattlers out of The Paradise, wondering about those words carved into the frame. A hunchbacked old woman was coming carefully up the steps of the porch, holding a large, blue plastic fly swatter.

'Suck cock!' she spat at them. 'Suck cock! Suck cock! Suck cock!'

Riot at Rock Hill

'You won't regret goin', Bunny. Reverend Plenty puts on a show and a half.'

'I'm lookin' forward to it, Lula. Been needin' to get away from the laundromat anyway. More'n even a two-armed woman can handle there.'

Lula and Bunny Thorn were riding in Lula's rented T-bird from Charlotte to Rock Hill to witness Reverend Goodin Plenty's first-ever sermon in South Carolina. His Church of Reason, Redemption and Resistance to God's Detractors had been running ads in every newspaper within two-hundred-fifty miles of Rock Hill for a month.

'How's your sex life, Lula? You don't mind my askin'.'

Lula laughed, looked quickly at Bunny, then back at the road.

'Well, OK, I guess,' she said, and with her right hand shook a More from an opened pack on the seat next to her, stuck it between her lips and punched in the dashboard lighter. 'How's yours?'

'Lousy, you don't mind my complainin'. Guys'll do it once with a one-armed woman, just for a kick, 'cause it's kinda unusual, you know. That's it, though. They don't come lookin' for seconds. I been wed to a rubberized dick for a year now. Least it don't quit till my arm give out. I'm considerin' joinin' some women's group just to meet some queer gals. Maybe they won't mind a two-hundred-twenty-pound washerwoman with one musclebound arm. And I almost lost it, too, tryin' to unjam a Speed Queen the other day.'

The lighter popped out and Lula lit her cigarette, took a couple of powerful puffs and laughed again.

'Bunny, you're somethin' fresh, I tell you. Sailor'd love you to death.'

'Yeah? Think I oughta come visit, stay at your house? Maybe get Sailor to give me a workout or two?'

Lula coughed hard and tossed the More out the window.

'Just jokin', hon'. Tried to get Beany to ask Bob Lee if he'd do it, but she didn't go for the idea. And she's my cousin! Guess I'll have to stick with Big Bill.'

The parking lot at the Rock Hill church site was full by the time Lula and Bunny arrived, so Lula parked the T-bird across the road. Since groundbreaking for the church building had not yet commenced, a giant tent had been set up and filled with folding chairs. Lula and Bunny managed to find two together at the rear. The tent was filled to capacity by the time Reverend Goodin Plenty, dressed in a tan Palm Beach suit with a black handkerchief flared out of the breast pocket, walked in and strode down the center aisle, hopped up on the platform, grabbed a microphone and faced the audience.

'My goodness!' Goodin Plenty said as he smiled broadly and sized up the crowd. 'Ain't this just somethin' spectacular! My, my! Not a empty seat in the Lord's house tonight. Ain't it grand to be alive and holdin' His hand!'

'Yes, sir, Reverend!' someone shouted.

'Tell us about it, Reverend!' said another.

Reverend Plenty smoothed back his full head of prematurely white hair with both hands, making the microphone squeal, then raised up his arms as if he were a football referee signaling that a touchdown had been scored.

'I am gonna give you somethin' tonight, people! The Church of Reason, Redemption and Resistance to God's Detractors is here in the great state of South Carolina, first to secede from the Union, to stay!'

'Maybe so,' shouted a tall, skinny, bald-headed man wearing a blue-white Hawaiian shirt with red and yellow flowers on it, who jumped up from the front row, 'but *you* ain't!'

The skinny man held out a Ruger Redhawk .44 revolver with a seven-and-one-half-inch scoped barrel and pointed it straight at the Reverend's chest.

'This is for Marie!' the man yelled, as he held the gun with both hands and pulled the trigger, releasing a hardball round directly into Goodin Plenty's left temple as he attempted to dodge the bullet. The shell exploded inside the Reverend's brain and tore away half of the right side of his head as it passed through.

A riot broke out and Lula and Bunny got down on their knees

146

and crawled out of the tent through a side flap. As soon as they were outside, they stood up and ran for the car.

'Holy shit!' said Bunny, as Lula cranked the engine and sped away. 'That was better than the Hagler-Hearns fight! Only thing, it didn't last as long.'

Lula put the pedal down and drove as fast as she dared.

'Uh-uh-uh,' Bunny uttered. 'That Marie must be some *serious* piece of ass!'

Shake, Rattle & Roll

Wendell Shake watched the Jimmy's oversized tires crawl through the mud ruts toward his farmhouse. He lifted the 30-06 semi-automatic rifle to his right shoulder and sighted down the four-power Tasco scope. At his feet, propped on end under the window, was a loaded eleven-and-three-quarter inch, forty-pound draw Ninja pistol crossbow with a die cast aluminum body and contoured grips. Wendell had come home to Mississippi and the Shake family farm two months before, after the fifth severed head had been found in a garbage can in the Bronx. That was the last of them, Wendell decided, one for each borough of New York City, to show the Jews, Catholics, and coloreds what he thought of their so-called civilization. Armageddon was about to commence, Wendell believed, and he was an operative of the avant-garde. It was his Great Day in the Morning, as he liked to call it, at last, after forty-eight years of silent suffering, witnessing the slaughter of the innocents. Now, however, the rest of the avenging angels were poised to strike, and the message Wendell had delivered was being read and discussed. Perhaps, Wendell thought, as he watched the Rattler brothers and Pace disembark from their vehicle, he was about to receive an acknowledgment of his effort.

'This place been abandoned for years,' Lefty Grove said to Pace, as the three boys walked up the path to the house. 'Daddy and us used it lots of times when we come up to visit Mama. Been about three, four months since we been here, I guess. Right, Smoke?'

''Bout that, Lef. You remember this gate bein' wired shut like this?' Smokey Joe placed his left hand on the post and vaulted himself up in the air.

Before Smokey Joe had cleared the top rail, a bullet smacked into the center of his forehead, knocking him backward, so that his legs looped over the front of the rail by the backs of his knees,

148

leaving the upper half of his body dangling upside down on the opposite side.

Lefty Grove and Pace both hit the ground and covered their heads. They heard the screen door of the house open and slam shut, footsteps coming down the porch steps and then on the path toward them. Neither of the boys dared to move. The footsteps stopped at the gate.

'Charity, gentlemen,' said Wendell Shake, 'ain't got nothin' to do with mercy. Even in a foreign land.'

Lefty Grove raised his head and saw a middle-aged man about six feet tall and two-hundred pounds, wearing a red and gray flannel shirt, red suspenders, black pants and low-cut, steel-toed, brown work shoes. His hair was almost completely gray, with dark patches at the front, worn very long, touching his shoulders. It was difficult to see the man's face because of his heavy red beard and the way his head was pressed down close to the rifle. The man's eye sockets seemed devoid of white.

'Suppose you say somethin',' Wendell said to Lefty Grove, 'and they ain't the right words?'

Wendell rested the rifle barrel on Smokey Joe's right knee, keeping the business end directed at Lefty Grove's head.

'Could be there'd be repercussions.'

Pace looked up and saw Wendell standing at the gate. A light rain was falling.

'Both you boys stand up,' Wendell ordered, and they obeyed.

Wendell flipped Smokey Joe's legs up with the barrel, causing the corpse's head to hit the ground before the rest of it pretzeled over. Lefty Grove and Pace got to their feet.

'Come in, gentlemen,' said Wendell, unfastening and opening the gate to admit them.

Wendell marched the boys up the steps into the house, where he motioned with the gun to a wooden bench against a wall of the front room.

'Sit yourselves down there, gentlemen, and tell me what's brought you this far.'

Pace sat down and Lefty Grove remained standing.

'Look, mister,' said Lefty Grove, and Wendell shot him through the heart.

The last Rattler brother collapsed on the floor next to Pace's

149

feet, made one slight lurch after he was down, then lay perfectly still. Pace closed his eyes.

'Didn't exactly sit, did he?' said Wendell, looking down at Lefty Grove's body, then up at Pace. 'That's a rhetorical question, son. You needn't answer. Open your eyes.'

Pace looked at the man. Wendell Shake had mud puddles where his eyes ought to have been, and he was grinning, exposing gums that matched his suspenders and a dozen crowded, yellow teeth.

'We'll wait together, son,' Wendell said. 'There are terrible things soon to be revealed, and man craves company. That's but one flaw in the design. Do you love the Lord, boy?'

Pace said nothing.

'Please answer.'

'I do, sir,' said Pace. 'I surely do love the Lord.'

'Then the Lord loves you.'

Wendell pulled up a goose-neck rocker and sat down, resting his 30-06 across his knees. He began to sing.

'I'm goin' to take a trip in that old gospel ship, I'm goin' far beyond the sky. I'm gonna shout and sing, till the heavens ring, when I kiss this world goodbye.'

Pace saw the pistol crossbow lying on the floor beneath a window on the other side of the room.

They decided to take two vehicles, Coot riding alone in his red Dodge pickup and Sailor with Jaloux in her metallic blue Chevrolet Lumina.

'All the top stock racers back home use these,' said Sailor, as Jaloux drove, following four car lengths behind Coot Veal's Ram.

'These what?' Jaloux asked. 'And where's back home?'

'North Carolina, born and raised. Luminas, they all run 'em. Quick, light, and powerful.'

'Kinda like me,' said Jaloux, laughing, 'only you don't know it yet.'

Sailor looked over at her. Jaloux was short, about five-three, with a sweet little figure that tempted Sailor to suck on her like he would a piece of hard candy, rub her smooth with his tongue until she disappeared. It wouldn't happen, though. There was no way Sailor wanted to risk breaking the bond between him and Lula. All he needed from Jaloux Marron was her help in finding his and Lula's son. This wasn't the time to get complicated.

'Mama's second husband, he was a welder,' said Jaloux. 'Kind of a criminal, though.'

'Yeah, what kind?'

'All I know's what Mama says, but Terrell – his name was Terrell Vick – he'd need somethin' extra, Terrell'd just go out at night and knock somebody over the head and take it. Never nothin' big, I guess, small-time. Maybe that's what prompted Mama to get rid of him.'

'What about your own daddy?'

'He was French. Not Cajun, real French, from France. Belgium, really, which is a place close to France. His family was all from there. Marcel Marron. *Marron* means chestnut, you know.'

'I didn't.'

'Yeah, he was livin' in Antwerp before he come to the States. Started sellin' hosiery for some New York company and wound up in New Orleans at a convention, where he met Mama. She was on her own by then, nineteen years old, and was sorta hard up for cash, I guess, workin' as a party hostess for this bunch of conventioneers at the Monteleone. 'Course all them boys, they just after a quick dip, and why not? That's how Mama met Marcel Marron and he got her pregnant, married her, and hung around NO until about two months after I was born, then run off. Mama says she never knew where to, and ain't never heard. Maybe back to New York, or Antwerp. Least I'm legal.'

'You mean legitimate.'

'Can't have it both ways, huh?'

'How'd you get started at the Fais-Dodo?'

'After high school, which I went three years, only work I could find was fast food places or checkin' in grocery stores. That weren't no decent money, so a guy I knew, Jim-Baby Fitch, tended bar at Inez's for a while, introduced me to the manager, Blackie Caddo, happens to be from Plain Dealin', where Mama grew up partly. He hired me and there you go.'

'Strange how them things turn out.'

Sailor switched on the radio and they listened to Eddie Floyd sing 'Knock on Wood' before the news on the hour.

'In Baton Rouge today, a man who two days ago shot and killed another man who had just shot and killed a woman in a shopping mall, turned himself over to the police.

'Enos Swope said he acted on impulse after seeing Kirkland Ray kill his former fiancée, Yvette Vance. Lieutenant Frank LeRoi, of the Baton Rouge police department, said, "Ray murdered this woman. She's down, she's wounded, and he goes and shoots her in the head again after she's down."

'Swope said that as he pulled into the mall's parking lot he saw Ray chase Yvette Vance, waving a revolver in the air. Swope took out his own gun, a forty-four caliber pistol, and shot at the back of Ray's car as Ray was pulling away, hoping to disable it. His second shot penetrated the door and struck the fleeing man, who slumped down in his seat. Ray's car went out of control and crashed into a light pole, toppling it over on to the top of a 1958 Cadillac Coupe De Ville, trapping seventy-eight-year-old Johnson Buckeye inside. Both Buckeye and Kirkland Ray were taken by ambulance to a hospital, where Buckeye is listed in stable condition. Kirkland Ray was pronounced dead on arrival.

'"I didn't want to kill him," said Enos Swope, a twenty-five-year-old washing machine repairman. "I was just trying to help a lady."

'Swope fled the scene, he told police, because he was afraid of being treated like a criminal. After reading in the newspaper that police were searching for a third person believed to have been involved in the incident, he came forward.

'"My life is a mess now," Swope said today. "I could lose my job, everything I own. I don't want to lose my gun. I paid dearly for it. I don't want my gun marked up. It's such a pretty gun. I love that gun."

'Police have decided not to file charges against Enos Swope, pending a grand jury's review of the case.'

Jaloux followed Coot Veal off the highway to a Short Stop convenience store.

'Hey, Sailor,' Coot said, before they went in for a coffee break, 'forget what I was sayin' before about them Shinin' Path people in Peru.'

'Why's that, Coot?'

'Well, I was just listenin' to the radio news?'

'Yeah, so was we.'

'Had a report that them guerrillas shot and killed nineteen peasants, nearly all of 'em women and children, in a small village up in the Andes. These peasants went there to escape the rebel attacks down below. Said some of the kids weren't no more'n two or three years old. Just like Nam.'

A young black woman, no more than fifteen years old, a bright yellow scarf wrapped around her head, holding an infant with one arm and a bag of groceries with the other, was coming out of the Short Stop. Sailor held the door open for her.

'Thanks, mister,' she said, passing Sailor without looking at him.

'No problem,' said Sailor.

Working in the Gold Mine

Carmine Papavero and Zero Diplopappus left the office of Bayou Enterprises at seven-forty-five A.M. Poppy slid behind the wheel of his powder blue BMW and punched up his home number on the cellular phone as he pulled into the commuter traffic on Airline Highway.

'H'lo.'

'*Buona mattina*, Perdita *mia*. I wake you up?'

'Uh huh.'

'Sorry, sweetheart, but I figured if I didn't call now I might not get another chance until late.'

'Got a busy day, huh?'

'Zero and I are going to Mississippi today, after we make a stop in town. We might not be back until tomorrow, tomorrow night.'

'I'm still pretty beat from all that flyin', honey, so I'll be sleepin' mostly. That Europe's OK, but it's too damn far away. Think from now on I'll just stick to Dallas or Palm Beach, I need somethin' special.'

'Whatever pleases you, honey. Get your rest and we'll have some fun when I return.'

'Hold ya to it.'

Poppy laughed. 'Sleep tight, baby,' he said, and hung up.

'You ought to get married, Zero. Change your outlook.'

'Only one I'm lookin' out for is me. Besides, I was married once.'

'Oh yeah? What happened?'

'Back in Tarpon Springs, when I was eighteen. A local girl, Flora Greco. She drowned on our honeymoon in Mexico.'

'I'm sorry, Zero. I didn't know.'

'I don't look back. Where we stoppin'?'

'Sonny Nevers needs a visit. We'll catch him at his jewelry store right when he opens at eight.'

Poppy guided the Beamer off Interstate 10 onto Claiborne and turned down Elysian Fields. He pulled in front of The Gold Mine and parked. He and Zero waited until Sonny Nevers pulled up the doorshade, then they got out and rang the bell next to the store entrance. Nevers recognized Zero and Poppy and buzzed them in.

'Don't even say it!' said Sonny, edging his five-feet four-inch, three-hundred-pound body around from behind the counter to greet the two men. 'I'll have it tomorrow, no problem.'

Poppy accepted Sonny's handshake and waved away the smoke from what was already the jewelry salesman's second Partagas Topper of the day.

'Wasn't expecting there'd be one,' said Poppy. 'You've always been a man of your word, Sonny.'

'Had a small cash flow difficulty here, just straightened it out. You can count on it. Want a cigar?'

'I know I can. No, thanks.'

The doorbell rang. Sonny looked out and saw two men in blue sports coats carrying briefcases.

'Salesmen,' said Sonny, who went back behind the counter and pressed the buzzer.

'What can I do for you gentlemen?' he asked, after they'd entered.

Both men were more than six feet tall, well-built, had blond hair and wore Carrera sunglasses. Each man pulled a .45 automatic from his briefcase and pointed it at Sonny and Poppy and Zero.

'We'll kill all three of you,' said the slightly taller of the two men in a calm voice, 'unless you give us what you've got in the safe.'

Nobody said a word as the taller man followed Sonny into the rear of the store. The other man kept Poppy and Zero covered while he pulled down the doorshade and reversed the OPEN sign to CLOSED. In less than five minutes, the taller man emerged from the back, carrying a large black satchel filled mostly with twenty-four-karat gold used for the manufacture of gold chain.

Sonny ran out and hurled his huge body at the man with the satchel. The other blond man turned and shot Sonny in the face, the slug going in under the nose, lifting off the top of the fat man's head. Sonny's corpse belly-flopped on the floor as an umbrella of blood spread around him. Zero and Poppy plastered themselves against the wall. The taller blond man turned toward them and fired twice. One round entered Poppy's open mouth, killing him instantly. Zero dropped to his knees, so the man's first shot missed entirely, shattering the plaster above his head. The second shot, however, was on target, gouging a large opening in the left side of Zero's neck, causing his oversized ears to flap furiously as he crumpled over on the cool, black-and-white-tiled floor.

The two blond men put their guns into the briefcases and left the store, the shorter man making certain that the door was closed securely behind them. The men walked swiftly to a new black Cadillac Fleetwood, put the satchel, containing nearly seventy-five pounds of gold worth three quarters of a million dollars, and the briefcases into the trunk, locked it, got into the car and drove away at a moderate speed. Inside The Gold Mine, Zero Diplopappus watched a ribbon of sunlight wriggle slowly through the front window and settle on what was left of Sonny Nevers's face. Zero did not live long enough to close his eyes.

Pure Misery

'You don't have to be afraid to talk to me, boy,' Wendell Shake said to Pace. 'Got somethin' to say, say it.'

'I ain't,' said Pace.

'This world's an awful cruel place, son. Worst place I ever been.'

'You remind me of a person I met once, named Elmer Désespéré,' said Pace, 'hailed from Mamou. He weren't so crazy for it, neither.'

'There's a few of us is sensitive to more'n the weather. Where's this Elmer now?'

'He was killed on the street in New Orleans.'

'Mighta guessed. It's the good go young, like they say. But there'll be one Great Day in the Mornin' before it's finished, I guarantee.'

'Sir?'

'Yes, son?'

'What is it exactly gripes you, you don't mind my askin'.'

Wendell grinned. 'Ain't worth explainin'. Best repeat what Samuel Johnson said: "Depend upon it that if a man talks of his misfortunes there is something in them that is not disagreeable to him; for where there is nothing but pure misery there never is any recourse to the mention of it."'

Pace stared at Wendell, who sat stroking his red beard.

Wendell stood up and said, 'Time to tend the garden. You'll stay put, won't ya?'

Pace nodded and watched Wendell walk out of the room. As soon as the madman was out of sight, he scrambled to his feet, ran over to the pistol crossbow and picked it up. Pace heard Wendell relieving himself in what he assumed was the toilet. He crouched under the window and waited. When Wendell reentered the room, Pace pressed the trigger that released a black dart into his captor's

157

left eye. Wendell fell down and Pace dropped the crossbow and ran out of the house, headed on foot the four miles to Miss Napoleon's Paradise.

Wendell Shake carried no identification of any kind, and when his body was found, along with those of the Rattler brothers, the only item discovered in his pockets by police was a personal ad torn from a newspaper.

> If any open-minded, good-humored men of any race wish to write, I'm here and waiting. BF doing a 60-year term for something that just came out bad.
>   Lamarra Chaney # 1213 P-17
>   Women's Correctional Facility
>   Box 30014, Draper, UT 84020

Paradise Revisited

Miss Napoleon, Jaloux, and Sailor were sitting in rocking chairs on the front porch at The Paradise, drinking iced tea. Coot had driven into Starkville to see if he could dig up any information on the whereabouts of Pace and the Rattler brothers. It was late afternoon, siesta time for the Lord's disturbed daughters, and things were quiet.

'It's the kind of thing happens if you hold the faith,' said Miss Napoleon. 'Tell the truth, I was worried about paying the bills for the first time in my life. We live modestly here at The Paradise, as Sister Domino insisted, but even so we had begun to struggle. When Mary Full-of-Grace came down those stairs last night and delivered into my hands that money, it was the answer to our prayers. Now we'll be able to continue as we've always done, and provide for more than just ourselves. I've thought about opening a haven for the homeless, which until last night didn't seem possible. The Lord has plans for us we cannot even imagine.'

'You always been the kind of woman make God or any man do for, Miss Napoleon,' said Jaloux.

'Child, don't you know the Lord's not a man? He's all things to all manner of people, and He provides best for those who provide for others. In this case, Mary Full-of-Grace was His instrument of mercy. Praise be.'

Just then, Coot Veal's Ram came tearing up the drive, and Sailor could see that Coot had a passenger with him. The truck stopped and Pace jumped out. Sailor dropped his iced tea, hopped down off the porch and embraced him.

'Boy was runnin' down the road, Sail,' said Coot, coming around the front of the truck. 'Couldn't believe it myself when I saw who it was. And you won't believe this, neither. Heard on the radio that Papavero and his henchman, Zero the Greek, been shot and killed in NO under mysterious

159

circumstances. Their bodies was found in a jewelry store on Elysian Fields.'

'The Rattlers is dead, too,' said Pace. 'We was gonna hide out at a abandoned farmhouse – least the Rattlers thought it was abandoned – and turned out a crazy man with a red beard was there. He shot both Lefty Grove and Smokey Joe. I was gonna be next, but he got to talkin' with me, all kindsa strange talk, and when he went to the head I got the drop on him with a pistol crossbow and let him have it. Then I run outta there fast as I could. Daddy, it was worse than what happened to me that time with the wild boy from Mamou.'

Sailor and Pace stood and hugged each other.

'It's OK now, son,' said Sailor. 'Looks like the Lord done pulled off another one.'

Miss Napoleon nodded and smiled and rocked in her chair.

'Come on up here, you two,' she said to Coot and Pace, 'and have a cold glass of tea.'

Famous Last Words

'Guess this means whatever's between us is gonna have to wait,' said Jaloux.

Coot and Pace were waiting in the truck while Sailor said goodbye to Jaloux in front of Inez's Fais-Dodo Bar.

Sailor grinned and brushed back his silvery black hair with both hands. Jaloux reached her right hand under the left sleeve of his white tee shirt and traced the large vein in his bicep with her index finger.

'Guess it'll have to, Jaloux. You been a giant help to me and my boy, and I ain't forgettin' it. I know I owe you.'

'Rather have it be voluntary, you know what I mean.'

Sailor laughed, leaned forward and kissed her above her left eyebrow.

'I do,' he said.

Coot drove the Ripleys home and they were surprised to see Lula's red Cressida wagon in the driveway.

'Jesus, Mama's home,' said Pace.

They got out of Coot's truck, and Pace ran into the house.

'Comin' in, Coot?' Sailor asked.

'No, Sail, thanks. I'm pretty well bushed, all this drivin'. Talk to y'all later'd be best.'

'Thanks, buddy. Couldn'ta done it without ya.'

Coot grinned, saluted and drove off.

'Sailor, honey!' Lula shouted, as soon as he walked in the door. 'You won't believe what happened! Reverend Plenty got assassinated in Rock Hill and Bunny and I barely escaped with our own lives! I been tryin' to call you-all but there ain't been no answer. I been wild!'

Lula rushed into Sailor's arms and held him tight. Pace was lying on the couch with his eyes closed.

'Sail,' Lula said, 'I'm afraid the devil got this world by the tail and he ain't lettin' go.'

Sailor smiled and kissed the top of Lula's left ear.
'Maybe so, peanut, but I ain't lettin' go of you, either.'
Lula almost swooned. 'Oh, Sail, that's what I needed to hear.'

Consuelo's Kiss

'There are two kinds of women: those who move to make room when you sit on the bed and those who remain where they are even when you have only a narrow edge.'

Edmund Wilson

Consuelo's Kiss

Consuelo Whynot licked idly at her wild cherry-flavored Tootsie Pop while she watched highway patrolmen and firefighters pull bodies from the wreckage. The Amtrak Crescent, on its way from New Orleans to New York, had collided with a tractor-trailer rig in Meridian, hard by the Torch Truckstop, where Consuelo had stopped in to buy a sweet. The eight train cars had accordioned on impact and the semi, which had been carrying a half-ton load of Big Chief Sweet 'n' Sour Cajun-Q Potato Chips, simply exploded.

'The train's whistle was blowin' the whole time and, Lord, it sounded like a bomb had went off when they hit,' said Patti Fay McNair, a waitress at the Torch, to a rubbernecker who'd asked if she'd seen what happened.

Consuelo Whynot, who was sixteen years old and a dead ringer for the actress Tuesday Weld at the same age, stared dispassionately at the carnage. The truck driver, a man named Oh-Boy Wilson from Guntown, near Tupelo, had been burned so badly over every inch of his body that the firemen just let him smolder on the spot where he'd landed after the explosion. His crumpled, crispy corpse reminded Consuelo of the first time she'd tried to make Roman Meal toast in the broiler pan of her cousin Vashti Dale's Vulcan the summer before last at the beach cottage in Ocean Springs. She never could figure out if she and Vashti Dale were once or twice removed. That was a result, Consuelo decided, of her unremarkable education. Venus Tishomingo would fix that, too, though, and the thought almost made Consuelo smile.

Four hospital types dressed in white and wearing plastic gloves slid Oh-Boy Wilson into a green body bag, zipped it up, tossed it into a van, and headed over to the wrecked Crescent, which had passenger parts sticking out of broken windows and crushed feet, hands, and heads visible beneath the overturned cars. Consuelo didn't think there'd be anything more very interesting to see, so she turned away and walked back to the truckstop.

'You goin' north?' she asked a man coming out of the diner.

The man looked at the petite young thing wearing a red-and-white polkadot poorboy that was stretched tightly over her apple-sized breasts, black jean cutoffs, yellow hair chopped down around her head like somebody had given it the once-over with a broken-bladed lawn mower, red tongue still lazily lapping at the Tootsie Pop, and said, 'How old're you?'

'I been pregnant,' Consuelo lied, 'if that's what you mean.'

The man grinned. He had a three-day beard, one slow blue-green eye and a baby beer gut. Consuelo pegged him at thirty.

'West,' he said, 'to Jackson. You can come, you want.'

She followed him to a black Duster with mags, bright orange racing stripes, Moon eyes and a pale blue 43 painted on each side. She got in.

'My name's Wesley Nisbet,' he said, and started the car. The ignition sounded like thunder at three A.M. 'What's yours?'

'Consuelo Whynot.'

Wesley laughed. 'Your people the ones own Whynot, Mississippi? Town twenty miles east of here by the Alabama line?'

'Sixteen, be exact. You musta passed Geography.'

Wesley whistled softly and idled the Duster toward Interstate 20.

'Where you headed, Consuelo?'

'Oxford.'

'You got a boyfriend there?'

'Better. I'm goin' to see the woman of my dreams.'

Wesley checked the traffic, then knifed into the highway and went from zero to sixty in under eight without fishtailing.

'This a 273?' Consuelo asked.

'Dropped in a 383 last week. You into ladies, huh?'

'One. What's the "43" for?'

'Number my idol, Richard Petty, ran with. Lots a man can do for ya a chick can't.'

Consuelo bit down hard on the outer layer of her Tootsie Pop and sank her big teeth deep into the soft, dark brown core. She sucked on it for a minute, then opened her mouth and drooled down the front of her polkadot poorboy. Wesley wolfed a look at Consuelo, grinned, and gunned the Duster past ninety before feathering back down to a steady seventy-five.

'You ain't met Venus,' she said.

Sailor and Lula at Home

'Who's gonna watch the worms?'

'Already taken care of, Sail, honey. Beany'll do it.'

'She's gonna be helpin' out at Gator Gone, too, you know, fillin' in for me.'

'Beany can handle more'n one thing at a time, darlin'. She can't get by one time, Madonna Kim will. She ain't doin' much between marriages.'

'Can't believe that girl, peanut. Only seventeen and put two men in the grave.'

'Bad luck is all it is, Sailor. Madonna Kim ain't no spider woman. Mean, Beany and Bob Lee raised her right.'

'Just glad Pace ain't never got hooked up with her.'

'How could he, bein' off in Nepal since before Madonna Kim got her first period?'

'We heard from the boy lately?'

'Month ago's the most recent. He was preparin' to leave Katmandu for the place in India the tea comes from?'

'Darjeelin'.'

'That's it. Was gonna be a long trek, he said, three months or so. Wanted to know when we was comin' over and go on a hike with him. Says he ain't gonna be doin' it forever.'

'I seen that Abominable Snowman movie more than enough times to know I ain't ever goin' near no Tibet, and Nepal's near it.'

'Don't know how Pace can take bein' in such a cold climate. Bad enough when it snows here in New Orleans once in the blue moon. Place just shuts down.'

'You know 'bout blue moons, peanut? I mean, what one is, really?'

'No, what? Just sometimes the way the sky is makes the moon look blue.'

172

'Uh-uh. It's when there's two full moons in the same month. Second one's the blue moon.'

'Where'd you hear this?'

'Woman named Jaloux Marron, used to work for Poppy Papavero, told me, long time ago.'

Sailor and Lula Ripley were eating breakfast in the Florida room of their house in Metairie. Sailor was on his second cup of Community and third Quik-Do raisin-nut muffin, and Lula was halfway finished with a peach, which was all she could handle before about noon. It was seven-forty-five A.M.

'Papavero was that gangster got shot in a jewelry store, right? Dozen years ago?'

'That's right, peanut.'

'And who was this Jealous woman?'

'Jaloux. Gal worked the bar at Inez's Fais-Dodo before it was shut down. Believe it's a fish place now. No, antique store, that's it.'

'So how'd you know her?'

Sailor sipped his coffee and looked out the sliding glass doors at the bird feeder.

'How come there ain't no seed in the feeder?' he asked.

''Cause there ain't no birds around.'

'Might be if there was somethin' for 'em to eat.'

'Didn't realize you was such a bird lover. Who was she, Sailor?'

'Told you, Lula. Girl worked for Papavero. Met her once I was at Inez's. Weren't nothin' more to it. I ain't seen her for twelve years.'

Lula popped a small slice of peach into her mouth and swallowed it without chewing. She sucked on her tongue and stared blankly at a photo of Ava Gardner wearing a low-cut dress that Sailor had clipped out of the *Times-Picayune* and tacked to the wall the day her obituary had appeared in the newspaper. Ava was a homegirl, one of North Carolina's finest.

'Don't seem possible I'll be fifty years old next week, does it, peanut? Never figured on lastin' this long. Might just last a while longer, now I come this far. What do you think?'

'Might could, you will,' said Lula. 'Dependin'.'

'Dependin'? Dependin' on what?'

'Dependin' on your keepin' the love of a certain good woman.'

173

Sailor laughed, put down his cup, and reached his right hand across the table toward Lula.

'I ain't about to mess with true love, Lula, you know it. I never have.'

She accepted Sailor's hairless hand into her own and smiled at him.

'I know that, darlin'. Just sometimes, even at forty-seven and a half years old, that ol' bug gets to squirmin' in my brain and knocks a wire loose. I love you, baby. Always have, always will. We're it, you know?'

Sailor nodded and squeezed Lula's slim left hand with the ruby ring on the third finger that she'd worn ever since Sailor had given it to her when she was sixteen years, six months and eighteen days old.

'I do know, peanut. Don't need no remindin', though it's OK you do it now and again.'

The telephone rang and Lula reached over with her free hand and picked up the receiver.

'Oh, hello, Mama.'

'You busy?'

'No, me'n my true love're just about to take off on a little trip to celebrate his first half-century on the planet.'

'He takin' you to the Bahamas again on one of them gamblin' junkets just so's he can piss away your home improvement savin's?'

Lula laughed. 'We're takin' a car trip, Mama, up to Memphis. Sailor always did want to visit Graceland, so we're goin' now. Be gone about a week.'

'What about your worms?'

'Beany and Madonna Kim'll keep an eye on 'em.'

'That Madonna ain't got the brains or morals of a worm. Didn't her last husband shoot himself after he come in on her screwin' his daddy?'

'That was the first one, Mama. Lonnie Wick? The Wick Wallpaper people? Second one hanged himself. Jimmy Modesta, had a beverage distribution company in Slidell. Used to get us all that Barq's and Dr Pepper for nothin'? That one weren't really all Madonna Kim's fault.'

'What you mean, Lula? I recall now she shamed him with a homeless person.'

174

'Man ran a shelter, Mama, there's a big difference. Anyway, them Modestas has a family history of chronic depression. Jimmy's brother, mother and a couple or three others took their own life before him.'

'No loss to this earth, I'm positive,' said Marietta Pace Fortune. 'Look, Lula, I'm glad I caught you on your way out the door because I want you to know I got a houseguest.'

'You call from North Carolina just to tell me you got a visitor? This another of your and Dalceda Delahoussaye's destitute Daughters of the Confederacy? Why can't Dal take in this one?'

'No, Lula, it's not. It's Marcello Santos.'

'Santos?! Mama, ain't he in jail for life?'

'Released him from Texarkana day before yesterday. He's sick, Lula, real sick. Heart's about to quit. Feds figured a sick old man can't cause them no more trouble.'

'Yeah, but Mama, Crazy Eyes Santos ain't just anyone. He was the crime king of the Gulf Coast since before I was born. You always said Daddy didn't trust him. What about that company of his he used as a front, Bayou Enterprises?'

'He ain't interested, Lula, really. Besides, no way after all these years the ones runnin' things'd let him back in. And he ain't got no crazy eyes no more, he's got cataracts both sides and can barely see. Your daddy didn't depend on Marcello's word, that's true, but Clyde Fortune didn't trust anyone, tell the truth, even me, probably. Anyway, Marcello had no place to go. Was stayin' at The Registry in Charlotte when he called me. I got him fixed up in my room. I'm usin' the study, had Johnnie Farragut bring over a cot. He and Marcello are in the front room together right now, watchin' "Wheel of Fortune." Marcello says it's the favorite show in the joint.'

'Life is full of surprises, Mama, ain't it? I thought he and Johnnie hated each other.'

'Johnnie been retired from the detective business ten years now, Lula. He's almost seventy-five and all he cares about is raisin' flowers. Dal and I got him comin' twice a week to the There But for the Grace of God Garden Club.'

'Mama, I got to hand it to you. Talk about the lion lyin' down with the lamb!'

Marietta cackled. 'Ain't no beast so fierce as time, Lula. It's time makes us all lie down in the here and now or the hereafter, one.'

'I'll check in with you-all when we get to Memphis. Meantime give my love to Dal and Johnnie. Santos, too, I suppose.'

Lula looked at Sailor, who was grinning. His teeth were several shades of brown from thirty-eight years of smoking unfiltered Camels. She figured his lungs must be several shades of black. Maybe if she quit smoking Mores, Lula thought, Sailor would quit Camels, and they wouldn't die of cancer or, almost worse, emphysema, where a person had to haul a machine around with him and keep tubes stuck up his nostrils so he could breathe.

'Love you, Lula,' said Marietta. 'You be careful on the road. There's serious enough devils every step of the way. You hear from my grandboy?'

'Pace is fine, Mama. He's off on a trek.'

'Don't know why he'd want to hole himself up way behind the Bamboo Curtain like this. Boy got a mind of his own, though, I'll give him that.'

'Mama, I'm goin'. I got Sailor Ripley to protect me, so don't worry.'

Lula smiled at Sailor and he raised his left arm and flexed the bicep.

'He ain't always done such a spectacular job of it, Lula, or can't you remember?'

'Bye now, Mama. Love you.'

Lula hung up.

'I know, peanut,' Sailor said, 'the world's plenty strange and not about to change.'

'Might not be worth gettin' up in the mornin' it was any different, Sail, you know?'

The Age of Reason

'Your folks know where you're goin'?' asked Wesley Nisbet, as he guided his Duster into the Bienville National Forest.

Consuelo had not looked at Wesley since she'd gotten into the car. She didn't feel like talking, either, but she knew it was part of the price for the ride.

'They ain't known where I'm goin' ever since I been able to reason.'

'How long you figure that is?'

'More'n seven years, I guess. Since I was nine, when me'n Venus got brought together in the divine plan.'

Wesley slapped his half-leather-gloved right hand hard on top of the sissy wheel.

'Goddam! You mean that woman been havin' her way with you all this time? Hell, that's sexual abuse of a child. How is it your folks didn't get this Venus put away before now?'

'They couldn't prove nothin', so they sent me away to the Mamie Franklin Institute in Birmin'ham. I escaped twice, once when I was eleven and got caught quick, and then two years ago I stayed gone three whole months.'

'Where'd you go?'

'Venus and me was shacked up in the swampy woods outside Increase. Didn't have no money, only guns, ammo and fishin' tackle. We ate good, too. Venus is about pure-blood Chickasaw. She can live off the land without askin'.'

'How'd you get found out?'

Consuelo snorted. 'Simon and Sapphire – those are my parents – hired about a hundred and one detectives. Still took 'em ninety days. Venus found us a pretty fair hideout that time.'

'What's she doin' in Oxford?'

'Got her a full scholarship to study the writin's of William Faulkner, the greatest writer the state of Mississippi ever provided the world. Venus is also a writer, a poet. She says I got the makin's, too.'

'You write poetry?'

'Not yet, but Venus says I got the soul of a poet, and without that there's no way to begin. It'll come.'

'You ever read any books by this fella she's studyin'?'

Consuelo shook her head no. 'Venus says it ain't important. 'Course I could, I want.'

Wesley kept his ungloved left hand on the steering wheel and placed his right on Consuelo's naked left thigh. She didn't flinch, so Wesley slid his leather-covered palm up toward her crotch.

'You wouldn't know what to do with my clit if I set it up for you on the dashboard like a plastic Jesus.'

Wesley's right hand froze at the edge of her cutoffs. He kept it there for another fifteen or twenty seconds, then removed it and grabbed the gear-shift knob, squeezing it hard.

'You're some kinda wise little teaser, ain't you?' he said.

Consuelo turned her head and stared at Wesley's right profile. He had a scar on the side of his nose in the shape of an anchor.

'How'd you get that scar?' asked Consuelo. 'Bet you was doin' such a bad job the bitch just clamped her legs closed on it.'

Wesley Nisbet grinned and took the Duster up a notch.

'I'm likin' this more and more we go along,' he said.

Men in Chairs

'You two need anything this afternoon? I'm goin' out.'

'No, Marietta,' said Johnnie, 'thanks. Marcello and me's doin' good.'

Johnnie Farragut and Marcello Santos were both seated in overstuffed armchairs with their feet up on needle-point footstools in the front room of the Fortune home, watching a talk show on the twenty-four-inch Sony. A practically naked woman was on the screen, her long, slender, tentacle-like legs seemingly about to entwine themselves around the shoulders of the show's male host, who was perched on a step below the chair in which his guest was seated. The fluffy-haired host held the microphone up in front of her dangling breasts, which were delicately contained by a slip of pink cloth.

'Who's she?' asked Marietta. 'Some X-rated movie actress?'

'Concert violinist,' Santos said. 'Just played Brahms's "Opus 25." Very nicely, too.'

'Never saw no violinist looked like that.'

'While back there was a woman played cello in the all-nude,' said Johnnie. '"Member her?'

'I don't,' said Marietta. 'I'll leave the cultural events to you gentlemen, then, you don't mind. Back after the Daughters meetin'. Dal's goin' with me, so you-all're on your own if you spill your milk or need your pants changed.'

'Bye, Marietta,' said Johnnie.

He and Marcello sat quietly for several minutes, listening to the inane banter between the violinist, whose right breast rested on the microphone, and the unctuous host, waiting for the woman to stand up again so they could watch her parade in her skimpy dress. The show broke for a commercial and when it resumed the female violinist was gone.

'Damn,' Johnnie said, 'woulda appreciated seein' them stems

179

once more. Only thing better to look at than a cluster of Cecil Brunners.'

'You're an amusing man, Johnnie,' said Santos, 'and a most fortunate one. Before my eyes began giving me such problems, I read a great deal. In the penitentiary, there isn't much else of a savory nature to help pass the time, as you, having been in the law enforcement business, certainly know. I most enjoyed reading the bulletins and studies issued by the Justice Department, which were made available on a regular basis by the prison library. One of the last I read revealed that in the United States approximately 640,000 crimes per year are committed that involve the use of handguns. More than 9,000 people per year are killed in the process, and another 15,000 are wounded. Also committed each year are over 12,000 rapes, 200,000 robberies and 400,000 assaults by individuals possessing guns. Three quarters of the perpetrators of these crimes are strangers to the victims.'

'Don't tell me that you, of all people, Marcello Santos, one of the most feared crime bosses of our time, is advocatin' gun control!'

Santos laughed. 'I'm boss of nothing any longer, Johnnie. Those days are long passed. Yes, I am against the easy availability of weapons. It's the amateurs that ruin the business. In the proper hands, these kinds of things don't happen. Certainly they do not happen so often.'

'There's a lot of guns in the world, but there's only one Johnny Rocco.'

'What's that?'

'Line from an old movie. Anyway, you got a point, Marcello. Funny how we end up wheezin' in armchairs like this, in the parlor of a woman we both been chasin' after for decades. Though you, of course, was necessarily out of the runnin' for a spell. And after bein' on opposite sides of the fence, so to speak, in our professional lives. Kinda creeps up on a person that there ain't much he can do to influence his outcome.'

Santos sat back in his chair with his eyes closed, his large, thick hands with the left thumb missing folded together in his lap.

'Tell me, Johnnie, have you had a happy life?'

'I guess so, Marcello. My regrets don't amount to much. Only thing is, I never made no mark as a writer, which is somethin' I'd always had in mind.'

'Do you believe in an afterlife?'

'You mean, like heaven? Or reincarnation?'

'Call it what you like.'

'No. Do you?'

Santos nodded his head slightly.

'I do. I'm looking forward to it. What I feel behind me is only pain.'

The two men sat without talking, neither of them really listening to or watching the television. Johnnie thought about a cat he'd had for a while when he was a boy, an orange tom his father had named Kissass. Kissass had been electrocuted one summer evening when a bolt of ribbon lightning struck a power line that lashed down over him as he streaked across the lawn in front of the Farragut house on Stivender Street in Bay St Clement. That was sixty-five years ago, Johnnie thought. He could remember Kissass's face an instant before the strike, and he stopped his memory right there.

Running into Darkness

Rather than take 10 into 55 around the lake, the fast way, Sailor decided to drive over the Lake Pontchartrain Causeway and head west just before Covington on Interstate 12, then pick up 55 north of Pontchartrain, which would take them all the way into Memphis. He and Lula had agreed to take their time, and Sailor kept the Sedan de Ville at a respectable sixty as they cruised across twenty-four scenic miles of the most polluted lake south of Erie.

'Ever tell you about the time I seen a corpse floatin' here?' he said.

Lula was adjusting her eye makeup in the visor mirror on the passenger side of the front seat. She'd had her eyelids tinted the day before and she wasn't sure that she liked the effect. They made her eyes look sunken or something, she thought. Lula studied them now and only half paid attention to what Sailor was saying.

'Tell me what, darlin'?'

'Me'n Slim Leake was takin' his nine-year-old nephew, Pharoah Sanders Leake, whose daddy – Slim's brother, Otis Blackwell Leake – teaches wind instruments at LSU, out for a boat ride, and here come a corpse up on the port side, bloated and fumin' like a abcess on a spaniel's belly.'

Lula frowned into the mirror, flipped up the visor and put her beauty utensils into her purse.

'Say what about a dog?'

'No, peanut, I'm tellin' you about a dead body we come across on Pontchartrain here one mornin'.'

'Whose body?'

'I don't know. Man drowned or was dumped. Looked like a purple balloon with bad air steamin' out all pores. Stank fierce.'

'Delightful. What'd y'all do?'

'Went on and rowed around a while, till Pharoah'd had enough, then took it in and told the dockmaster.'

'What'd he say?'

Sailor slipped a Camel from the open pack in his left front shirt pocket, stuck it between his lips, pulled out a black book of matches with a white skull-and-crossbones on it under the words PURVIS PETTY'S PIRATE LOUNGE, flipped the cover and lit the cigarette with one hand, tossed the match out the window, inhaled deeply, and dropped the matchbook back into his pocket.

'Said floaters was a regular feature of the lake and there weren't no extra charge. Didn't seem to excite him none, though before we left I noticed he'd uncovered the NO in front of the SWIMMING ALLOWED sign on the dock. Slim Leake – you remember, back then he was the Gator Gone distribution manager in Port Allen? Slim said the pollution level of the lake was checked daily, and dependin' on the readin', swimmin' was allowed or not.'

'Wouldn't never get me in this sewer. Whatever happened to Slim Leake, anyway? He reminded me a little of that movie actor, the one looked like a cute bloodhound. Harry Dean Stanton.'

'Yeah, I remember him. He's the one in *The Missouri Breaks* is ridin' with some old boys from Montana into Canada when they hear some horrible animal noise they can't ID, and Harry Dean says, "The further north you go, the more things eat your horse." Whoever wrote that line had a real talent. Always thought that was a pretty fair analysis of the human condition, myself.'

'So what about Slim Leake?'

'Not real certain. He and Nelda Bea divorced, of course, his work went to hell in a hurry, he was drinkin' a lot and Bob Lee had to let him go. Last I heard he was up north in Ohio, managin' a trailer park.'

'Nice man like Slim deserved better'n Nelda Bea. She was one impatient type of woman.'

Sailor inhaled and exhaled a stream of smoke from his nostrils without removing the cigarette from his mouth. Lula looked at him and wondered how many thousands of times she'd seen Sailor pull on a Camel.

'Man might be better off without what he ain't been without since he can't recall,' Sailor said, 'only there ain't no way he can imagine bein' without it.'

Lula nodded. 'You know, honey, I'm givin' up smokin'. I got a pack of Mores with me but I ain't gonna crack 'em. This trip's a good occasion to quit.'

'More power to ya, peanut. You quit forty, fifty times before. It prob'ly ain't impossible.'

Lula stared out the window at the water. Thirty years ago she and Sailor had been on the move like this, only then they were running into darkness. She could recall the feeling all too well, and there hadn't really been a day since that she'd been entirely free of the memory. They were rolling in the light today, though, and Lula knew she should be thankful for it, but somehow the thought of that crazy, out of control time shook her in a way nothing else could.

'Feels fine bein' back on the road, peanut, don't it?'

Sailor tossed his half-burned butt out the window.

'Ain't no substitute,' said Lula. 'Rest of the world other than what's outside the windshield fades right out. Like yesterday? I was readin' in the paper about a ninety-five-year-old man murdered a eighty-eight-year-old woman in her apartment in New York City.'

'How'd he do it? Hammer her with his crutch?'

Lula nodded. 'Knocked her out with a lead bar he used for therapy.'

'Musta been he caught her with a younger man of ninety-two.'

'Uh-uh. Said she'd tried to kill him on orders from the ashes of her dead husband, which she kept in a box on her bedroom dresser. Man accused her of poisonin' fifteen people and practicin' voodoo. Said she'd put a curse on him preventin' him from havin' proper sexual relations and causin' his wheelchair to rust.'

'Guess there's no guarantee of goin' gentle into the good night, or however that poem says.'

Lula looked at Sailor and smiled. 'After all these years, Sail, darlin', you're still capable of surprisin' me.'

Sailor laughed. 'What you mean, sweetheart?'

'Quotin' poetry and all. I like it.'

'Well, I like you.'

'I know it, Sailor Ripley. I surely do. And I really do think that despite ever'thin's happened to us, we got a charmed life.'

Lula reached up and tied her long, gray-black hair back into a ponytail and put on a new pair of fake tortoise-shell Ray-Bans she'd purchased the day before at the Rexall. A huge beige pelican fell out of the sky, bounced off the roof of the car and tumbled over the passenger side into the lake.

Every Man a King

'Just want to say one thing,' said Wesley Nisbet, 'before we get to anywhere, and I don't mean for you to get the wrong idea.'

'What's exactly a wrong idea?' asked Consuelo. 'Tough enough tellin' right and wrong in doin', here you come with thinkin'. You talkin' 'bout believin' evil?'

Wesley passed a gray-primered Dodge Shadow that had the driver's flabby left arm hanging out the window.

'Only a man can make a real woman out of you, is all.'

'You a medical man, I take it.'

Wesley shook his head. 'Was a woman in Greenville, guess it was, convinced herself the King of Sweden was in love with her. Took to tellin' everyone she met how the King of Sweden was comin' to town soon to take her away with him and they'd live in his snow palace over there in Europe. She wrote to him every day for years, even though she never got no answer. Ever'body figured she was just a harmless person and was pretty well amused by her obsession.'

'How you know all this?' Consuelo asked.

'Read it in a book about sexual behavior written by a doctor. So guess what happened? The King of Sweden, she finds out, is comin' to Memphis to visit Graceland durin' a goodwill trip. Turns out he's a big fan of Elvis. The woman tells ever'one she's meetin' the King in Memphis, closes up her house, takes her money out of the bank and drives to Tennessee. On the day the King of Sweden shows up at Graceland, there she is at the gate, waitin' for him. Naturally, he don't notice her and goes right on in.'

'She couldn't go back to Greenville after that.'

'Sticks by the gate, gettin' crazier by the minute, and when the King comes out, she pulls a gun from her purse and tries to shoot him, only her aim ain't no good and the bullet hits a tourist from France.'

'They musta locked her up for good.'

'Uh-uh. She beat 'em to it. Put the pistol in her mouth and blew her brains back to Miss'ippi, right in front of the King of Sweden and ever'body. Doctor who wrote the book said someway the woman had developed a strange condition called De Clerambault's Syndrome, meanin' she was way out of line concernin' her object of affection. I copied out the name of her disease and memorized it.'

'Why you tellin' me this, Wesley Nisbet?'

'Your feelin's directed toward this Venus ain't normal, either. There's prob'ly a name for it, too.'

Wesley sped up and passed a powder blue BMW with California license plates being driven by a woman wearing a blond wig and large, orange-tinted sunglasses. The woman gave Wesley the finger as he went by.

'Nice folks, them California people,' he said.

'Why you so concerned about me?' asked Consuelo. 'You don't even know me, and you ain't gonna get to, neither.'

'It's Venus I'm mostly curious about. I'm thinkin' I'd like to meet her. Maybe we three can have us a party.'

'Wesley, you're givin' me a ride and all, which I appreciate, but I got to say you ain't nearly the answer to nobody's dreams.'

Wesley laughed. 'Just could be we'll find out there's any truth to that, Miss Whynot, honey.'

Consuelo arched her back and stretched her arms behind her, which made her nipples perk up under the polkadots. She held the pose long enough for Wesley to notice, then relaxed.

'Death and destruction ain't never more than a kiss away,' she said. 'Woman shot at the King of Sweden knew that much.'

Red Bird

Sailor and Lula sat in a tan Naugahyde booth in Rebel Billy's Truckstop off 55 near Bogue Chitto, eating bowls of chili and drinking Barq's. Sailor was reading the *Clarion-Ledger* he'd bought from a box out front.

'Guess we been real lucky with Pace, peanut,' he said.

Lula looked over the red lumps on her tablespoon at the top of Sailor's head and noticed that the bald spot on his crown was growing larger. Sailor was supersensitive about losing his hair. Whenever Lula said anything about it, like suggesting he get a weave or try Monoxidil, he got upset, so she ignored the urge to reiterate her feelings regarding the situation.

'Why you say that, sweetheart? I mean, you're right and all, but what made you think of it?'

Lula stuck the spoon into her mouth.

'Item here in the Jackson paper. Headline says, "Sorrow Ends in Death," and underneath that, "Boy, 12, Hangs Self after Killing Red Bird." Story's out of San Antonio.'

Lula retracted the spoon. 'Nothin' good happens in Texas, I'm convinced.'

'Here it is: "Conscience-stricken after he had shot and killed a red bird, Wyatt Toomey, twelve years old, hanged himself here last night. The body was found by his sister. A signed note addressed to his parents told the motive for the act." This is what he wrote: "I killed myself on account of me shooting a red bird. Goodbye mother and daddy. I'll see you some day."'

'Jesus, Sail, that's a terrible story.'

Sailor folded the newspaper to another page.

'Hard to know what a kid's really thinkin',' he said. 'Pace had himself a few scrapes, of course, but he got clean, thank the Lord.'

'Thanks to you, too, Sail. You been a fine daddy. Want you to know I appreciate it.'

187

Sailor smiled, blew Lula a kiss and leaned back in his corner of the booth and lit up a Camel.

'Hope you don't mind my smokin', peanut. I may be a good daddy but I ain't always such a clean liver.'

A waitress came over carrying a pot of coffee.

'Need refills?' she asked.

Sailor covered his cup with his left palm.

'I'm peaceful,' he said. 'Peanut?'

Lula nodded. 'Don't mind a drop.'

'Folks don't drink so much coffee they used to,' said the waitress, as she poured. 'Don't smoke, neither.'

The waitress carried a good one-hundred-eighty-five pounds on her five-feet two-inches. She was about forty-five, Sailor guessed, and she reeked of alcohol. Sailor figured her for a nighttime cheap gin drinker. Five minutes after she was in her trailer door after work, he imagined, she'd be kicked back in her Barcalounger watching the news, four fingers of Gilbey's over a couple of cubes in a half-frosted chimney in one hand and five inches of menthol in the other.

'My wife's tryin' to quit,' he said.

'I got thirty years' worth of tar and nicotine in me,' said the waitress, 'too late to stop. Anyway, I like it. This health thing's gone just about far as it can now, I reckon. What with AIDS and the Big C, not to mention heart disease and drug-related crimes, might as well let yourself go a little and get some pleasure out of life. My son, Orwell, he's twenty-two now, was born deaf and with a withered-up left arm? He won't eat nothin' but raw vegetables, no meat or dairy. Runs three miles ev'ry damn mornin' before seven, then goes to work at the telephone office. In bed by nine-thirty each night. You'd think Orwell'd want to cut loose, 'specially after the cards he been dealt, but he figures he might could live forever he don't smoke or drink liquor and sticks to eatin' greens. What for? That ain't livin', it's runnin' spooked. Can't stand to see it, but half the world's in the coward's way at present. You folks take care now. Highway's full of God's worst mistakes.'

She left the check on the table.

'Gimme a drag on that Camel, willya, Sail?'

He handed his cigarette to Lula and watched her suck in Winston-Salem's contribution to the good life.

'Feel better?' Sailor asked, as she exhaled and handed it back to him.

Lula nodded. 'It's terrible, but I do love tobacco. Must be it's in our blood, comin' from Carolina.'

''Member that woman kept a vigil out front of the Lorraine Motel in Memphis for three years, place where Martin Luther King got shot? She was protestin' it bein' made into a civil rights museum, 'stead of a medical clinic or shelter for the homeless.'

'Kinda do, honey. What happened to her?'

'Cops dragged her away, finally. Don't know where she went after.'

'Why you askin' now, Sailor? That was a long time back.'

'Oh, I'm thinkin' it might be interestin', long as we're in Memphis, go look at the Lorraine, maybe see the spot James Earl Ray aimed from. I mean, it's our history.'

'Think James Earl Ray ever shot a bird when he was a boy?'

'He did,' said Sailor, 'don't guess it bothered his mind none.'

Burning Love

'Had me a buddy for four or five years named Felix Perfecto,' said Wesley Nisbet, as his Duster finished off Rankin County. 'Perfecto family come over to this country from Mariel, Cuba, on the boatlift in '81. Guess they musta settled in Miami or somewhere in Florida for a while before movin' to Miss'ippi, which is where we met, right here in Jackson. Felix was a good-lookin' cat, dark-skinned with blond hair and blue eyes, which he got from his mama, who was of German extraction. Think her grandaddy was a Nazi fled to Cuba end of WW Two. All the girls went for Felix Perfecto. "Señor Perfect" they called him. Boy had more women than Madonna had push-up bras. That's why what happened to him's such a tragedy.'

Consuelo shifted her left leg out from under her and folded in her right. She couldn't wait to get away from Wesley and was relieved to see the Jackson city limits sign, but she relaxed, knowing it wouldn't be long now, and decided to humor him.

'Somethin' bad happened, huh?'

Wesley whistled softly through his front teeth.

'It ain't pretty.'

'*Dit-moi.*'

'*D* what?'

'French for tell me. Venus been teachin' me.'

'Felix was goin' steady with a girl name of Felicity Tchula. Señor Perfect and Miss Felicity was quite the couple around here for a good while. She was a red-haired beauty, too, full of freckles with big green eyes and a figure like nothin' this side of Sophia Loren when she was young. Ever see her in that movie, *Boy on a Dolphin*, with Alan Ladd, who had to stand on a box to be as tall as her? She don't wear nothin' but a thin, wet shirt, stays plastered to her tits. Hope Alan Ladd had a bite or two on them bullets.

'Anyway, Miss Felicity's parents weren't altogether keen on her

190

hangin' out with Felix Perfecto, since his main source of income come from dealin' dope. Nothin' serious, mind you. Felix sold reefer, is all, and maybe some pills once in a while, but no crack or ice or hard stuff. He started dealin' in high school and just stayed with it afterward, so's he wouldn't have to work for nobody. He was a happy guy, Felix Perfecto, and didn't never hurt people. They was sorta an ideal couple. Felicity was studyin' to be a registered nurse.'

'We're almost to where I'm gettin' off,' Consuelo said, 'so you'd best tell me the terrible part.'

'DeSoto Tchula, Felicity's daddy, decided to try and persuade Felix to break off with his daughter. He went to see Felix with three or four of his employees, construction workers from off one of the Tchula Buildin' Company jobs. Felix told DeSoto to get fucked and the goons broke both of Felix's legs, ruptured his spleen and kicked him so many times in the balls that one of 'em had to be surgically removed. Felix knew it wouldn't do no good to bring charges against the man, seein' as how DeSoto Tchula was so powerful in the town, so he waited until he healed up good as could be expected before he got his revenge.'

'What'd Felicity do after her daddy mangled Perfecto?'

'Felicity's mama, Pearl, took her on a long trip to Europe. When they come back, Felix was about fit, and Felicity went to see him. He hadn't wanted to see none of his friends while he was recuperatin', includin' me, and he didn't let Felicity in, neither. Told her to go home, but warned her not to ride in a car with either of her parents.'

'I can guess now what happened. Real burnin' love business, like me'n Venus.'

'Uh huh. First, Pearl Tchula's T-bird blew up with her in it in the parkin' lot of the Winn-Dixie on Natchez. Couldn't tell her brains from the canteloupe parts. Quarter-hour later, DeSoto Tchula bit metal in his Lincoln Town Car when he started it up to leave a construction site out at the Ross Barnett Reservoir.'

'The cops catch Felix Perfecto?'

'He was already gone by the time the bombs went off. Hijacked a private plane from the airfield, a baby Beechcraft belonged to Tchula, and headed for Cuba. He got there, too, at least in the sky over Havana, but the Cubans wouldn't let him land, sayin' they'd shoot him if he did. He told 'em he was runnin' out of fuel, but they didn't care.'

'He explain about his bein' born in Cuba, and all?'

'Suppose he tried, but whatever he said apparently didn't do no good, 'cause the Beechcraft went down a few minutes later in Havana harbor. Felix never got out, drowned inside the cockpit.'

'What happened to Felicity?'

'Inherited her parents' money, married a banker from Memphis and moved there. Has three kids, includin' a son name of Felix.'

'Fittin',' said Consuelo. 'You can drop me up here, at the A&W.'

Wesley pulled into the drive-in and let the engine idle.

'Sure you don't want to hang out a bit, get to know me better?' he asked.

Consuelo opened the door and got out.

'You prob'ly ain't such a bad guy, Wesley, but I got my own agenda, you know? 'Preciate the lift,' she said, and walked off.

Wesley leaned over and swung the passenger door closed. Something about the girl made him twitch where it hurt but felt good at the same time, and he made the not-so sudden decision to make sure this one didn't get away.

Banter at Bode's

Marietta Pace Fortune and Dalceda Hopewell Delahoussaye were in the corner nook in Bode's Diner sipping sour Cokes following the Daughters meeting. The nook had been their regular spot at Bode's for more than sixty years, since they were little girls and used to go there with their mothers. The diminutive Misses Pace and Hopewell had been special favorites of W. Saint Louis Bode, the original owner. Saint Lou, as he was popularly known, made it a habit to present a brand-new copper penny to each child who came into his diner to spend in the gumball machine next to the huge old National cash register. Marietta and Dalceda once figured out that during their girlhoods, Saint Lou had gifted them with approximately two thousand pennies apiece.

W. Saint Louis Bode had retired when the girls reached sixteen, and his only son, W. Cleveland Bode, known to the residents of Bay St Clement as Mister Cleve, had run the place for the next forty years, until his death, fourteen years ago. Mister Cleve, who had discontinued the policy of passing out pennies to kids after Saint Lou's death three years following his retirement, had never married, and following his funeral the diner was sold by his heirs, cousins who lived in Pensacola, Florida, to the P. L. Ginsberg Group, which owned most of the real estate in downtown Bay St Clement. To the relief of regular patrons, such as Marietta and Dalceda, who despaired at the thought of doing without their sour Cokes and quiet chats in the corner nook three or four afternoons a week, the Ginsberg people decided to keep the place as it always had been, at least for the time being, which, as Marietta pointed out, was the only time one could count on.

'Clyde wouldn't mind, Dal, do you think? I mean about Santos stayin' at the house.'

'Ain't worth thinkin' about, Marietta. Clyde's dead too many years now for what he mighta thought to matter. The world changes, don't it? He'd had to change his thinkin', too, along with the rest of us driftin' souls. If Louis Delahoussaye the Third was still alive, he'd have him a firm opinion, I know.'

'And what might it have been?'

Dal sucked some sour up through her straw and let it slosh around her bottom teeth before swallowing.

'That you was disgracin' Clyde's mem'ry. But Louis was a fool far's them things go, Marietta. Best parts about him was his earnin' power and love of small animals.'

'You don't really miss him, Dal, do you?'

'Like a old rug was always lyin' in the same spot on the floor till it got walked over so many times it needed replacin'.'

'You never replaced Louis.'

'Turned out the floor looked better uncovered, after all.'

Both women laughed and bent to their straws.

'Amazin', though, how well Marcello and Johnnie keep company, Dal, don't you think?'

'Neither of 'em got much teeth left, Marietta. One's a widower and mistress murderer with nothin' but down-time to show for the past couple decades, and the other's a lifelong bachelor who never had the guts to take what he thought he wanted.'

'You're a tough enough nut, Dal. Why I always admired you.'

'Only been cracked once, which is plenty.'

'You mean Truxno Thigpen?'

Dal nodded. 'That boy had lived, my life mighta been a whole sight different. I ain't complainin', though. We had our moment.'

'You ever visit his grave?'

'Not for fifty years, Marietta, a whole half-century. Ain't that somethin'?'

'Sailor Ripley's gonna be fifty next week. He and Lula are goin' to visit Graceland for the occasion.'

'Trux done one thing for me I never will forget.'

'What's that, Dal?'

'After my dog, Clark Gable, died – 'member him, the golden retriever? – Trux brought one white rose to my house every day for a month and left it in front of the door.'

'You never told me that.'

Dal's eyes clouded up. 'Never told anyone. My mama and daddy didn't even know who done it.'

194

'How'd you know?'

'Didn't, really. I mean, I didn't see him bringin' the flowers, but I guessed it was Truxno. Couldn'ta been nobody else. Meant to ask him if he was the one, but then that bolt of ball lightnin' scorched the life out of him on the par-three golf course used to be over by the dump before Ginsberg built them apartments, and I never had the chance.'

'Dal, I'm thinkin' I might marry Marcello. He ain't got long to go.'

Dalceda looked at Marietta and smiled. Her eyes sparkled despite the water in them.

'I got just the dress for you,' she said.

Pickup

'I have a collect call for Venus Tishomingo from Consuelo Whynot. Is this Venus Tishomingo?'

'Yes, it is.'

'Will you accept the charges?'

'Yes, I certainly will.'

'Go ahead, please.'

The operator cut out.

'Hi, Venus, I'm on my way.'

'Where you, Suelo, sweets?'

'Next to a A&W in Jackson. Just hitched a ride here from a weird dude in a nasty short. No boy wants to believe a girl ain't simply dyin' to lick the lint off his nuts.'

'He make a attempt?'

'Not directly. Told him you was my dream woman and I didn't need no further stimulation.'

'Sapphire and Simon know you split?'

'Don't think yet. Was a big train wreck in Meridian, I was there. Fireman on the scene said it's the worst in Miss'ippi hist'ry. Rescue squad'll be pullin' people's parts out of that mess for hours. Prob'ly be findin' pieces in the woods around for days.'

'I know, it's on the news here. How long you gonna be?'

'Depends on when I can get a lift. I'm gonna have me a root beer and a burger and catch another ride.'

'What happened to the hotrod boy?'

'Made him leave me off. He'd been trouble I woulda asked him to take me up to Oxford. Figure I'll make it in by midnight, I'm lucky.'

'OK, precious. I'll be waitin' up. You call again, there's a problem.'

'I will, Venus. Love you dearly.'

'My heart's thumpin', baby. Be careful, you hear?'

196

They both hung up and Consuelo left the phone booth, which was on the side of the road, and walked up to the window of the drive-in.

'Cheeseburger and a large root beer, please,' she ordered from the fat man behind the glass.

'Ever'thin' on it?' he asked.

'No pickles.'

'Three dollars,' said the fat man, as he slid a bag through the space in the window.

Consuelo dug a five dollar bill out of her shorts, handed it to him, and he gave her back two dollars, which she folded in half and stuffed into her right front pocket.

'Y'all hurry back,' the man said, his gooey, small hazel eyes fixed on her breasts.

Consuelo smiled at him, tossed her blond chop and pulled back her shapely little shoulders and expanded her chest.

'Maybe,' she said.

The A&W was only a few hundred yards from the on-ramp to the Interstate, and Consuelo sipped at her root beer as she headed toward it. She took out the cheeseburger, dropped the bag on the ground and ate it as she walked. Next to the on-ramp was a Sun Oil station, and Consuelo spotted Wesley Nisbet's Duster, the hood raised, parked at a gas pump with Wesley bent into it, eyeballing the engine. She hoped he wouldn't see her. She also noticed a road-smudged white Cadillac Sedan de Ville with a man and a woman in it, about to pull away from the pump opposite the one occupied by Wesley's vehicle. Consuelo wolfed down the rest of her burger, wiped her right hand on her black jean cutoffs and stuck out her thumb as the Sedan de Ville rolled her way. The car stopped next to Consuelo and the front passenger window went down.

'Where you goin'?' Lula asked.

'Oxford,' said Consuelo. 'I'm a student at Ole Miss and I got to get there tonight so's I can make my classes in the mornin'.'

'Guess we can take you far's Batesville,' said Sailor, leaning over against Lula. 'You'll have to catch a ride east from there on route 6.'

'Good enough,' Consuelo said, and opened the right rear door and climbed in, careful not to spill her root beer.

Sailor accelerated and guided the heavy machine on to 55

North and had it up to sixty-five in twelve seconds. Wesley Nisbet watched the white Cad disappear and snickered. He gently closed the Duster's hood and slid behind the steering wheel. He wouldn't have a problem keeping a tail on that whale, Wesley thought.

'What river's this?' Consuelo asked, as the Sedan de Ville crossed a bridge just before the fairgrounds.

'The Pearl, I believe,' said Sailor. 'Where you-all from?'

'Alabama,' said Consuelo. 'I been home on vacation 'cause my grandmama died.'

'Sorry to hear it, honey,' said Lula, who was turned around in her seat studying the girl.

'Yeah, we was real close, me and my grandmama.'

'You didn't take no suitcase with you, huh?' Sailor asked.

'No,' Consuelo said, 'I only been gone a few days. Don't need much in this close weather.'

Lula examined Consuelo, watching her sip her drink, then turned back toward the front. She looked over at Sailor and saw the half-grin on his face.

'You let me know the AC's too strong for you, Miss,' said Sailor. 'Wouldn't want you to get a chill in that outfit.'

'Thanks, I'm fine,' Consuelo said. 'And my name's Venus.'

The Suitor

As Wesley Nisbet trailed the white Cadillac by a discreet one eighth of a mile, he thought about his family. It wasn't too often that the Nisbet clan occupied Wesley's mind. Most of them that he'd known were dead now, anyway, buried alongside the Bayou Pierre near Port Gibson. His mother, Althea Dodu, and his father, Husbye, had been killed in a car wreck when Wesley was four years old. They'd been returning from Pine Bluff, Arkansas, where Husbye had robbed a liquor store of four hundred dollars and a fifth of Jack Daniel's. He was sucking on the Jack when the oncoming Pacific Inter-mountain Express truck, into whose lane Husbye had allowed his and Althea's Mercury Monarch to drift, slammed into them head-on.

Wesley had been raised thereafter by Husbye's maiden sister, Taconey, in Weevil, Mississippi, where Wesley did his best to avoid going to school and church, preferring to spend his time under the hoods of trucks and cars and exploring the nearby woods, shooting at things with his Sears .22 rifle. Aunt Taconey had died when Wesley was seventeen, and he'd left Weevil at that time, traveling first to McComb, where he worked for a few months in a filling station, then to Memphis, where he was arrested for stealing a battery out of a new Mustang. He did ninety days in the city lock-up and, following his release, drifted down to Meridian, where he got a job as a gravedigger at the Oak Grove Cemetery.

Wesley had had an argument the day before with the foreman at Oak Grove, Bagby Beggs. Beggs, whose father, Bagby Beggs, Sr, had been a guard for twenty years at the prison farm at Parchman, had reprimanded Wesley for having left the tool shed door unlocked the previous night. Even though nothing had been stolen, Beggs told Wesley, this kind of oversight went a long way, in his opinion, toward revealing a man's true character. Beggs went on to inform him that there were plenty of able bodies in the state of Mississippi willing to work and properly acquit themselves of the responsibilities attendant to the job if the challenge proved too exacting for this particular Nisbet.

At first Wesley had tried to wriggle out of it by saying that he thought someone else had already locked the shed, but when he looked directly into Bagby Beggs's square red eyes Wesley knew the foreman wasn't about to buy it, so he apologized and promised not to let it happen again. When Wesley drove away from the job after working a half-day on Saturday, Beggs's last words echoed in his cerebrum.

'There's two sides to me, Mr Nisbet,' Beggs had said, 'just like there's two sides to ever'body. The side you see's the side you get, 'cause if you don't see that side you won't see any. If I tolerate you, you'll see me. If I don't, you won't.'

Wesley decided as he drove that his career as a gravedigger was about done. Not necessarily because of anything Bagby Beggs had said, but because Wesley felt that life had more to offer him than a position as a caretaker of the dead. He'd enjoyed being able to pay his daily respects to Jimmie Rodgers, the Singing Brakeman, whose remains resided in Oak Grove, but it was time to move on. Maybe he could convince this vixen Consuelo Whynot to take off with him to Charlotte, where he'd begin a career at the Speedway as a stock car racer. First, though, he wanted to check out the lesbian Chickasaw. There were plenty of things his Aunt Taconey hadn't known about, and she'd been no worse off for it, he thought.

One of these days, too, Wesley promised himself, he would go back to Meridian, creep up on Bagby Beggs, and bash his head in with a shovel. Then he'd bury the foreman in an unmarked grave, whether Beggs was already dead or not. It would probably be better not to tell Consuelo about this plan, Wesley decided, at least not right away.

Confession

'There's one thing I been meanin' to ask you about, Marcello.'

Santos was propped up in the fold-out bed in the study with two fluffy pillows behind his head. Marietta was sitting in her grandmother Pace's straight-backed mahogany chair on his right side. Johnnie had gone home an hour before, after the three of them had eaten dinner and watched a rerun on television of one of the original 'Twilight Zone' episodes, the one about the last man left on earth after a nuclear blast.

This story was a favorite of Johnnie's, who at one time in his life had aspired to being a writer of bizarre fiction. In it, the actor Burgess Meredith portrays a Milquetoast bank clerk whose only real passion in life is for reading, an activity for which, due to work and a nagging wife, he never has enough time or peace to enjoy. When the cataclysmic explosion occurs, he is alone in the bank's vault, and he survives. The clerk, who must wear glasses with Coke-bottle-thick lenses, stumbles out into the light and surveys a rubble-filled landscape. After a painstaking search through the city, he realizes he is the only person around. He goes to the library, is overjoyed to find that the books have been spared, and contemplates a leisurely lifetime of reading without disturbance. Reaching for a book, however, his glasses fall off, and in his effort to retrieve them, inadvertently steps on the lenses, crunching them beyond repair. Helpless without his glasses, his future is shattered, too.

Marietta thought the story was just plain mean and didn't want to hear anything Johnnie thought about irony.

'What do you mean, "irony"?' Marietta said. 'Whenever I hear that word, all I can think of is pressin' Clyde's shirts.'

After so many years of friendship, Johnnie Farragut knew better than to argue an abstract point with Marietta Fortune, so he laughed it off and said good night. She'd then fixed up Santos's bed and helped him into it. His condition was worsening visibly day by day, and she didn't see how he could get much weaker and continue living at her house. He was one close step away from an IV feeder and a breathing machine.

'You mean Mona, yes?' Santos said, his voice no more than a tiny croak.

'I hate to ask,' said Marietta, "specially considerin' your heart and all, but I just gotta know, Marcello. Did you have Mona Costatroppo killed?'

Santos sighed heavily. He had been sent to prison for arranging the murder of his mistress, Mona Costatroppo, who had threatened to testify against him in a federal court in New Orleans regarding a variety of criminal charges. The Feds were supposed to have given her a new identity in a distant city as part of the government witness protection program, but she had been shot to death in a hotel room in Chicago by a hitter from Detroit.

'You know, Marietta, my wife, Lina, before she died five years ago, wrote me a letter telling me that she forgave me everything, all of my sins against her and the children, none of whom, of course, will now even acknowledge that I am alive, however barely this is so. I wrote her back, informing her that had I desired absolution I would have remained a Catholic and paid a priest to perform this service. Clergy do not work for nothing, you know. The larger the alleged sin, the larger the church's bite in exchange for removing an obstacle on the path to heaven.'

'Marcello, honey, I ain't interested in Lina, or any letters she mighta wrote. Far's I know, she died of natural causes culminatin' in cirrhosis of the liver.'

Santos nodded slightly. 'That's what I was told.'

'It's this other business I need to satisfy myself about, we're gonna take a step. Answer me, Marcello.'

Santos's eyes, once fiery, unsettling-to-look-into combinations of red and green, now floated on either side of his nose like opaque yolks in viscous, swampy yellow puddles. He blinked them several times, causing the puddles to overflow their containers and streak stickily down the sides of his face. Marietta took a tissue from a pocket of her robe and wiped away the effluent.

'I did, Marietta. I ordered the death of Mona Costatroppo. It was a terrible moment for me, when I realized what I had done, and that it was too late to prevent it. Mona knew it would happen, sooner or later, when she agreed to testify against me. She telephoned me one night, after she had gone into hiding. "I have always been willing to die for you, Marcello," she said, "and now I am willing to die because of you." Then she hung up. Now that you know, Marietta, what difference can it make?'

'It's the truth matters to me, Marcello. You had your reasons for doin' what you done, or had done for you, and I can live with that. I was just hopin' you wouldn't lie about this, is all. Murder ain't no more or less than a imperfect act of desperation, and ain't none of us is perfect. Nothin' to forgive or forget.'

Marietta leaned over and kissed Santos on the forehead. He smiled at her and covered her left hand with the four remaining fingers of his own.

'I am a happy man tonight, Marietta. For the little it is worth, you have won the undying love and respect of an old, dying gangster.'

'It's worth plenty, Marcello.'

Marietta kissed him again on the forehead, stood up and grinned down at the once mighty Crazy Eyes Santos.

''Night, killer,' she said.

Weird by Half

'Wake up, honey,' Lula said to Consuelo, 'we're about at the Batesville junction.'

Consuelo blinked hard a few times and pinched her cheeks. Her mouth tasted dry and sour. She wished she had an ice-cold soft drink.

'Had me a awful strange dream just now,' Consuelo said. 'I went into my brother Wylie's room in the middle of the night, to check on him and see if he was all right. He was only about six years old in the dream – in real life he's fourteen and a half – and he was sleepin' sound. But then I looked over and there was this other bed kinda perpendicular to Wylie's, a single mattress, maybe, on the floor, and there was my cousin Worth, who drowned in Okatibbee Lake when he was twelve and I was eleven. Worth looked the same as he did then, with his reddish-brown hair cut short on the sides and floppin' on his forehead. He sat up in the bed and looked at me, and I said, "Worth, that you?" And he said, "Who do you think it is? 'Course it's me." And I reached out my right hand and touched him with my fingers. I really felt him, and I jumped back, 'cause it was such a spooky feelin'. Then I woke up. Worth was real as y'all. Too damn weird by half.'

'I don't dream so much any more, now I'm older,' said Lula. 'Least I don't remember 'em the way I used to. How 'bout you, Sail?'

'Dreamed more in the joint than anywhere,' Sailor said. 'Prob'ly 'cause I was always catnappin', and my thoughts stayed close to the surface.'

Sailor steered the Cadillac off the interstate and stopped at the State Highway 6 intersection.

'Here you go, Miss Venus. Oxford's due east twenty-five miles. Shouldn't have much trouble gettin' a ride to the university from here.'

''Preciate it much. Oh, by the way, my name's really Consuelo. Consuelo Whynot, from Whynot, Miss'ippi. It's my best friend's name is Venus. She's a Chickasaw Indian. Always wanted to know what it'd feel like to have someone call me by her name, not knowin' it wasn't really mine. Anyway, thanks again.'

Consuelo got out of the car, closed the door and walked off. As Sailor pulled his Sedan de Ville across the road and headed down the return ramp to the Interstate, Wesley Nisbet's black Duster crept off at the Batesville exit. He spotted Consuelo, drove up alongside her, leaned over and rolled down the passenger side window.

'Don't I know you?' he said. 'Them polkadots is difficult to forget.'

'What in blazes you doin' here now?' said Consuelo.

'Thought I'd take me a college tour. I ain't never been to one.'

'You're followin' me.'

'Just goin' the same way, is all. Hop in.'

Consuelo stood on the side of the road for a minute and considered the situation, then she opened Wesley's car door.

'It'll be OK, Consuelo,' Wesley said. 'Y' always burn a few tiles on reentry.'

Out of Body

In Memphis, Sailor and Lula checked into the Robert Johnson Regency, where Hilda Rae, Sailor's secretary at the Gator Gone Corporation, had made them a reservation on the recommendation of Sailor's boss, Bob Lee Boyle, who always stayed there on business trips to the city. It wasn't a fancy place, but it was clean and patroled around the clock by visibly armed security guards. A large sign at the registration desk proclaimed, THE MANAGEMENT SUGGESTS THAT GUESTS LOCK THEIR VALUABLES IN THE HOTEL SAFE DURING THEIR STAY.

'Not much of a view,' Lula said, looking out the window of their third-floor room. Across the street was a dilapidated row of mostly abandoned brown brick buildings.

'Didn't come to Memphis for the view, peanut,' said Sailor. 'Just us and Elvis's home place is all we need.'

He came up behind Lula, hugged her with his large arms folded across her breasts, and kissed her gently on the nape of her neck.

'Harder, Sail, honey. Bite me there on the neck how I like it.'

Sailor gnawed harder on the lower part of Lula's neck and the tops of her shoulders, which made her moan. She bent backward into him, then forward, dipping her head as she lifted her skirt and lowered her panties.

'Stick it in, Sailor,' she said. 'Find a hole and drill me.'

After they'd made love and showered, Sailor and Lula went downstairs to find a restaurant. Sailor was about to ask the desk clerk if he knew of a good place when Lula grabbed his arm and pointed to a man standing just inside the front entrance.

'Do you recognize him?' Lula asked. 'Ain't that Sparky? You remember, he and his friend Buddy was stranded with us in Big Tuna, Texas.'

'It sure is, Lula. Holy shit. You know, some years back I thought

206

I saw him on the late-night cable TV sellin' hair restorer. Wasn't certain, though.'

They walked up behind the man, who was facing the street, and Sailor tapped him on the right shoulder.

'Hey, pardner, you ever been stuck in the Big Tuna?'

Sparky, who was wearing a straw half-Stetson similar to the one he'd worn in Texas almost thirty years before, turned around and grinned broadly when he recognized the couple.

'Well, look at this! It sure is good to know some of us poor white trash has somehow survived the ravages of time.'

Sparky and Sailor shook hands and Lula gave him a big hug.

'Sailor Ripley, I presume,' said Sparky. 'I thought we'd seen the last of you, along with Bobby Peru and Perdita Durango. Got yourself in with a tough twosome down there. Good to see you made it out.'

'Barely did, but here I am. Here we are. Me'n Lula been together again almost eighteen years now.'

'Lula, you're just as sweet-lookin' a young thing as ever. Still got that real black hair and big gray eyes with violet lakes in 'em I ain't never forgot.'

Lula laughed. 'I ain't young no more, and the eyes are real, OK. But I kinda have to cheat now and then on the hair, which is threatenin' to go the way of my eyes.'

'Me'n Buddy used to handle hair products back when we had the House of Santería in Waggaman, Louisiana. I could still get you some good dye, you want it.'

'I thought that was you and Buddy one time doin' a commercial on the TV!' said Sailor.

Sparky smiled. 'We did that for a while, till the FDA come after us. Before that we owned a bar in Dallas. Never did make it back to California.'

'Where's Buddy?' Lula asked.

'Waitin' for him now. Better standin' inside the Me'n the Devil Motel here than catchin' a stray slug in the street. Memphis is a unpredictable town.'

'What are you-all doin' in Memphis?' Sailor asked.

'Got us a new business, prosperin', too.'

Sparky took a card out of his Madras sports coat pocket and handed it to Sailor.

'"S&B Organ Retrieval Service,"' Sailor read out loud. '"Only the best parts."'

'We got a 800 number, you'll notice.'

'Organ retrieval?' said Lula. 'What in hell's that?'

'Vital body pieces,' Sparky said. 'Heart, kidneys, eyes, even livers, though real useful ones is difficult to come by, given the Southern disposition toward Rebel Yell and Wild Turkey.'

'Sparky, you jokin'?' Lula asked.

'Nope. We got us some steady customers in the private sector. Keep that card, Sailor. Might come in handy. What about you folks? What's been happenin' all these years? And why're you in Memphis?'

'Sailor's vice-president of the Gator Gone Corporation now, produces alligator and crocodile repellent. It's a worldwide operation, even in India.'

'Sell a bunch over there, that's the truth,' said Sailor.

'We have a house in Metairie,' Lula said, 'by New Orleans. Our son, Pace, is livin' in Nepal, leadin' expeditions in the Himalaya mountains.'

'Man,' said Sparky, 'life fools me right and left.'

'We come up to visit Graceland,' said Sailor. 'Never been here before.'

'Tomorrow's Sailor's birthday, his fiftieth. We're celebratin'.'

'Guess you know about what the King's widow and daughter're doin' with mostly all the proceeds from the estate now, don't ya?'

'No,' Sailor said, 'what's that?'

'All goes to the Church of Myrmidon, that mind-control cult headquartered in San Diego. The widow and the kid're whole hog in the grip of that fake prophet calls himself Myrmidon, claims to have visited Venus and Mars and wrote all them books about out-of-body experiences. Man lives on a three-hundred-foot yacht, cruises the Greek Islands and the French Riviera. Saw in the newspaper where he was at the Cannes Film Festival last week promotin' a movie about his life. Can't set foot on US soil or the Feds'll feed him into the shredder.'

'Heard of the Church of Myrmidon,' said Sailor, 'but I didn't know they was suckin' the blood out the King's afterlife.'

'Yeah, the Colonel bled him while he was alive, and now this Phelps Bonfuca, calls himself Myrmidon, drains his heirs.'

'You say Phelps Bonfuca?'

'Uh huh. Myrmidon's real handle.'

'I was in the joint with him,' said Sailor. 'At Huntsville. I did a dime standin' up for that stunt with Bobby Peru, and for four of 'em Phelps Bonfuca was in the same cell block. He was in on some bunco beef. Pyramid scam, I think. Milkin' suckers.'

'Still at it,' said Sparky. 'Only on a big-time basis.'

Sailor shook his head. 'This don't make me feel so good now about goin' to Graceland, knowin' the money's endin' up in Phelps's pockets.'

'It don't matter, Sail, sweetheart,' said Lula. 'Could be worse. The fam'ly might be donatin' the proceeds to the Cath'lic Church, or the Mormons or somethin'. One cult's same as another.'

'Kinda disappoints me, is all.'

'Don't matter what people do with their money,' said Sparky, 'long as they spend it, keep it comin' around where the other guy can reach in, he gets the chance, and grab him a fistful. Say, you folks hungry? Here's Buddy now.'

Sailor and Lula looked through the glass door and saw a brown Plymouth Voyager pull up in front. The words S&B ORGAN RETRIEVAL SERVICE – ONLY THE BEST PARTS were stenciled in white on the side.

'We was just about to find us a restaurant when we seen you,' said Lula.

'Come on, then,' said Sparky. 'We'll get some ribs. I know a place they take 'em off the body for you!'

Professionals

Venus Tishomingo was six feet even and weighed a solid one-hundred-seventy-five pounds. Her hands were each the size of an infielder's glove, and she wore a 12-D shoe. Her hair was chestnut brown and very thick, and hung down loose past her waist. She wore at least one ring on every finger other than her thumbs. They were cheap, colorful rings she'd bought in pawn shops in Memphis. Her eyes were clear, almost colorless stones set deep in her skull. Most people had a difficult time staring into them for very long before becoming uncomfortable and having to look away. At first glance, Venus's eyes resembled pristine pebbles in a gentle, smooth-flowing stream, but then they came alive and darted toward whomever's eyes met hers. She sat in her one-bedroom cottage in a gooseneck rocking chair, wearing only a well-faded pair of Wrangler blue jeans, reading the *Oxford Eagle*, waiting for Consuelo to arrive or call. An item datelined Jackson caught her eye.

'Pearl Buford, of Mockingbird, accused of trying to sell two of her grandchildren in an adoption scam, has pleaded innocent to charges in federal court here. Buford, 34, who told authorities she used to baby-sit professionally, also pleaded innocent to six counts of mail fraud involving solicitation of offers for the children. She is currently unemployed. Her daughter, Fannie Dawn Taylor, 16, a dropout after finishing 8th grade at Mockingbird Junior High, pleaded innocent to one count of mail fraud.'

Venus had it in mind to adopt a child that she and Consuelo could raise together. Maybe more than one. It was too bad, Venus thought, that Pearl Buford hadn't contacted her about taking on Fannie Dawn's kids.

Venus massaged her left breast with her right hand, tickling the nipple with the second and third fingers until it stood out taut and long as it would go. She had large breasts that were

210

extremely sensitive to touch, and Consuelo knew perfectly how to suck on and fondle them. Venus dropped the newspaper and slid her left hand down inside the front of her jeans and rubbed her clit. She closed her eyes and thought about a photograph of a cat woman she'd seen in a book in the Ole Miss library that afternoon. It wasn't really a cat woman but two negatives printed simultaneously, one atop the other, of a cat and a woman, so that the face was half-human, half-feline, with long white whiskers, weird red bolts for eyes and perfect black Kewpie doll lips. Venus came quickly, bucking sharply twice before relaxing and slumping down in the chair. She removed her left hand and let it drape over the arm of the rocker. Her right hand rested in her lap. Venus was almost asleep when Consuelo knocked on the door.

Venus jumped up and opened it. Consuelo threw herself forward onto her naked chest.

'I'm starved, Venie,' Consuelo said. 'I need your lovin'.'

'Got it comin', baby,' said Venus, stroking Consuelo's wheat-light hair with a large brown hand.

Venus heard a car engine idling, looked over Consuelo's left shoulder out the door and saw the black Duster in front of the house.

'Who's that?' she asked.

'Wesley Nisbet, the one I told you about. He's a pest, but he give me a lift here. Followed the ride I caught outta Jackson, picked me up again in Batesville.'

'He truly dangerous?'

'Maybe, like most.'

'He figurin' you're gonna invite him in?'

Consuelo swung her right leg backward and the door slammed shut.

'Just another mule kickin' in his stall,' she said.

When Wesley saw the door close, he shifted the Duster into first and eased his pantherlike machine away. He drove into town, parked on the northwest side of the square in front of a restaurant-bar named The Mansion, got out of the car and went inside.

'J. W. Dant, double,' Wesley said to the bartender, as he hopped up on a stool. 'One cube, splash water.'

A toad-faced man with a greasy strand of gray-yellow hair falling over his forehead sat on the stool to Wesley's left. The man was wearing a wrinkled burgundy blazer with large silver buttons over a wrinkled, dirty white shirt and a wide, green, food-stained tie. He wobbled as he extended his right hand toward Wesley.

'Five Horse Johnson,' the man said. 'You?'

'That a clever way of tellin' me you got a short dick or's it your name?'

The man laughed once, very loudly, and wiped his right hand on his coat.

'Nickname I got as a boy. Had me a baby five HP outboard on a dinghy, used to go fishin' in Sardis Lake. Can't hardly remember my so-called Christian one, though the G-D gov'ment reminds me once a year. Hit me up for the G-D tax on my soul, they do. Strip a couple pounds a year. Forty-five G-damn years old. Amazed there's any flesh left to cover the nerves. You ain't from Oxford.'

'No, ain't.'

'Then you prob'ly don't know the local def'nition of the term "relative humidity."'

Wesley picked up his drink, which the bartender had just set in front of him, and took a sip.

'What's it?'

'Relative humidity is the trickle of sweat runs down the crack of your sister-in-law's back while you're fuckin' her in the ass.'

Five Horse Johnson grinned liplessly, exposing six slimy orange teeth, then fell sideways off his stool to the floor. Wesley finished his whisky and put two dollars on the bar.

'This do it?' he asked the bartender, who nodded.

Wesley unseated himself and stepped over Five Horse Johnson, who was either dead or asleep or in some indeterminate state between the two.

'Professional man, I'll guess.'

'Lawyer,' said the bartender.

'I known others,' Wesley said, and walked out.

Sprinkle Bodies

Sailor and Lula spent most of their first afternoon in Memphis having lunch with Sparky and Buddy in the Hound Dog Cafe on Elvis Presley Boulevard across the street from Graceland, a place that specialized in Elvis's favorite sandwich, peanut butter and banana on white. The four of them passed on 'The White Trash Blue Plate,' as Buddy called it, and ate hamburgers as they listened to old Sun 45s by the Killer, the King, Roy Orbison, Charlie Rich and Carl Perkins on the jukebox, and filled each other in on their respective activities over the past quarter of a century and more. After lunch, Sailor and Lula exchanged addresses and telephone numbers with Sparky and Buddy, who went back to work at Organ Retrieval, and then browsed the Elvis souvenir shops.

Sailor was reluctant to tour Graceland now that he knew about the connection to Phelps Bonfuca, alias Myrmidon, and he told Lula he wanted to think it over some more. He was tempted to go through Elvis's private jet, the *Lisa Marie*, which was on display in the Graceland parking lot, but he resisted the urge, since that cost money, too. He did buy a few postcards and two Elvis tee shirts – both decorated with photos from *Jailhouse Rock*, his favorite Elvis movie – at a shop called The Wooden Indian, because he figured Elvis's heirs didn't own it.

Back in their room at the Robert Johnson Regency, Sailor and Lula lay on the king-size bed in their underwear, smoking and talking. Lula had fallen off the cigarette wagon in the Hound Dog Cafe, having fished a More from her purse and fired it up before she'd even realized what she was doing. She puffed happily away and put any thoughts about the possible consequences into a dark corner of her mind.

'Sail, you know, we really been alive a long time now.'

'Sometimes it feels long, peanut, other times not much. Why you say that?'

213

'Oh, thinkin', is all.'

Sailor lit a fresh unfiltered Camel off an old one and stubbed out the butt on the letters RJR in a round glass ashtray.

'Bet Robert Johnson never stayed in no hotel fancy as this,' Sailor said.

'Robert who?'

'Johnson, man this hotel's named for. Blues singer from Miss'ippi died young. Record comp'ny brought him to the city, right off the plantation, I believe. Think Dallas, or San Antone. Cut some tunes then got killed, shot or knifed or somethin', so there ain't much to listen to. What he done was outstandin', though. Kinda spooky, some of it. That's what Sparky was referrin' to when he called this place the Me'n the Devil Motel. "Me'n the Devil" was one of Robert Johnson's songs. Another good one was "Hellhound on My Trail."'

Lula inhaled hard on a More and then blew a big gusher of smoke into the air where it hovered over the bed like a cumulus cloud.

'Shit, Sailor, you know so much more'n me about things? I mean, strange, about unheard of details, like what happened to Robert Johnson.'

'Anybody's interested in the music knows about him, honey. Ain't nothin' special.'

'Not just this, Sail. You got tons of information tucked away in every part of your brain you never even gonna use. It's a gift.'

Sailor laughed. 'Ain't the same as bein' smart, though. I'd been smart, never woulda spent a dozen years of my life behind bars. Only real smart thing I ever done was realize you're the best, peanut. I mean that more'n anythin'.'

'Sailor?'

'Huh?'

'Don't laugh at me now, OK? When I say what I'm goin' to say?'

'How do I know if I'll laugh or not? What if it's funny?'

'No, you gotta promise or I can't say it.'

'OK, peanut, I promise.'

'You think when a person dies, he just fades away? Mean, there ain't really no heaven or even no hell and it's just all over? Tell me the truth now.'

'Thought you figured this out back when you was part of the Reverend Goodin Plenty's flock in the Church of Reason, Redemption and Resistance to God's Detractors.'

'You know I ain't been to church since Bunny Thorn and I seen Goodin Plenty shot to death in the tent at Rock Hill. His answers didn't hold up, neither.'

''Member that ol' Buddy Holly tune, "Not Fade Away"?'

'Yeah?'

'There's your answer.'

'Splain yourself.'

Sailor raised himself on one elbow and stubbed out his cigarette.

'I'll tell you,' he said, 'but now you gotta promise not to laugh.'

'I do.'

'Well, I believe that when folks die all their energy just disperses in the air and flies off like sparks through the universe. Their spirit shoots out of their body and sprinkles back over ever'thin'. That way nobody dies, 'cause their vital self enters into what's left.'

'You talkin' 'bout reincarnation, like in India, where a person can come back in another life as a insect? Or you mean that past lives stuff?'

'Uh-uh. Some people in India figure if they live holy enough, next time around they'll be an American. No, just what I said. I call it the "sprinkle body" theory. Sometimes maybe because of the way the earth's spinnin' or somethin', more of someone gets transferred into a newborn baby or a bee or a rose, but prob'ly that's pretty rare. I figure it's sorta like tossin' a handful of sand into the sky and lettin' the grains blow into eternity.'

Lula lay still and didn't say anything.

'Peanut, you think I'm crazy, thinkin' this?'

'No, Sail, I think you're smart, real smart. About some things, I mean. Mostly important things, and this is one. Wasn't totally your fault you went to prison. There's plenty of bright boys locked up for one reason or another.'

Sailor lay back on his pillow, picked up his pack of Camels, shook one out and lit it.

'Can't figure it any other way,' he said.

'Sprinkle bodies,' said Lula.

'Yeah.'

'It makes sense, don't it, Sail? It truly does.'

The room was almost completely dark, and Sailor stared at the burning end of his cigarette.

'This is the only chance we got to be who we are, Lula, to have all of ourselves in one package.'

'I believe you, Sailor. I believe in you, too. But I guess you must know that by now.'

Lula turned toward Sailor and fit her head into his right armpit.

'I love you, too, peanut,' he said. 'And you know what?'

'Huh?'

'Neither of us ain't never had another choice in this world.'

Lula nuzzled in even closer.

'Listen, Lula,' said Sailor, 'I want you to have engraved on my tombstone: "Dear Peanut, I love you to death," and underneath just my name.'

'Oh, Sail, don't be depressin'. You ain't about to die anytime soon.'

'Prob'ly Elvis, even though he was a overweight drug addict, didn't think he was gonna go at forty-two, honey. Just remember, OK?'

'Course I will, sweetheart, it's what you want. Just you remember I love you to death, too.'

A World of Good

'OK, peanut, guess we might just as well do it, even if Phelps gets the money.'

'Don't matter anyway, Sail. This bein' your birthday you should do what you want. It'll be fun visitin' Graceland. Elvis didn't die there, did he?'

'Yeah, he OD'ed sittin' there on a toilet.'

'Prob'ly if he'd always stayed in Memphis, or got him a spread down in that beautiful area around Hernando, Miss'ippi, he'd've lived a whole lot longer. Elvis was outta his true element in California, I believe. Read a Elvis-on-Other-Planets Weight Chart was in a *Enquirer* or somewhere, said that since he weighed 255 when he died, Elvis woulda weighed 648 pounds on Jupiter but only 43 on the moon.'

Sailor and Lula had awakened early on the morning of his fiftieth birthday. They'd each gone to the bathroom, peed and brushed their teeth, then gone back to bed and made love. Ordinarily Lula had a hard time coming when they did it so soon after waking, but today she'd been able to get the calf out of the chute so easily that it gave her the giggles.

'What's so funny?' Sailor asked.

'Nothin', honey, just feelin' nice and warm, is all. Look, bring that big bad thing up here where I can treat it right.'

Lula grabbed Sailor's cock and pulled him up so that he straddled her chest. She guided him into her mouth, placed her hands on his buttocks and let him move himself forward and back until the hourglass-shaped vein on his penis swelled to bursting and her throat was flooded.

'Still works good, don't it, peanut?' Sailor said, getting off the bed.

'I'm a lucky girl, all right.'

Sailor went into the bathroom to take a shower and Lula

217

switched on the TV. The news was on and Lula cranked up the volume in order to hear over the running water.

'In Oxford, Mississippi, last night,' the young, African-American woman newscaster said, 'a man was shot and killed with his own gun by a half-naked woman, who was then run over and killed by the man's car when it went out of control. Police in Oxford are calling the incident the "Lesbian Indian Murders." The killings were apparently the result of a love triangle involving the man, who has been identified as Wesley Nisbet, address unknown, and the woman, Venus Tishomingo, a Chickasaw Indian who was a student at Ole Miss, and a sixteen-year-old girl named Consuelo Whynot, who was present at the scene. Miss Whynot, who was unhurt, is being held in protective custody at the Lafayette County Jail in Oxford.'

'Sailor! Sail, come here! You won't believe this!'

Sailor turned off the water and grabbed a towel.

'What is it, peanut?' he said, running in and dripping everywhere.

'You know that girl hitcher we picked up and drove from Jackson to Batesville?'

'Yeah?'

'She's in jail in Oxford. Near as I could make out, a man and a woman were fightin' over her and killed each other. Cops got her in custody.'

Sailor ran the towel over his head, under his arms, around his back, down his legs, daubed his feet and tossed it on the bed. He started to put on his clothes.

'Let's get down there, peanut. She might could use some help.'

'What could we do for her? Besides, it's your birthday and we're goin' to Graceland.'

'Don't matter what day it is. Just think it's what we oughta do. Fuck Graceland, anyway. I re-decided I don't want none of our money filterin' down to no Church of Myrmidon.'

Lula got up and began to pack. The telephone rang and Sailor answered it.

'Ripley speakin'.'

'Sailor, this is Dalceda Delahoussaye.'

'Hello, Mrs Delahoussaye. Why you callin'? How'd you know we was in Memphis?'

'Marietta told me. Is Lula there?'

'Yeah. You rather speak to her? She's packin' 'cause we're about to leave.'

'Don't really matter, I s'pose. Marietta wanted her to know that Marcello Santos had heart palpitations yesterday and is under doctor's care at the Sister Ralph Ricci Convalescent Center here in Bay St Clement. Marietta's stayin' by his side and won't leave.'

'That so? Look, lemme put Lula on.'

Sailor handed her the phone.

'Dal? Mama all right?'

'Yes, Lula, Marietta's fine, but Santos is havin' serious chest pains and's in Sister Ralph's. Marietta's there with him, holdin' his hand and readin' him chapters from his favorite book, Eugene Sue's *Mysteries of Paris*.'

'That's Mama. He gonna pull through?'

'Don't think he's got long to go, Lula, but he might could hang on, bein' he's one tough Sicilian. There's somethin' else, though.'

'What's that?'

'Johnnie Farragut's kidneys just completely quit on him this mornin' early, and he's over at Little Egypt Baptist plugged into a dialysis machine. Marietta don't even know yet. I ain't told her since she's got her hands full with old Crazy Eyes. Doctor at Baptist says unless Johnnie gets a transplant soon he's done.'

'Sweet Jesus, Dal, what a phone call.'

'Sorry to be the one, Lula, but I thought you'd want to hear the news sooner'n later.'

''Course, Dal, I 'preciate it. Sailor and I are leavin' here now. We got a stop to make in Oxford, then we'll head for home, I guess. I'll call you when we get to Metairie.'

'OK. Take care drivin'.'

'We will, Dal. Bye.'

'Bye, hon'.'

Lula hung up and said, 'Shit hits the fan, it splatters.'

'You don't care 'bout Santos, do you?'

'Not one way or another, but Dal says Johnnie Farragut's got kidney failure and needs a new one or he's a goner. He's rigged to a device at Little Egypt Baptist.'

Sailor picked up the telephone.

'You got that card Sparky give you?' he asked.

Lula found it in her purse and handed it to Sailor, who read the number on it and dialed. A machine answered.

'You've reached S&B Organ Retrieval Service,' said Sparky's recorded voice. 'Leave a message and we'll do what we can to

219

accommodate your needs. It might cost you some, but at least we won't charge an arm and a leg! Just a little humor there, of course. We stand by our motto: "Only the best parts!" Be talkin' to ya. Here comes the beep.'

'Sparky, Buddy, this is Sailor Ripley speakin'. Listen, Lula's mama's old friend Johnnie Farragut is got kidney failure and's hooked up to a tube or somethin' at Little Egypt Baptist Hospital in Bay St Clement, North Carolina. He needs a transplant real quick or he's gonna die. If you can help out with this, Lula and I'll find a way to pay you back. We're checkin' out of the hotel now. I'll call you again later.'

He hung up, opened his suitcase and threw in his clothes. The phone rang and Sailor answered it.

'Sailor? It's Buddy.'

'I just called you.'

'I know, we heard the message. We never answer ourselves. Never know who it might be. Anyway, we're on the case. Sparky's contactin' our best retrieval man, John Gray, on the other line. Prob'ly we can get a part on its way to your friend by tonight. And don't worry about the price, it's free of charge. For old times' sake.'

'This is awful large of you guys,' said Sailor. 'Awful large.'

Buddy laughed. 'Sparky's standin' here talkin' in my other ear now. Hold on, Sailor.'

'Sailor? Sparky here.'

''Preciate this, Spark. You guys are beyond outstandin'.'

'Anything for veterans of the Big Tuna! You tell Lula's mama not to worry. We gotta run now, we're gonna get this part out.'

'We're goin', too. *Adiós, amigo.*'

'*Ciao!*'

Sailor hung up.

'What'd they say, Sail? Tell me!'

'Boys have it covered, peanut. They're sendin' a new kidney to North Carolina tonight.'

'Gonna cost a arm or leg, I bet.'

Sailor laughed. 'No, sweetheart, it ain't. It's free.'

'Them two're somethin' else. Shows you how much good there still is left in the world, Sail. Just gotta know where to look.'

'Don't know about good, Lula, but could be Johnnie Farragut'll be able to take a real piss again one of these days.'

220

The Proposal

'"When the phantoms cease for a moment to pass and repass on the black veil which I have before my eyes, there are other tortures – there are overwhelming comparisons. I say to myself, if I had remained an honest man, at this moment I should be free, tranquil, happy, loved, and honored by mine own, instead of being blind and chained in this dungeon, at the mercy of my accomplices."

'"Alas! the regret of happiness, lost by crime, is the first step toward repentance. And when to this repentance is added an expiation of frightful severity – an expiation which changes life into a long sleep filled with avenging hallucinations of desperate reflections, perhaps then the pardon of man will follow –"'

'Marry me, Marietta,' said Santos.

Marietta stopped reading, closed the book and looked up at him. His face was green and puffy and his eyes were closed.

'Marietta Pace, will you marry me?'

She squeezed his right hand, the one with a thumb, with her left.

'Yes, Marcello,' said Marietta, 'I will.'

Poison

'I still ain't sure we're doin' the right thing. I mean, we ain't even relatives.'

'Maybe there ain't nothin' we can do, peanut, but I got a feelin' this is a lost girl could use a hand.'

Sailor had just turned the Sedan de Ville on to Highway 6 toward Oxford.

'Sail, look how these trees is bein' strangled by kudzu. Them vines strap around 'em like boas on bunnies.'

'No stoppin' it, I guess. Kudzu's nature's version of The Blob.'

'Wonder if Beany's rememberin' to turn my worms.'

Sailor turned up the radio.

'In Miami yesterday,' said a newscaster, 'a man and a woman died after drinking a six-pack of a Colombian soft drink laced heavily with cocaine. Pony Malta de Bavaria, an imported beverage that has been available for sale in limited quantities in independent grocery stores in the area known as Little Havana, was removed from shelves this morning by order of the Greater Miami Board of Health.'

'Used to be Co-Cola had cocaine in it, didn't it, Sailor?'

'Think maybe the first few batches did, till the government figured out a better way to make money off it.'

Oxford came up fast and Sailor slowed the Cad as they entered the town. He drove in on Old Taylor Road and followed the signs to the square, where he stopped and asked an old man for directions to the police station.

'They holdin' the "Last Kiss" girl there, you know,' said the man. 'I been over but they ain't lettin' nobody in.'

The old man was wearing a faded, torn yellow tee shirt that had the words FREE BYRON DE LA BECKWITH on it in black block letters. The man had no hair and no visible teeth, and as he

222

pointed across the square with his left hand, Sailor noticed that the index finger was the only remaining digit on it.

'Lafayette County Jail's just yonder, past the square. Follow around and it'll be on your right. Tickets to view a poison pelt like her'd move faster'n jumper cables at a nigger funeral, I'll guarantee.'

Sailor nodded at the man, drove to the jail and parked on the street in front. In the space ahead was a Mercedes-Benz 600 sedan with a Lauderdale County personalized license plate that read WHY NOT.

'Bet that belongs to her parents,' said Lula.

'We'll find out,' said Sailor, as he opened his door.

As soon as Sailor and Lula entered the station, Consuelo Whynot, who was standing with a well-dressed middle-aged couple and a sheriff, shouted, 'They're the ones picked me up in Jackson! They'll tell you 'bout how I was runnin' from that deranged boy!'

'That true?' asked the sheriff, walking toward Sailor and Lula.

'It's true we give her a lift from Jackson to Batesville,' said Sailor, 'but we don't know nothin' 'bout no boy.'

'Why you here?'

'Heard about the incident on the TV news in Memphis, where we was stayin',' said Lula. 'Today's my husband's fiftieth birthday, which we was plannin' to celebrate, but he thought it'd be best we drove down and see she needed help.'

'You-all sure I didn't tell you 'bout that hor'ble Wesley Nisbet?' asked Consuelo.

'Not that I recall,' said Sailor. 'You?' he asked Lula.

'Uh-uh.'

'I give him one kiss, is all,' said Consuelo. 'I swear. Said he'd leave me'n Venus be if I did. Had a gun, that boy. Then he told us unless we did a act of love while he watched, he was gonna kidnap me. That's when Venus took after him and the cat caught the chicken. Mama, you got a cigarette?'

The well-dressed woman took a pack of Mores from her purse, removed one and handed it to Consuelo.

'Need a blaze,' Consuelo said.

Her mother produced a gold lighter with the initials SOW on it and lit Consuelo's cigarette.

'Sailor, look,' said Lula, 'she smokes the same brand as me.'

'So you folks don't know nothin' 'bout this Nisbet?' asked the sheriff.

'We don't,' Sailor said.

'Look, sheriff,' said the well-dressed man, 'none of this really matters, does it? Consuelo will be with us if you need her. We'll make sure she don't leave home again until this case is cleared up satisfact'rily.'

'You can take her,' the sheriff said. 'Ain't nothin' I can charge her with. It's you and your wife might have a problem, bein' she's a minor.'

'Old enough to get married without nobody's permission,' said Consuelo. 'Though there ain't a man alive can replace Venus in my affections.'

'Let's go, Sail,' Lula said. 'Nobody needs us here.'

'OK, peanut. So long, Consuelo. Good luck.'

Consuelo took a deep drag on the More and pushed her free hand back through her brushfire of hair. She pursed her lips and exhaled, then smiled at Sailor.

'Elvis has left the buildin',' she said.

Solo

John Gray lived, ate and worked alone. He had risen only several minutes prior to the phone call from S&B Organ Retrieval, his best customer. The day had begun well for John Gray, and he hummed the tune of 'Just a Closer Walk with Thee' while he shaved. John Gray was forty-five years old, he was slightly more than six-feet three-inches tall, weighed two-hundred-ten well-muscled pounds, wore a bushy black hair weave, and a thick Mexican *bandido*-style mustache that he coated with black Kiwi shoe polish. His eyes were light green, although on a bright afternoon, when he wasn't wearing dark glasses, they turned almost yellow. He wore a three-piece, Wall Street gray Brooks Brothers suit every day, with a red handkerchief in the breast pocket, and black Reebok dress shoes.

John Gray knew where to go for product. He kept his supercharged, midnight blue 5.0-liter Mustang under control as he glided through the Memphis streets. When he arrived at the corner of Murnau and Lewton, he slid to the curb and let the engine idle while he waited. The neighborhood appeared deserted, with abandoned buildings on all sides, but within thirty seconds, two teenaged boys appeared, both wearing Bart Simpson tee shirts, black Levi's and Air Jordans. They came over to the Mustang.

'Got ice, bro',' one of the boys said, as they both leaned their heads toward John Gray, 'blow you away.'

'No,' said John Gray, as he brought up the nine-millimeter machine pistol he'd been holding on his lap, 'blow *you* away.'

He shot both boys point-blank once each in their foreheads, got out of the car, picked them up, placed them carefully in the trunk and wrapped a heavy brown blanket tightly around the bodies.

As he drove at a modest speed toward the S&B office, John Gray began to sing 'Angelo castro e bel' from Donizetti's *Il Duca d'Alba*. Though not a true tenor, John Gray did his best to mimic Caruso's interpretation of the piece, imagining himself as Marcello de Bruges pouring his heart out for Amelia d'Egmont, who is at that moment on her way to meet him.

Life As We Know It

Sailor and Lula stopped to eat at the Mayflower Cafe on Capitol Street in Jackson on their way home. Most of downtown Jackson had been recently torn down, including the grand old Heidelberg Hotel, and replaced by faceless state government buildings and parking lots. Not that most of the city was that old, Sherman having torched everything that would burn on his march to Atlanta during the unpleasantness known unpopularly as the War Between the States. About the only building left standing after the Yankees left had been the old Capitol. Since the demise of Tom and Woody's Mississippi Diner, the Mayflower was pretty much the end of the line for the downtown restaurant business.

'Same two Greek brothers been operatin' this place since forever,' Sailor said to Lula, as they seated themselves in a red leather booth.

He pointed to two ancient-looking, bald-headed, big-nosed men sitting at a Formica table by the cash register. Above the register on the wall was a framed photograph of a man whom both brothers resembled closely.

'That picture's prob'ly of their daddy,' said Sailor. 'Food's as good here as at the Acme, I recall. Ain't been in since them few months we was apart followin' my release from Huntsville. Those were dark days for me, peanut.'

'I know, Sail. They were for me, too.'

Sailor shook his head. 'Never will forget workin' in that lumberyard in Petal, and livin' in that crummy furnished room over the St Walburga Thrift Store in Hattiesburg. Whew, that was a bad deal. Come through here and stayed a few days after I left you and Pace in NO.'

'Let's not talk about it, Sailor. Them days is long gone. Look at the good life we created together since then.'

Sailor reached across the table and put his hands over Lula's.

227

'I'm fine, peanut. You don't hear me complainin'. Hate seein'
a bad fam'ly situation like the Whynots, is all.'

'Won't be no easy road for that Consuelo. Least not for
a while.'

'She's wild in the country, OK.'

A waitress came over and Sailor ordered fried oysters, shrimp,
onion rings, fries and two glasses of iced tea.

'That should do it,' he said. 'What you gonna have, Lula?'

After they'd eaten, Sailor suggested that they not drive all the
way home that night, and Lula agreed. They got a room at the
Millsaps Buie House on North State Street, a Victorian relic that
had originally been the residence of Confederate Major Reuben
Webster Millsaps, founder of the local Methodist College, whose
house was now operated as an inn. Lula loved the elegant old
bed and breakfast place, and she and Sailor slept late the next
day, neither of them being in a particular hurry to find out what
disastrous occurrence came next.

It was Lula who made the discovery a few minutes after they'd
gotten home.

'Sailor! Come see these worms! They're all dead!'

'How could that be, peanut?' Sailor said, running into the
backyard, carrying a letter in his right hand. 'Thought you told
me Beany was watchin' 'em.'

'She musta left the hose on the rose bushes too long, and the
water seeped into the worm bin and drowned 'em. Sailor, this is
the worst!'

'Maybe not, peanut.'

He handed Lula the letter.

'It's from Pace,' she said.

Sailor nodded. 'Go on and read it.'

Dear Mama and Daddy,
    I am just back from the trek and am writing to tell you the best
news of my life. I have met a great girl, a woman I should say,
from New York. Actually she is from Brooklyn which is about the
same place she says. Her name is Rhoda Gombowicz and yes, she
is Jewish. She is about the first Jewish person I have ever known
to my knowledge. Rhoda is very beautiful with hair kind of like
yours Mama and big brown eyes. Also she is incredibly smart.
Sometimes she talks too fast for me and I have to tell her to slow
down but she doesn't mind my telling her that. She says everyone
in New York talks that way which is one of the reasons she likes

228

me so much she says because I don't. Any way Rhoda and I are in love now and I asked her to marry me when we were on a peak in the Himalayas. She said no woman would say no being proposed to in that spot so she said yes. The one problem is that Rhoda's parents won't let her marry a man who is not Jewish so I have agreed to convert to the Jewish religion. The only religions I know about are Baptist, Buddhist, and Bonpo, so why not? We will leave in a week for New York to meet her family and where I will find out what it takes to become Jewish. I will call or write to you from there. Rhoda says we should live in Brooklyn because that is where her family is. Rhoda is a mental therapist who helps people with their problems by talking to them not a physical therapist who performs rubdowns. You'll like her I know. She is 32 years old five years older than me and never married. Rhoda says if I want I can work in the diamond business with her father and four brothers. I told her I would wait and see about that part. Don't worry about me or anything. The next time you hear from me will be from Brooklyn!

Love, your favorite (and only) son,

Pace Roscoe Ripley

Lula looked up at Sailor but said nothing.

'What you think, peanut?'

'I can't think yet, Sail. I need a minute.'

The telephone rang.

'I'll get it,' said Lula, who carried Pace's letter with her into the house and held it in one hand while she picked up the receiver with the other.

'Hello?'

'Lula? It's Dal.'

'Hi, Dal. How's Santos and Johnnie?'

'It was beautiful, Lula. I wish you coulda been there.'

'Been where?'

'At the weddin'. Your mama and Marcello Santos was married this mornin' at three A.M. by a priest at Sister Ralph's. Santos died at ten past three. He was a happy old gangster when his heart quit.'

'How about Johnnie?'

'That's the most beautiful part. Johnnie Farragut was the best man. He was strapped down in his bed and taped to a portable piece of equipment moved over from Little Egypt Baptist. After the ceremony, they rushed him back to the hospital where he had a kidney transplant operation. Marietta and I got word from the doctor two hours ago that he thinks it was successful. Doctor said it was a miracle they were able to locate a healthy kidney so quick. Came in on a private jet from Memphis, he said.'

'And Mama? How's she holdin' up?'

'Woman's a rock, Lula. You be proud you're her daughter. She's with the mortuary people now, makin' arrangements for Santos's burial. She told me to let you know about ever'thin's gone on and tell you she'll call first chance after she's rested. How's things there?'

'Not quite spectacular as your news, Dal, but other than Beany lettin' the worms die while we was away, the big story is that Pace is gettin' married.'

'Well, glory be! Not to one of them Hindu women, I hope.'

'No, Dal, to a Jewish girl from Brooklyn, New York. Think she's kind of a doctor. He's movin' there from Nepal.'

'You want me to tell Marietta?'

'Better let me do it. Mama's got enough on her mind just now. Give her my and Sailor's love and same to Johnnie Farragut. Thanks for bein' there, Dal. Love you, too.'

'Been here all my life, Lula. Bye now.'

'Bye. Take care.'

After she'd hung up the phone, Lula read Pace's letter again, then put it down on the kitchen table. She looked out through the sliding glass doors into the backyard and saw Sailor standing next to the flooded worm bin smoking a Camel. A huge blue jay landed on the grass about ten feet away from Sailor. He flicked his cigarette at the bird and it screeched and took off.

'Ain't no way human bein's can control their own lives,' Lula said out loud, 'and ain't no way they ever can stop tryin'.'

It suddenly occurred to Lula that she had forgotten to give Sailor a birthday present.

Bad Day for the Leopard Man

'Maybe what makes life so terribly fatiguing is nothing other than the enormous effort we make for twenty years, forty years, and more, to be reasonable, to avoid being simply, profoundly ourselves, that is, vile, ghastly, absurd.'

– Louis-Ferdinand Céline,
Voyage au Bout de la Nuit

Short of Heaven

'Lula, you won't believe this.'

'Won't believe what, Sail, honey?'

'Article in the *Times-Picayune* I'm readin', says thirty-seven per cent of Americans believe in the devil.'

'Don't know why that should surprise you none, havin' knowed so many people as you have durin' your sixty-three years on the planet. Count sounds about right to me.'

'Peanut, all the trouble this world's seen since the beginnin' of time ain't been the doin' of no devil. It's been the result of two things, organized religion and greed.'

'What about sex?'

'Lust I lump with greed.'

Sailor Ripley was sitting in his cracked red leather armchair in the front room of the house in Metairie, Louisiana, that he and his wife, Lula Pace Fortune, had lived in for thirty years. Lula, who was three years younger than Sailor, lay on the ecru shag carpet doing stretching exercises. She was still slim-figured at sixty, thanks to what she liked to call 'the vain woman's never-endin' struggle against stone-cold nature.' Sailor, pot-bellied, mostly bald and slightly arthritic, though otherwise in fair shape, had given up the fight long ago, and not unhappily. He was semi-retired from his vice-presidency of the Gator Gone Corporation, which was now the world's largest manufacturer and distributor of alligator and crocodile repellent. He went into the office in New Orleans two or three times a week to help out his friend Bob Lee Boyle, the company's founder and owner. Sailor read a great deal these days, mostly history and historical fiction, and the newspapers, which were still his greatest source of amusement. He was comfortable in his chair.

'Now here's one, peanut,' he said. 'Police in Shreveport are mystified, it says, by a series of car bombin's been goin' on

237

over a year. Sixteen people killed the same way and none of the victims seem to be connected. "Unrelated Murders Stump Cop Braintrust" is the headline.' Sailor laughed. 'Don't take much, that's sure.'

Lula rolled over from her right side to her left and began a scissors motion with her right leg.

'If you was gonna blow up a car, Sail, how'd you do it? Wire a bomb to the ignition? Bet ol' Crazy Eyes Santos done that lotsa times.'

'He mighta did, but that's too obvious. Best way is to insert a BB in a gelatin capsule filled with cyanide and drop it in the gas tank. The weight of the BB'll cause it to sink to the bottom of the tank where the small amount of water settled there'll eat away at the capsule. Within a half-hour the cyanide'll be released and ignite the gasoline. Boom! There you go.'

'Sailor, you're somethin' else, knowin' somethin' 'bout practically ever'thin' the way you do. Where'd you learn that precious piece of information?'

'Same place I picked up most of my practical knowledge, in the pen. Believe it was a fella named Party-Time Partagas, a Marielito, taught me that at Huntsville. He was an old professional killer had been in a Havana prison for years before Castro boatmailed all the Cuban criminals to Key West back in '81. Party was a senior citizen when I knew him. Musta died behind them Texas walls.'

'Boy, Sail, that seems so long ago you were inside. Almost like it never happened.'

'Wish it hadn't, peanut, but I come through.'

'Thank the Lord.'

'The Lord ain't always done such a exemplary job, honey. Listen to this: Out in California a guy claimed God told him he could drive his truck through cars, so he drove it into eighteen other vehicles on a freeway durin' the mornin' rush hour. Injured dozens, killed four and stopped traffic for half a day.'

Lula switched back to her right side and scissored with her left leg.

'Sounds like more of the devil's doin' there, darlin', not the Lord's.'

Sailor laughed. 'Guess you're in the thirty-seven per cent.'

238

'Old beliefs ain't easy to quit,' said Lula. ''Specially when there ain't nothin' better to replace 'em with.'

The telephone rang and Lula sprang up like a young girl to answer it.

'Hello?'

'Hey, Mama, it's Pace.'

'Don't nobody else call me Mama, son. I'd know it's you just by your breathin' anyway. Where you callin' from?'

'Hollywood. I got a job workin' for a director, the fella I told you I met two years ago over in Paris, where I went after me and Rhoda got divorced.'

'What exactly are you doin' for this director person?'

'Man's plannin' a new film. He's pretty famous for some horror pictures he made awhile back. I'm his factotum.'

'His what?'

'Factotum, Mama. Means I'm his chief assistant, right-hand man. I do what's necessary.'

'Pace Roscoe Ripley, you're forty years old. Don't you think you oughta be settled in a real job by now?'

'This is a real job, Mama. And didn't I spend eight miserable years in the diamond business in New York with Gombowicz and Sons, or are you forgettin'?'

'That was Rhoda's family's business, son. I mean somethin' of your own.'

'Mama, I'm doin' what I want now, like when I was leadin' treks in Nepal. I'm learnin' about the film world.'

'Long as you're happy, I guess.'

'How're you and Daddy?'

'Oh, we're inchin' by at about the same rate your daddy's hairline's recedin'. His arthritis is caused him to lose some strength in the left arm lately, though. He can't lift nothin' heavier'n a egg with it, and we don't eat eggs 'cause of the cholesterol.'

'Reason I'm callin' now, Mama, is to tell you we might be headin' to New Orleans next week to do some research for a screenplay. Wanted to know if you and Daddy were gonna be around.'

'Where else we gonna be? Ain't been anyplace in four years but that time Sail insisted on takin' me to Maui the month after your Grandmama Marietta passed away.'

239

Lula's eyes watered at the thought of her mother.

'Mama, you cryin'?'

'No, I ain't. Just hard to believe Mama's gone, is all.'

'How's Auntie Dal?'

'Dalceda Delahoussaye got a iron constitution to match her outlook on life. She's hangin' in, far's I know. We spoke day before yesterday and Dal was organizin' the Bay St Clement chapter of the Daughters of the Confederacy in a protest against a court order bannin' smokin' in restaurants. Can you imagine that? In North Carolina, of all places. Auntie Dal is eighty-five years old and she's still suckin' in a pack a day. Mores, just like me, only I cut down to 'bout half a pack you'll be glad to know.'

'I am, Mama. Want to keep you around long as possible. Tell Daddy I'll be home soon.'

'You-all want to stay with us?'

'Thanks, Mama, but prob'ly we'll be at a hotel in NO. That way we won't be disturbin' nobody.'

'You ain't no disturbance, Pace, you're our only child. And tell your director friend he's welcome here, too.'

''Preciate it, Mama. Love you.'

'Love you, son. Take precautions, you know?'

Pace laughed. 'I do. Bye, Mama.'

'Bye.'

'The boy all right?' asked Sailor, after Lula had hung up.

'Sounds dandy,' she said. 'He's in LA, learnin' the movie business. Says he may be here in a week or so with a man he's workin' for.'

'You don't sound like you're so happy about it. I mean, his bein' in LA.'

'That Hollywood lifestyle's a long ways short of heaven, Sail, you know?'

Sailor laughed. 'Peanut, what ain't?'

Bad Day for the Leopard Man

The Leopard Man's name was Philip Reãl. He was called the Leopard Man behind his back by others in the movie business because of the gothic nature of the films he'd directed and written during the past two decades. Val Lewton, a producer at RKO in the 1940s, had made a series of low-budget horror pictures, including one titled 'The Leopard Man.' In a review of Phil Reãl's startling first feature, 'Mumblemouth,' made when Reãl was twenty-three, the Los Angeles *Times* critic had compared the look and feel of the film – heavy shadows and deep suggestions of off-camera hideous goings-on – to Lewton's black and white B's that most film historians considered classics of the genre. At the time, it was construed as a compliment, but as the years wore on, and Reãl repeated himself with such efforts as 'Death Comes Easy,' 'Face of the Phantom,' 'The Slow Torture and Sexual Re-education of Señor Rafferty' and others, culminating in the universally maligned 'Dog Parts,' which featured a denouement wherein two Pit Bulls brutally dismember a pregnant Collie bitch and devour her fetus, Phil Reãl had become unbankable and persona non grata in Hollywood.

He had gone to Europe, living first for two years in France, then for three in Italy, where he directed and acted in a cheapie called *Il Verme* ('The Worm'), a soft-core pornographic version of the myth of Cadmus, before returning to LA. Since his return, he had been living alone in a house in the Hollywood hills, working on an original screenplay called 'The Cry of the Mute,' based on his own experiences in the industry.

Phil let the telephone ring three times before he picked up.

'Happy birthday, darlin'! How's it feel to be fat and fifty?'

'My birthday was yesterday, Flower, and I'm forty-eight. But thanks, anyway.'

'Sorry, sugar. Least you know I'm thinkin' about you.'

241

'I thought you were in Kenya, with Westphal.'

'Picture wrapped a month ago, Philly. Where you been keepin' yourself?'

'Right here by my lonesome. I stopped reading the trades and I do my own cooking.'

Flower laughed. 'You still writin' on that "Moot" script, huh?'

'The word is "Mute," Flower, and yes, I am. What do you have in the works?'

'Well, you do know me'n Jason got divorced?'

'No, I missed that.'

'Yeah, he's livin' with Rita Manoa-noa now, the top whore outta Tahiti that was brought over by Runt Gold to be in the re-make of "Captain Cook's Revenge" that never got made? Final decree came through just after I got to Africa. Let me tell you, Philly, they don't call it the dark continent for nothin'. People there're the blackest I ever seen anywhere, includin' Alabama.'

'Africa wasn't called the dark continent because of the color of the skin of most of its inhabitants, Flower. It's because it was one of the last places the Europeans got to. "Dark" referred to unexplored and unknown.'

'Phil, you always know about everything.'

'That's why I'm such a popular guy.'

'Oh, sugar, everyone thinks you're the smartest man in Hollywood.'

'As Daffy Duck said, "Ridicule is the curse of genius."'

'Anyway, I'm seein' Clark now.'

'Westphal? What happened to Suki?'

'He thrown her out before Africa. She's suin' him now, of course. But they weren't never married so he says she can't get much. Clark made her sign a paper while they was livin' together said she couldn't make no claims on him. He done it with all his women.'

'I think Clark may be just a tad brighter than I am.'

'He sure has more money, Philly, that's the truth. Not as much hair, though.'

'He can buy some.'

'Don't need to, now the natural look is in. Thinnin' hair is a sign of maturity, you know.'

'Spell maturity for me, Flower.'

She laughed. 'Sugar, ten years ago when I came to California

242

from Mobile, I had me a choice between practicin' spellin' or keepin' my lips over my teeth when I give head. Can't have it both ways in this town.

'Look, I gotta run,' Flower said. 'Clark's takin' me down to his place in darkest Mexico tonight, the house he bought from Jack Falcon, the famous old director who died last year?'

'I know who Jack Falcon was, Flower.'

'Oh, of course, you do. Prob'ly you and him went boar huntin' together and everything.'

'As a matter of fact, I think I still have my boar rifle around here somewhere.'

'I got to go shop now, honey. Happy birthday, even though it's the wrong day. I'll call you when I'm back from Mexico. You still hangin' at Martoni's?'

'Once in awhile.'

'We'll meet for drinks. Bye!'

Flower hung up, so Phil did, too. He suddenly flashed on the bathtub scene in 'Señor Rafferty,' where Flower Reynolds, as the crazed transsexual Shortina Fuse, wearing only a pair of red panties, tosses the sulfuric acid into Rafferty's face. The camera remains fixed on Flower's red triangle while she laughs and Rafferty screams, holding until the final fade. It was Flower's laugh people remembered later, not Rafferty's screams. She had a great laugh. Phil had always regretted not having used it in 'Dog Parts.'

Artificial Light

Phil had an 11:30 with Arnie Pope at Five Star. The meeting had been set up for him by Bobby Durso, who, during Phil's European hiatus, had become a powerful agent despite his lack of affiliation with an established agency. Bobby operated on his own and specialized in handling writers. Actors, he'd decided, were – with few exceptions – essentially undependable and insecure; dysfunctional people, his shrink called them. Writers, Bobby found, were the hardest-working, most clearly focused and dedicated individuals he'd ever known.

Bobby had been Phil Reãl's AD on 'Death Comes Easy,' then gone back to UCLA, where he'd earned a degree in American history, worked as a bartender for a couple of years, gotten married and begun his present career by representing his wife, Alice, who wrote screenplays. The first script of Alice's that Bobby Durso sold, 'Goodbye To Everyone,' wound up grossing over two hundred million for Paramount, and the sequel, 'Hello To Nobody,' did equally well. Since then, every producer in town found time to talk to, if not openly court him.

Bobby was not intending to represent Phil Reãl, however. At least not in any official capacity. The meet with Arnie Pope had been arranged as a favor, and that's where Bobby wanted to leave it. He hadn't even read Phil's screenplay, if he had one yet, or allowed Phil to describe the story. Phil, Bobby knew, would want to direct the picture himself, and there was no way a studio would allow that. Bobby dealt exclusively with the majors, he didn't touch the independents, and he'd explained his position to Phil, who said that he understood completely.

Arnie Pope was Bobby's brother-in-law – Alice was Arnie's sister – he and Bobby got along all right, and when Bobby asked him to take a meeting with the Leopard Man, no strings attached, he said OK. After all, Arnie figured, the man was a kind of legend in the business, and it could be interesting. Arnie told his assistant, Greta, to re-schedule his shiatsu for 11:45.

Phil appeared in Arnie Pope's outer office at 11:29. He did not bring the screenplay with him. Greta buzzed Arnie, who asked her to show in Mr Reãl.

'This is a real pleasure, Mr Reãl,' said Arnie, as he stood up and leaned across his desk to shake hands.

'Phil, please.'

'Arnie. Sit.'

They both sat down.

'This is really great,' Arnie said. 'I can still remember the first time I saw "Face of the Phantom." At the Riviera in Chicago, when I was fourteen. Scared the piss out of me. My girlfriend wouldn't even look at the screen. Kept her head buried in my right shoulder the whole time.'

Arnie rubbed his right shoulder with his left hand. Phil noticed Arnie's diamond pinkie ring.

'It was great, great,' said Arnie.

Arnie smiled and Phil nodded.

'So, what's this Bobby says you've got? Have to tell you, though, that since the Germans bought Five Star, all we've been able to push through are one-namers.'

Phil looked puzzled.

'You know: Rheinhold, Dirk, those guys. Muscle men. Put a title underneath, like "Death Driver," all that's necessary. So, it's 11:31:35. Tell me.'

'This is a special picture.'

'They're all special, Phil.' Arnie again looked quickly at his watch. 'Got a title?'

'"The Cry of the Mute."'

'A mute's someone can't talk, right?'

Phil nodded. 'The title is meant to be ironic.'

'Ironic, yeah, sure. I got it. So, what happens?'

'It's about a writer-director who was at one time very successful, when he was young, and then his career slipped away from him. He drinks, takes drugs, he travels, and finally returns to make one last picture. Nobody believes in him any more except for a girl, a woman, who began her acting career in his early films. She's become a big star and gets him a deal, based on her agreement to play the female lead.'

'Good. I was waiting for the girl. What does she do?'

'Sells tickets.'

'I know. I mean in the story. She helps the guy get back on his feet, cleans him up, marries him, what? Where's the big play come in?'

'He shows he can still pull it off. The picture's both a critical and box office success.'

'What about him and her? In the end?'

Phil shook his head. 'They don't get together. She marries someone else.'

Arnie Pope looked at his watch and stood up.

'When Nick Ray made "In A Lonely Place" he had Bogart,' Arnie said.

'Gloria Grahame made the picture work,' said Phil.

'Phil,' Arnie stuck out his hand as he came around the desk, 'I gotta be Japanese in five minutes. Less. Have Bobby send me the script. I promise I'll read it.'

Phil stood and let Arnie pinch the fingers of his right hand. Greta appeared.

'Almost time, Arnie,' she said.

'Greta,' said Arnie, 'when Phil's script arrives, read it right away.'

Arnie turned and looked directly into Phil's eyes.

'I'll never forget "Face of the Phantom," Phil. Never. It's a classic.'

Arnie nodded and grinned. 'Janet Coveleski,' he said. 'That was her name.'

'Whose name, Arnie?' asked Phil.

'The girl I took to see your picture at the Riviera.'

Arnie walked out of his office, followed closely by Greta. Phil stood without moving for twenty seconds. He remembered the last frame of 'Phantom,' where the man who has never slept with his eyes closed finally closes them, knowing he'll never wake up. Phil closed his eyes.

Wrangler's Paradise

Nobody in Hollywood has a past that matters. What counts is what someone is doing right now or might be doing tomorrow. The film business is open to anyone, and that was the great thing about it, Phil thought, as he drove home from Five Star. A person could be a multiple murderer escapee from prison or a lunatic asylum but if he or she had a bright idea that was considered do-able, and the proper pieces fell together in the right hands at the right time, that person, certifiedly depraved or otherwise, could have a three-picture deal in less than the lifetime of a Florida snake doctor.

If one of them is a hit, the escapee could be running a studio within a few months, and as long as the people kept buying tickets the studio lawyers would do everything they could to keep the authorities at bay. A big enough flop, though, and the *wunderkind* would no doubt be back doing laps inside a padded cell before it went to video. Phil loved the strangeness of it, he really did. Hollywood was a wrangler's paradise: the cattle either got to market or they didn't. Rustled, died of thirst, train derailed, didn't matter. No excuses, no prisoners. That was the law of the bottom line.

Driving along La Brea, Phil decided to stop at Pink's. He parked his leased Mustang convertible around the corner on Melrose, got out and joined the line at the outdoor counter. When his turn came, he ordered a double cheeseburger with chili and a black cherry Israeli soda. As he waited for the food, Phil looked across the street. A middle-aged bum had disrobed and begun doing jumping jacks on the sidewalk, his long hair and beard flopping around. Pedestrians passed on either side of him. A swarthy man came out of the convenience store on the corner and walked swiftly toward the naked bum. The swarthy man, who wore a thick black mustache and a square of hair in the center of his chin, pulled a small caliber revolver from a pocket, pushed the nose of it into the bum's left ear and pulled the trigger. The bum fell down and blood gushed from his head. The swarthy man ran back toward the convenience store.

Phil picked up his cheeseburger and soda, paid the Mexican girl who'd served him, walked to his car, got in and drove away. The bum had looked familiar, Phil thought. He made a mental note to check the newspaper the next day for the story, to see if the bum had been someone he'd known in the old days.

The Cry of the Mutilated

Phil was typing when the telephone rang.

'Pick that up, Pace, will you?' he shouted.

'Philip Reãl's line,' said Pace.

'Pace, it's Bobby Durso. Phil there?'

'Just a moment, Mr Durso. Phil, Bobby.'

Phil stopped typing and picked up his extension.

'Hey, Bobby.'

'How'd it go with Pope?' Bobby asked.

'Thanks for your help but my take is that Five Star wants something I don't have.'

'And what's that?'

'A brain-eater.'

'A brain-eater? What's a brain-eater?'

'Bobby, I'm about the devil in disguise to Arnie Pope and his people. And it ain't much of a disguise, either.'

'Meaning what?'

'Meaning they see right through me the same way I see through them.'

'Phil, I love the way you talk but I don't always get the message so easily. I take it you and Arnie didn't get along.'

'Oh, on the contrary. Turns out he's had a crush on me forever. But it's one of those two cars-at-a-stoplight romances. We checked each other out but then he took a right and I was in the left lane.'

'So?'

'Light turned green and the cars lined up behind me were honking, so I did the only thing I could.'

'Yeah?'

'Drove straight ahead and here I am, same as ever. Not even a fender bender on the way back.'

'Well, I tried.'

'I appreciate it, Bobby, I really do. You know, I had a dream last night where I was driving an old pickup truck that had "Al and Popeye's Hauling Service" painted on the door. I only had one arm, my right, so when I shifted gears I had to be quick about grabbing the steering wheel again. It was hot outside, in the dream, and the breeze through the rolled-down window hit directly on my left armpit, there not being a bicep to block it. I was real cool.'

'Phil, you are cool, but I don't know what to tell you.'

'Tell me about what, Bob?'

'How you're gonna make it now in this town. If you think I can help, call me.'

'Sure thing, Bobby. I'm taking off for a little while but I'll talk to you when I get back. Thanks again.'

Phil hung up and closed his eyes. Slowly he raised his left arm until it was entirely vertical and let the air hit his armpit. He reopened his eyes.

'Pace, you make our arrangements for New Orleans?'

'Done, Phil. We leave tomorrow out of LAX at one. Be in NO in plenty of time to have dinner at Dooky's. Have Miss Chase make us somethin' special.'

'Where are we staying?'

'The Rinaldi, on Gravier, just off the Quarter. Got you a junior suite and me a room.'

'Speak to your folks?'

'Mama says they're lookin' forward to meetin' you.'

'Maybe they can help me fill in some background for the story. I figure New Orleans is a properly exotic location for "The Cry of the Mute."'

'Spend enough time down there you just might want to change the title to "The Cry of the Mutilated."'

Phil grinned. 'I like that, Pace. I like how your rebel brain works. You and your parents have much in common?'

Pace laughed. 'Prob'ly more'n necessary, Phil.'

The Museum of Opinion

Sailor awoke at four A.M. from a vivid dream wherein he had taken a job as curator of the Museum of Opinion in Sweden. Located on a spit of land in the far northern reach of Scandinavia, the museum existed as a sanctuary for certain individuals whose ideas, as expressed either in some public form, such as books, newspapers or via electronic media, or simply by letter to the museum, were deemed by the curator as worthy of recognition and an open-ended invitation to reside in one of the houses maintained by the Foundation of Opinions.

In the dream, Sailor's position as curator entitled him to extend or revoke permits to the society of fellows, as museum residents were called, and to decide all matters of consequence. It was his opinion that counted the most. The only requirement of the fellows was that they regularly post their opinions on the Central Hall bulletin board, so that they could be discussed at mealtimes. Since the breakfasts, lunches and dinners were often – not unexpectedly – volatile affairs, residents were also provided foodstocks in their private rooms. Casual digestion was never a hallmark of the society.

Sailor picked up the pen and notebook he had lately taken to keeping on his bedtable and wrote down the essential belief of the Museum of Opinion as had been dictated to him in the dream: 'A man alone is the epitome of conflict.'

He lay in bed thinking about the turns his life had taken. It was at such moments, usually in the middle of the night, that he succumbed to a very low opinion of himself. This condition always passed quickly, however, as it did now, and Sailor lay there, listening to Lula's even breathing. He picked up a pack of Camels and the matches that were on the table next to his notebook and lit a cigarette.

251

He had recently read a biography of Pierre Loti, the 19th-century French writer whose real name was Julien Viaud. Loti had dressed himself variously as a Bedouin, a Pasha and a circus acrobat, had converted to Islam, and conducted countless sexual liaisons with both men and women. 'No matter what,' Loti wrote, 'I am always a déclassé, playing a part.'

Sailor thought about what Loti had meant by that. When he was a boy, Sailor had for a time fantasized himself as a character called the Black Phantom, leaping from rooftop to rooftop to rescue persons in distress, then escaping without a word back into the darkness. It was a part he had invented, he realized now, to escape from the constant alcohol-fueled arguments waged nightly by his parents. That had been an ugly time in his life, Sailor thought, almost as ugly as the time he'd spent in prison, away from Lula and Pace.

It was Sailor's opinion that without the ability to escape inside the mind there would be even more murders and suicides than there already were. Hadn't he read somewhere that Sweden had one of the highest suicide rates in the world? Sailor took a hard drag on the Camel, then made a note to look up the meaning of the word epitome.

Longevity's Victims

'My mama and Dalceda Delahoussaye used to meet like this at least four afternoons a week at Bode's in Bay St Clement most all their lives. They was close friends for three-quarters of a century, Beany, can you believe that? Even went to boardin' school together. Miss Cook's, in Beaufort.'

'Don't look now, Lula, but you and me is creepin' up on bein' friends for *half* a century ourselves.'

Lula shook her head. 'It's a comfort and frightenin', both, you know.'

'I do know,' said Beany. 'When I think about Madonna Kim turnin' thirty-one next month, it's like, how'd that happen? And Lance is thirty-seven!'

'Which makes Pace forty. Time gotten right out of control, Beany, no doubt about it. We're victims of longevity is what we are. By the way, Pace is comin' home next week.'

'To stay?'

'Uh uh. He's workin' with a director out of Hollywood and they're comin' to NO for research, Pace said.'

'Pace livin' in LA now?'

'I guess.'

'That boy been about everywhere, Lula. 'Specially since he and Rhoda busted up.'

'Weren't the divorce I minded, it's that they didn't make no family. You know how much I been lookin' forward to havin' grandkids. You're damn lucky, Beany. You got six.'

Beany sighed. 'Yeah, they're somethin' else, all right. Each of Madonna Kim's four is by a different father, and Lance's two are by his two wives. He's engaged again, did I tell you?'

'No. Who to?'

'Gal named LaDonna, capital L, capital D. She's twenty-two, blond – natural or not I don't know, since I ain't met her – wants

253

to be a singer of some kind. Lance told me they met in Phoenix two months ago when he was at the computer convention there.'

'What's her last name?'

'Flynn. Her daddy's Manny Flynn, guy Lance is thinkin' 'bout goin' to work for. Man built a software empire that's headquartered in Arizona. Lance'd have to move there, which he don't mind, seein's how he's burned out on Atlanta. Only thing, both his ex-wives, Zoe and Charlene Rae, are there, so it'd be tough on him and the kids. Also, don't know if marryin' the boss's daughter's a good idea or not.'

'Time'll tell.'

Lula and Beany Boyle were lingering over coffee following a salad lunch at Foissoner, their regular Thursday afternoon meetingplace in the French Quarter. The chef and part owner, César Foudre, was the father of Madonna Kim's next-to-last offspring, also named César, and he never allowed the ladies to pay. A tiny man with a thick red whiskbroom-shaped beard, César came out of the kitchen and greeted them.

'Madames Boyle and Ripley, a pure *plaisir*,' he said, smiling, though his lips were well-hidden, '*comme toujours*. The *repast* was satisfactory?'

'We got most the rabbits beat, César,' said Beany. 'It was fine.'

Lula smiled and nodded her agreement.

'I am teaching Little César now to cook,' said César. 'It is like swimming, I believe. One is never too young to learn. He is four years old and already he can bake the bread. By the time he is six, he will have learned the sauces.'

'That's swell, César,' said Beany, 'maybe he'll teach Madonna Kim how to fry an egg.'

César laughed. 'For this he will have to first master sorcery, not sauces!'

Beany and Lula laughed, and César excused himself.

'He's not such a bad fella,' said Lula, 'and he has a good business. Too bad Madonna Kim couldn't settle down with him.'

'Lula, there's no use talkin' about my daughter's matin' habits. Soon as César pulled out, she hooked into Roberto Roatan, the jockey got banned for life after fixin' races at Louisiana Downs. Remember him?'

'Madonna Kim always has gone for short ones. You notice that?'

Beany raised her eyebrows and shook her head.

'Asked her about it once. She said little men are more intense.'

After they'd finished their coffee, Beany and Lula walked along Burgundy toward the parking lot across Canal, where they'd left Lula's car. At Iberville Street, a giant black man waving an Israeli flag over his clean-shaven skull strode past them, shouting, 'Jews is saved! Jews is saved! Great God Almighty, the Jews is saved!' Following close behind him, carrying short lengths of pipe and sawed-off baseball bats, were a half-dozen skinheads wearing green tanker jackets, leather gloves and combat boots.

'Don't fret,' Beany said to Lula, 'I don't go no place without a gun.'

That's What I Like About the South

Pace and Phil were sitting in the lobby of the Rinaldi waiting for Sailor and Lula. It was cold and rainy in New Orleans, early January, so both Pace and Phil wore tan Burberry trenchcoats, cowboy boots and Great White Hunter hats.

'I'll bet you fellas either in oil or from Hollywood.'

Pace turned around and saw Sailor's grin.

'Hey, Daddy!' Pace said. He jumped up and they embraced. 'This here's Philip Reãl, my employer.'

Phil stood up and shook hands with Sailor.

'Pleased to meet you, Mr Reãl. Hope Pace is givin' you your money's worth.'

'Call me Phil, and if it's all right with you, I'll call you Sailor.'

'You bet.'

'Pace is rapidly becoming indispensable to me, Sailor. I was very fortunate to have found him.'

'Where's Mama?' asked Pace.

'Waitin' in the car. She's dyin' to see you, son.'

The three men started together toward the main entrance but before they had gone three steps a shot rang out. Sailor and Pace immediately hit the deck.

'Phil!' Pace yelled. 'Get down!'

Sailor grabbed Phil's left arm at the wrist and dragged him to the floor. Several more shots were fired and Sailor looked up just enough to see a tall white man wearing a New Orleans Saints jacket and a black woman in a red dress run across the lobby and out the door. The man and the woman each held a gun in their right hand and a black and white shopping bag in their left. Nobody in the lobby screamed or yelled. Like Sailor, Pace and Phil, they had taken cover and wondered what was going on. There was the sound of a vehicle's tires squealing, a brief roar of an engine, then silence. The inhabitants of the lobby cautiously came out of hiding, stood up and looked around.

'What in blazes was that all about?' asked Phil.

A doorman came running in and shouted, 'They got away in a black Cadillac! Had a white woman behind the wheel!'

Sailor ran out, followed closely by Pace and Phil.

Two police cars zoomed into the hotel driveway and four cops got out with their guns drawn. The doorman who had made the announcement came out and repeated what he'd said. A young woman dressed in a dark blue business suit stumbled out after the doorman and collapsed on the top step of the hotel entryway. There was blood in her light brown hair and on the left side of her face. One of the cops kneeled down next to her.

'They took everything from the safe,' she said. 'All the money and jewelry. Jeffrey's dead, the black girl shot him. The man hit me in the head with his gun.'

'Lula!' Sailor shouted at the cops. 'They stole my wife! She was in the car!'

Two of the cops grabbed Sailor and shoved him up against a pillar.

'You say your wife was drivin'?' said one.

'I'm tellin' you,' said Sailor, 'my wife was in the car they drove off in! She been kidnapped!'

'Hold him,' one cop said to the other. 'I'll check out inside.'

'You sure your wife wasn't in on this deal?' asked the cop who was holding Sailor.

'You must be crazy!' yelled Pace. 'Why don't you get after them thieves got my mama?!'

More squad cars pulled into the hotel roundabout and a dozen policemen leaped out. Half of them ran over to where Sailor was pinned against the pillar and pointed their weapons at him.

'Look,' Phil said to one of the cops, 'this man didn't do anything! Some people robbed the hotel and used his car to get away. His wife was in it.'

Before Phil could finish his last sentence, the cop had him face down on the ground with a hammerlock on his right arm. Phil's hat fell off and rolled into the roadway.

'This is Philip Reál!' Pace shouted. 'The famous director!'

A cop pushed the barrel of his .38 into Pace's stomach and told him to shut up. The left side of Phil's face was pressed into the cold, wet concrete, and it was from this perspective that he watched the right front tire of a New Orleans police car crush his Great White Hunter hat that two days before he had paid $159 for at Banana Republic on Melrose.

The Horror

'I hope you understand, Mr Ripley, and you, too, Mr Reāl, my men were just doin' their job. No harm intended, and you got my sinceremost apology for the rough stuff. What we gotta do now is make sure Mrs Ripley's returned to you soon and safe as possible.'

Police Captain DuMont 'Du Du' Dupre, who was in line to become commissioner when the current top gun, Eddie Fange, who had held the office for fifteen years, retired, looked carefully first at Sailor then at Phil, who were seated on folding metal chairs on the other side of the desk from the Captain in his office at police headquarters in the new windowless Louis Armstrong City Government Building across from the Superdome on Poydras. Pace stood behind Sailor's chair, his right hand gripping his father's right shoulder. A telephone on the desk rang and Dupre picked it up. The folds of his fat, froglike face alternately contracted and relaxed as he listened and spoke.

'Yeah, Eddie, I heard,' said Du Du. 'I told them Army boys we wasn't gonna touch it, which they was happy to hear. Shootin' cats in the head to study gunshot wounds don't bother me particular, but I can see how it's bound upset some folks. Uh huh. Let the politicians handle it, I agree. Yeah, Eddie, was about 700 felines altogether, 'cordin' our reports. Yes. Yes. They was anethesized, sure. Okay, Eddie, I just goin' refer 'em to the state hereafter. By the way, how your lung doin'? They gonna have to cut it more?'

Du Du winked his liquidy red left eye at Sailor and held up the index finger of his right hand.

'That good,' he said, nodding and rolling back his purple upper lip by pushing under it with his lower. 'Best to hang on what little we got left so long as possible, I agree. You still got that Enfield .30-06 at Barataria? Right.' Du Du laughed. 'You know it's same model old Delay Beckwith supposed to used when he shot Medgar

259

Evers. Sure is. You might could get a price for it now. OK, Eddie, you take care now.' Du Du hung up.

'We on this like white on rice, Mr Ripley,' said Du Du, 'and there ain't no quit in a case includes murder, armed robbery, kidnappin' and car theft. We'll keep you up on the investigation. Call me personal, anytime.'

'I can't just sit still,' Sailor said. 'There must be somethin' my son and I can do to help.'

The creases deepened in Du Du Dupre's rubbery face.

'Don't be gettin' no brave ideas here, Mr Ripley. We dealin' with people ain't shy 'bout shootin' off more'n their mouth. Best you-all remain at home, let us take care of it.'

On the street in front of Louis Armstrong, Pace said, 'Daddy, no way I'm waitin' on the blue.'

'I'm with you, too, Sailor,' said Phil. 'Why don't we go back to my suite at the Rinaldi and make a plan?'

'Better to stay at the house,' Sailor said, 'case Lula calls, or the kidnappers. Might be they'll try to ransom her.'

'You're right, Daddy. Knowin' Mama, it's possible she could talk her way out of this.'

'Anyone can, it's Lula.'

The three men got into Phil's rented white Lincoln Town Car. As Pace drove, memories of all of the years that he and Lula had spent together whizzed through Sailor's mind. A picture of Lula at seventeen flashed in his brain and he held that image. Lula was sitting on the top rail of the wooden fence that bordered the yard of the Fortune house in Bay St Clement. Lula wore a checked shirt and a short white skirt, and her thick black hair was tied back with a ribbon. She was smiling and the longer of her large two front teeth was snagged on her lower lip, giving her face a slightly anxious expression. Sailor could picture the indentation line on Lula's lip caused by her overbite and he felt his heart flutter. He knew he would die before he ever stopped looking for Lula.

Cat People

Oretta 'Kitty Kat' Cross, black female, twenty-five, black hair
with two dyed red braids, black eyes – the left with a slight
strabismus, or cast – five-five, one hundred-ten pounds, no
tattoos, rode shotgun.

'Don't see why we had to do this, Kitty Kat. Now we up for
kidnappin', too.'

Archie Chunk, white male, twenty-eight, sandy-brown hair cut
short, blue eyes, five-nine, one hundred-sixty pounds, broken
nose, two-inch horizontal scar middle of forehead, fire-breathing
dragon tattoo right biceps, anchor tattoo with snake entwined
back of left hand, squirmed around in the back seat of the
Cadillac. He kept turning to look out the rear window.

'You prefer we be walkin'?' said Kitty Kat. 'The woman be right
there. Nobody chasin' us, Arch. Relax.'

Archie twisted toward her. 'How I gonna relax you shot
the dude?'

Kitty Kat vaulted into the back seat, shoved Archie over so
that she could sit directly behind Lula, shifted the Colt Python
she was holding into her left hand, unzipped Archie's trousers
with her right, took out his penis and started jacking him off.

'You stay on 23 to West Pointe à la Hache,' Kitty Kat said to
Lula, sticking the barrel point into the soft spot at the back of
Lula's head, holding it there for several seconds, 'then I tell you
what to do.'

Archie let his head roll back and closed his eyes as Kitty Kat
caressed him. She put her thick lips to his left ear and purred like
a cat, making a soft, rumbling growl in the back of her throat.
Archie's penis, at first touch tiny and flaccid, soon swelled to its
full four-and-one-quarter inches and filled with blood so that it
resembled a Montecristo Rojo. Kitty Kat growled louder and
increased the speed and intensity of her caress. A few seconds

later, Archie came, splattering the back of the front seat and dribbling onto his pants. Kitty Kat released her hold on him, reached over and pulled the gold and black leaf-patterned scarf off Lula's neck and used it to wipe up Archie's emission.

'Feelin' better now, peach?' asked Kitty Kat, cleaning her hand with Lula's scarf, then tossing it on the floor.

'Some,' Archie said. 'Wish I could do for you.'

'It OK, I ain' nervous. Seen on *Geraldo* bunch of bitches called theyselfs non-orgastic, or somethin'. They same as me. Ain' like havin' the AIDS or cancer. Bet this old bitch she come easy. Hey, old bitch, you come easy, I bet.'

Lula had not said a word since Archie and Kitty Kat had jumped into the car and the woman had put a gun to her head and commanded her to drive fast. She tried to respond but could not.

'Bitch!' shouted Kitty Kat. 'Ask you nice does you come!'

Lula nodded. 'Yes,' she said softly, 'I do.'

'Easy? It easy comin'?'

'Not always.'

Kitty Kat poked the tip of Archie's shrunken penis with the barrel of her Python.

'Zip up, peach,' she said. 'There ladies present.'

'This situation brings back some bad memories,' said Sailor, 'about the time Pace was kidnapped.'

Sailor, Phil and Pace were sitting in the Florida room of the Ripley home in Metairie, drinking Jameson straight from shot glasses and waiting for the telephone to ring.

'You've never mentioned that episode, Pace,' said Phil. 'What happened?'

'I was ten years old,' Pace said, 'and a crazy teenaged boy grabbed me while I was playin' in Audubon Park. He hid me in his room in a boardin' house located in a bad part of New Orleans, told me how he'd been searchin' for the perfect friend, which he hoped I'd be, but I wasn't, of course. He'd murdered his father and brother and cut 'em up in a hundred pieces, then buried their parts on the family farm in Evangeline Parish. I escaped, though.'

'Jesus,' said Phil, 'how'd you get away?'

'Elmer – that was his name, Elmer Désespéré – went out one night after lockin' me in a closet, so I made a fuss, kicked at the door and stomped around, until the landlady, I guess she was, came in and let me out. I hightailed it straight down the stairs and into the street, found a cop and that was the end of the ordeal.'

'What happened to this Elmer?'

'Street gang chewed him up,' said Sailor. 'He wandered into the wrong neighborhood and he got took apart. Tell you, though, the up side to Pace's abduction was that it brought me'n Lula back together.'

'How so?' asked Phil.

'I'd done some hard time, ten years to be exact, for armed robbery, durin' the commission of which a man was killed. Pace was born while I was inside, and when I got out things was kinda overwhelmin' for me'n his mama. Lula never did come to visit me durin' my stretch, which didn't much please me, though she did write a lot and send photos of her and Pace.'

'I didn't know this, Daddy,' Pace said. 'I mean, that Mama never once came to see you.'

Sailor nodded. 'It weren't all her fault, though. See, I was put away at the prison in Huntsville, Texas, and Lula and Pace were in North Carolina, with her mama, Marietta. Marietta never did think real highly of me, and due to the way I was actin' in them days I can't say how I could blame her. I'd done a couple years before that at a work camp in North Carolina for manslaughter, so Marietta pretty much had me pegged as a worthless badass from the get-go.'

'But you got nailed unfairly, Daddy, what Mama's always said. You were defendin' her in a bar and the man you hit banged his head on a table or somethin' and died. Man name of Lemon, right?'

'Bob Ray Lemon, right. Anyway, Lula's mama was dead set against her takin' up again with me when I got out, but Lula was eighteen by then and there weren't nothin' really legal Marietta could do about it, though she tried. After my release, Lula met me at the gate and we took off for California, though of course we didn't get more'n half that far. Marietta hired a private detective friend of hers to track us down, but by the time he did I'd pulled the dumb stunt in West Texas that subtracted a decade of my freedom. Marietta pretty much kept Lula prisoner for a while, which weren't too difficult for her to do, seein's how Lula was pregnant at first, and then with Pace bein' an infant it weren't so easy for Lula to travel. After Pace was growed some I guess it was just too hard for Lula to face me behind bars.'

'This is a wild story, Sailor,' said Phil. 'How did Pace's bein' kidnapped figure in your getting back together with Lula?'

'I went to see Lula and Pace soon as I got out, of course, but like I said, we couldn't neither of us handle it. There was too much hard feelin's and pain and all on both sides, though I didn't blame nobody but myself for what'd happened. I took off and went to Mississippi for six months, worked in a lumberyard by Hattiesburg, but I couldn't stop thinkin' about Pace here, and Lula, and how we should all be together. I was in my thirties by then and was finally beginnin' to understand a bit about how the world really works and what a man's gotta do to be a man and find his way. It's one real strange voyage.'

'I remember meetin' you, Daddy, with Mama, right after you got out. You just walked away from us.'

'I couldn't help myself, Pace. I didn't know what else to do. You didn't know me, weren't used to havin' me around, and I thought maybe you'd be better off without me. I was dead wrong, naturally, and it was just luck that brought me and Lula in contact again. I quit the lumberyard job and took a bus to New Orleans. I got a newspaper to look for a job and there was the article about Pace bein' abducted. Lula had come to NO with him to visit her childhood friend, Beany Thorn, whose husband, Bob Lee Boyle, later hired me to work for his company, Gator Gone, which is now the world's largest manufacturer of crocodile and alligator repellent. Wound up workin' for Bob Lee for thirty-ought years.'

'So you and Lula found each other again and lived happily ever after,' Phil said.

'Couldn'ta guessed you was from Hollywood, Phil,' said Sailor. 'There been a few detours along the way but we been able to hold our own.'

'Quite a romance, Sailor. Like Romeo and Juliet only nobody dies.'

'It ain't over, Phil,' Sailor said, and swallowed two fingers of Irish whiskey. 'Lula always used to say the world is wild at heart and weird on top, and sometimes it's tough stayin' out of the way of the weirdness. Kinda like a tornado, you never know where it'll set down or what'll be left in place after it blows through.'

'We'll get Mama home safe, Daddy,' said Pace.

'You'll pardon me for thinkin' out loud, Sailor,' said Phil, 'especially at a time of crisis like this, but I think there's a marvelous story here that would make a great film. It's a true romance, Sailor, and there aren't many of those. I came down here to research an incident that took place back in 1957. A black GI shot and killed a prominent white businessman during Mardi Gras and wound up on death row for twenty-five years. Through the efforts of a young white attorney who had never even tried a case, it was finally proven that the victim had provoked the shooting. Witnesses had been suppressed, paid off, and the black man spent more than half of his life in prison for defending himself. The attorney got him out.'

'Sorta like you, Daddy, defendin' Mama against Bob Ray Lemon.'

'Not quite, son, but maybe if I'd been black they woulda tried to fry me, too. Sounds like a good one, Phil. And you got yourself a happy endin'.'

'It's been done before,' Phil said, 'which doesn't mean the picture shouldn't be made, but you and Lula have something special, Sailor, and I think the world should know about it.'

Sailor smiled slightly. ''Preciate your sayin' that, Phil. You want to take a run at it, go ahead. Pace here can help you out on the details. You'll forgive me, though, I don't seem too enthusiastic at the moment, seein's how I'm mostly concerned with gettin' my wife back from the Lord knows who's got her.'

Phil poured himself a fresh shot of whisky and took a sip. Flower Reynolds would be perfect for Lula, he thought. That snake Clark Westphal could be a problem, though. He might try to influence Flower against working with him. A movie about the Romeo and Juliet of the Deep South could do it, thought Phil, it could put Philip Reāl back on top. What was it Sailor said Lula used to say? The world is wild at heart and weird on top, that's it. 'Wild At Heart' would be a great title, all right. Phil nodded to himself as he sipped the Jameson's. Or maybe just 'Strange Voyage.' His private title, though, would be 'Revenge of the Leopard Man.' It would pave the way for him to make 'Cry of the Mute.' Even Arnie Pope, Phil knew, if he was still at Five Star by that time, would be begging to pay for it.

Ball Lightning

Lula looked around the room. Tacked to the walls were pictures severed neatly from magazines, books, calendars and newspapers of different types of lightning. There was one of a rainstorm with a single vertical bolt of cloud to ground lightning in a purple sky and a bright pink spot atop the bolt that marked its exit spot; a flame-like ribbon of ball lightning looping through a bloody backdrop; triple ground lightning over Las Vegas that looked like a flaming match head waved over a black bat wing; lightning striking behind a ridge line, its meandering main stem resembling the Mississippi River; an anvil-shaped, violet-tinted storm cloud disclosing a scorpion-like excretion onto a barren landscape; double ground lightning with the secondary channel striking more than five miles away from the primary route; slow-moving air discharge lightning outlining the state of Florida; and double bolts from a monstrous magenta thunderhead.

She sat on a nude, high-backed wooden chair, the only chair in the room, which she guessed to be about fifteen feet by fifteen feet. It was devoid of any other furniture. There were three windows, one in each wall other than the one containing a door, which was closed and, Lula presumed, locked. She was unbound but sat still, waiting for her abductors, to whom she had not spoken excepting the brief exchange with the woman in the car. Lula thought about opening one of the windows and running away, but she was not young anymore, she certainly could not run very fast or very far, and she did not want to antagonize the two captors, who, it seemed to Lula, were unpredictable types. She needed a cigarette. Her Mores were in her purse, which she had last seen on the floor under the front seat of the Cadillac. The door opened.

'You like the pictures, lady?' asked Archie Chunk, walking in. 'I love lightnin'. Back in Broken Claw, where I was born and mostly raised – that's in Oklahoma – is the best electrical storms. Come

August, I'd stand in the field behind my granny's house and pray for the lightnin' to hit me. Never did, though, even when I held up a five iron.'

'Can I have a cigarette?' asked Lula.

Archie took a pack of Marlboros and a book of matches from the breast pocket of his Madras shirt, shook one out to Lula and lit it for her before doing the same for himself.

'Kitty Kat and me don't mean to keep you in suspense,' he said, replacing his cigarettes and matches in the same pocket, 'but you're a sorta unplanned-on part of the deal, you know? We gotta do one of three things: let you go, kill you, or ransom you. Them're the options.'

The black woman came into the room. She was holding a thick, foot-long clear plastic dildo in her right hand and the Colt Python in her left. She walked over to Lula and showed her the dildo, the head of which was smeared generously with some kind of salve.

'You ever use one of these?' Kitty Kat asked.

Lula shook her head no.

'Here,' Kitty Kat said to Archie, handing him the gun.

He took it and Kitty Kat hiked her skirt up over her naked crotch, bent her knees slightly as she spread her legs wide enough to admit the instrument into her vagina, then manipulated the dildo with both hands, inserting it slowly, a half-inch at a time, until most of it was inside her. Kitty Kat stood directly in front of Lula while she pumped the toy into and part-way out of herself. She began to sweat heavily, even though the temperature in the room was only fifty-three degrees. Lula felt the Marlboro burning down between the first and second fingers of her left hand, so she dropped it onto the floor. Archie Chunk stood by intently watching Kitty Kat work out.

'Master! Master!' cried Kitty Kat. 'Master, make me! Make me, master!' she shouted, plunging the dildo deeper and harder.

Suddenly she stopped and extracted it, breathing hard, her legs quivering. Kitty Kat held the wet tool out to Archie.

'Gimme the gun now,' she said, and they exchanged weapons.

Kitty Kat inserted the barrel of the Python into her cunt and massaged herself.

'Got to be gentle with this,' said Kitty Kat. 'Torn myself before.'

Lula remained motionless. Archie Chunk held the slimy stick in his left fist and grinned.

'Wish I could pull the trigger,' Kitty Kat whined. 'Wish Kitty Kat push it up pussy, pull trigger. Pull pussy trigger. Open pussy, up pussy, pull trigger.'

Kitty Kat Cross swayed, shuddered, her mouth open, made a gagging sound and held the stainless blue steel cylinder tight to the left side of her cunt. She trembled and whinnied, then her contractions slowly tapered off until they ceased entirely. Kitty Kat withdrew the Python's nose and stood up straight. She held the gun to her mouth and ran her tongue along the barrel, first one side, then the other, licking it clean.

'Close as Kitty Kat get,' she said.

Long Distance Call

'You and Mama amaze me, Daddy.'

'How's that, son?'

'Way you been able to stay together all these years. Me and Rhoda didn't make it, and same goes for most couples I know or know of. Seems to me you-all're still in love, too. How you manage it, Daddy?'

It was one o'clock in the morning. Phil was asleep on the couch in the front room, a copy of *Obras completas de Federico García Lorca* folded open on his chest, his right thumb over the words, '*En mi pecho se agita sonámbula/una sierpe de besos antiguos.*' Pace and Sailor were still in the Florida room, unable and unwilling to sleep, sipping whiskey and talking.

'Your mama's a special kind of woman, Pace. She don't hardly ever consider herself first. She's most always been concerned about how other folks around her are feelin' and what they need, not what she wants. That ain't to say she don't know how to please herself or even to get what she wants or needs. She'll take time for her own purposes, but Lula's always been the single most unselfish person I ever have known.'

'Grandmama Marietta wasn't that way, though.'

Sailor laughed. 'Not nearly, though she had her good points, I suppose. She was always lookin' out for Lula.'

'How come you and Mama never had no kids after me?'

'Well, when you was born, of course, I was in the joint, and after I got out and Lula and I eventually come back together, there was a whole long time Mama and me just required to get to know each other again. We was in our thirties by then, and I guess my own priority was makin' up for all the time I'd lost with you, too. Tell the truth, we just didn't even give it a thought, plus Lula didn't get pregnant. By the time we mighta had another child we was older'n we woulda liked to be if we were gonna have

270

to look after an infant. It was enough just bein' alive and the three of us bein' together. That's about all I could dream about them years at Huntsville. Sometimes I didn't think it was ever gonna happen.'

'I guess me and Rhoda just didn't love each other enough to make our marriage work,' said Pace. 'Neither of us is as givin' a person as Mama, that's for sure.'

'Tough to figure, son. Lovin' and bein' in love is two different things, of course. Best if you can keep both in the house, but it's love that keeps it goin'. People fall in and out of love regular, oftentimes with the same person. Your mama put up with a bunch from me, but I ain't never really lost sight of what it is attracted me to Lula in the first place. I don't mean looks, neither. That means more to some than to others.'

'If Rhoda hadn't kept so close to her family, I believe we mighta had a better chance. The Gombowiczes is fine people, Daddy, don't get me wrong, and they was swell to take me into the diamond business with 'em, but between Rhoda's therapy work and havin' to be with her folks so much, it didn't leave hardly no time just for us. Then her bein' spooked about bringin' kids into the world, always talkin' about how there's so many maniacs runnin' around loose and how some sand niggers is gonna get their hands on a nuclear device and blow up the planet anyway, shit. That tore it after too long for me.'

Pace poured himself a fresh shot of Jameson's and knocked it back.

'I was sure sorry when it didn't work out, boy, but with you and Rhoda bein' of such diverse heritage and all, can't say as I was entirely surprised. Your mama was surprised it lasted as long as it did, then she was upset about the divorce. You ain't the only victims of the seven year itch.'

'Eight, Daddy. We lasted eight years. I still think we'd of had kids it woulda worked out different.'

The telephone rang. Sailor and Pace looked at each other and let it ring a second time. Before it rang again, Sailor lifted the receiver.

'Sailor Ripley speakin'.'

'Hello, Sailor? This is Rhoda. I'm sorry to be calling so late.'

'Rhoda, darlin', how're you? Pace and I just been talkin' about you.'

271

'Is Pace there?'

'Big as life.'

'I didn't know where he was, Sailor. We haven't been in touch lately. I was calling you to find out. For some reason all of you have been on my mind the last two days and finally I just decided to call, even if it is past two A.M. here in New York. Is everything all right?'

'As a matter of fact, Rhoda, things ain't all right. Lula been kidnapped durin' a armed robbery. We don't know where she is, so me'n Pace been waitin' by the phone. I thought maybe you was her or the ones got her.'

'Oh, Sailor, that's terrible! I'm so sorry.'

'Pace is right here. You want to speak with him?'

'If it's all right for a minute. I won't tie up your line.'

'It's OK, Rhoda, we got call-waitin' now.'

Sailor handed the phone to Pace.

'Hello, Rhoda. How you been doin'?'

'Something made me call, Pace. The feeling was too strong to ignore. I didn't know where you were.'

'I'm livin' in LA now. Was in NO on business when all this happened. Your mental powers ain't diminished none.'

'I feel terrible about what's happened to Lula, Pace. I wish there were something I could do to help.'

'Don't even know what our move's gonna be yet, Rhoda, but thanks.'

'Pace?'

'Uh huh.'

'Do you ever think that perhaps our separating was the wrong thing to have done?'

'We ain't just separated, Rhoda, we're divorced. And this ain't precisely the greatest time to be bringin' up this subject, seein' as how my mind's mainly on Mama right now.'

'Of course, Pace, certainly. I understand absolutely. I would very much like to talk to you about things, though, when this is all over and Lula's safe. Would you at least consider that?'

''Course I will, Rhoda. You OK otherwise?'

'Yes.'

'How's the family?'

'There's nothing you need to hear about. Please call me as soon as there's news, all right?'

'OK, Rhoda.'

'Good night, Pace. Give my love to Sailor.'

'I will. Good night.'

Pace hung up and looked at his father.

'Rhoda says to give you her love.'

Sailor nodded and scraped his right hand across his mostly bald head.

'Gotta admit, son, the girl has a gift, feelin' somethin' was up.'

'Likely just coincidence, Daddy.'

'Could be, boy, but keep in mind it don't never pay to underestimate a woman, 'specially one knows your sleepin' habits.'

Origin of the Species

'Been brought to my attention by Eddie Fange, the commissioner, that felonious crime, kidnappin' in particular, ain't altogether unfamiliar to you, Mr Ripley.'

Sailor had telephoned Du Du Dupre to find out exactly what steps the police were taking to find Lula. It was ten-thirty in the morning.

'What's it got to do with locatin' my wife, Captain Dupre? Past is past.'

'You got two convictions of a significant nature, manslaughter in North Carolina, for which you done a deuce, and armed robbery in Texas, includin' a parole violation and a kidnappin' charge was dropped when you went down for a sawbuck on the AR beef. Then a woman you was involved with, a certain Señorita Perdita Durango, drove the getaway vehicle for you and your gun-totin' cohort at the time, Mr Robert Peru, deceased, durin' this robbery attempt, from which she avoided prosecution, still got a federal warrant out on her for kidnap and torture of two college kids some thirty years back. Mexican authorities wanted her for murder, too.'

'I don't know nothin' about any of that.'

'Finally, your son, Pace Roscoe Ripley, was his self kidnapped thirty years ago. Five years later he was implicated in a armed robbery and murder right here in New Orleans, and another killin' or two in Miss'ippi, both charges he was cleared of 'count of his bein' held captive and forced to participate. Now your wife been taken prisoner durin' a violent crime. I didn't know better, Mr Ripley, I'd be mighty tempted to conclude kind of a pattern been developin' here.'

'Ever'body's a prisoner of some kind, Dupre. People who learn some correct detail about another person's life are always drawin' conclusions from it ain't accurate, then they start seein' in this one

274

fact an explanation of things ain't got no connection with it at all. A famous dead French author wrote that.'

'Can't argue the fact you had plenty time to read, Ripley, all them years you spent behind bars. I ain't been nobody's guest, so I've had to make do with less high-toned material, like newspapers and police bulletins, which I can't hardly get to as it is, bein' that I'm kept pretty busy tryin' to protect citizens from one another.'

'I take it you ain't got no line on Lula.'

'We're workin' on it, Ripley. I got your number. They contact you, call me right away, let us handle it. Don't do nothin' stupid. I'm hopin' you got quit of that cowboy shit now you're a senior citizen.'

Dupre hung up before Sailor did. For some reason, Sailor suddenly remembered the first time he had ever called Lula 'Peanut,' his favorite nickname for her. He had driven over to Bay St Clement High School in his yellow 1958 Buick Limited, the one his cousin, Jesse Stitch, later totalled in Rocky Mount while Sailor was serving his sentence at Pee Dee, to pick up Lula when classes let out. As soon as she'd spotted his car, Lula ran to it, opened the passenger door and slid into the front seat practically on top of Sailor, where she curled up with her head burrowed hard into his chest.

'Oh, Sail,' she had said, closing her eyes and pushing her nose into the black cotton Fruit of the Loom tee shirt that covered his upper body, 'I'm so happy you came to get me! You just thrill me to death.'

Sailor had laughed, wound Lula's long black ponytail around his right hand and tugged gently on it. Lula was sixteen years old and Sailor sincerely believed that she was the most beautiful creature he had ever seen, a belief he had never come to doubt. Folded up on his lap the way she was had made her seem so small, so fragile.

'Hell, Lula,' Sailor had said to her then, 'you look like a perfect little peanut.'

'I ain't so very little,' Lula had said, 'but I am your peanut, for now and forever.'

That had been forty-four years ago, Sailor calculated. The telephone rang, startling him. His right hand was still on the receiver and he picked it up.

'Sail, is that you? It's Lula!'

'Hello, peanut,' he said.

Kitty Kat Calls

"Nough, woman!'

Kitty Kat snatched the telephone from Lula.

'This her old man?' she shouted into it.

'That's my wife you got,' said Sailor, 'if that's what you mean. You fixin' to turn her loose?'

'Check this out one time, daddio, 'cause I'm gone make it shit simple. Prob'ly she cost you plenty so far an' now she gone cost you some mo'. Ain't sayin' you gots to pay, though. You say no, OK, we put the barrel up her nose, pop go the weasel, then dump in a bayou. You listen?'

'How much?'

'Hun' thou, sma' bill. Put it in a duffel, kind you get in a army surplus. Forty-eight hours from now, this same time, one-thirty, you leave the bag front the gate Judge Perez Park in Arabi. That in St Bernard Parish, past Tupelo Street. You think you be able find it?'

'It'll be there. What about Lula?'

'Oh, she be turn up theyafter. You leave the money, go 'way. Cops come, y'own posse, anyone, your wife, instead she turn up the *here*after.'

The line went dead.

'What's the price, Daddy?' asked Pace.

Sailor hung up the phone.

'A hundred thousand.'

'You got that much?'

'Between what we got in the house and what I can borrow from Bob Lee, prob'ly I can raise it.'

'You gonna call Dupre?'

'Ain't sure, son. Figure I'll sleep on it and decide in the mornin'.'

'Wish our ol' huntin' companion Coot Veal was still alive,'

Pace said. 'He'd help us out. Coot's the one taught me to shoot.'

Sailor nodded. 'I sure do miss that old boy. Couple others, too, who're no longer around, who I could count on. Sparky and Buddy, friends of your mama's and mine from way back. They was damn resourceful.'

'Them the ones located the kidney donor for Uncle Johnnie, weren't they?'

'Uh huh. Just after Lula and I run onto 'em in Memphis. Them two guardian angels kept turnin' up in our lives in some mighty strange circumstances. They both prob'ly passed on by now, though.'

'Phil's a stand-up guy, Daddy. Three of us can handle it.'

Sailor lowered his head to the table and buried it in his folded arms. Sailor fell asleep and Pace sat there, listening to his father breathe. After a few minutes, Pace leaned over and kissed Sailor on the top of his head.

'I love you, Daddy,' Pace said. 'Even without Mama you ain't alone in this world.'

Kitty Kat Talks

'I tell you how people like me an' Archie Chunk come up, maybe you get the picture. My mama worked as a aide in a nursin' home, cleanin' after old folks' dirt. Had me an' my two brothers to care for herself after our daddy disappeared. Mama out cleanin' up piss, shit, vomit, wipin' drool off they half-dead faces, proppin' 'em in they wheelchairs for next to no money an' no benefits. She was too proud to take the welfare, she wanted to work. Wouldn't let the state take her kids for no foster homes. She was for keepin' the fam'ly together, even when Daddy gone.

'Mama made us go to school long as we'd mind. We lived in a closed-down motel without no runnin' water or heat. Had us a wood stove but no ice box. Mama got up four ev'ry mornin' fix our clothes, breakfast. She an' me sleep together in one bed, Yusef an' Malcolm in another. We walk with Mama five miles each mornin' in rain an' dark to school. I get sick an' tired walkin' in rain an' dark.

'When Yusef break his arm, fall through a hole in the floor, Mama had to pay cash to fix it, but after his cast come off he never had no pin put in keep the shape, like he suppose to, 'cause Mama ain't had enough money. His arm bent wrong and dangle weird.

'I was twelve a drug dealer hung out around the motel got me pregnant. After I had the baby, I leave it with Mama and go. Malcolm, he drown. Mama, Yusef and my baby, girl name Serpentina, burn to death when the motel catch fire one night.

'Ain't was no diff'rent for Archie. Black or white don't make no diff'rence you down so far. He be on the street since he six, chil' alcoholic. Stealin' all he know, or lettin' some ol' sick fool pinch his peepee fo' a meal at Mickey D.

'I know you scared, lady. Maybe this work out. It don't, least you know there tougher roads than one you been on.'

The Business

'This is 3099. Any messages?'

Phil was checking in with his answering service in Hollywood.

'Yes, sir. There's one from a Miss Reynolds. She'd like you to call her at your earliest opportunity.'

'That's all?'

'Yes, sir.'

'Thanks.'

Phil direct-dialed Flower's number. She answered on the third ring.

'Philly, where are you?'

'In New Orleans, Flower. What's up? How was Mexico with Westphal?'

'That's what I called you about, Philly. I happened to mention to Clark that you were back in town and he got all excited and started talkin' 'bout how you always been a hero of his and how he'd love to work with you. I just couldn't believe it!'

'I find it a little difficult to believe myself. So?'

'So, he wants to set up a meeting. When y'all comin' back?'

'I'm not sure. We've kind of run into a situation here. Maybe I can talk with Westphal on the phone.'

'It'd be a good idea, Philly. I ain't certain Clark got much of an attention span.'

'Why do you say that?'

'Just one of my correlations. Attention spans is linked up with sexual habits, I think. Clark comes too quick, so my guess is he got the attention span to match.'

'Exactly what did he say, Flower?'

'Just if you had a good idea, he'd listen. You got somethin' beside that "Mute" story?'

'Actually, I do. A love story, like Romeo and Juliet, sort of, only the characters are older.'

'Could Clark and I do it together?'

'You two might just be perfect.'

'Oh, Philly! Do I get to laugh? You know how much I love to laugh.'

Phil laughed. 'Of course. What would a Flower Reynolds picture be unless you laughed in it?'

'I didn't get to in "Dog Parts."'

'That was a mistake not to be repeated. Give me Clark's number, Flower. I'll call him.'

Phil wrote it down and said, 'This is nice news, honey. It's a good thing you had such good-looking parents.'

'You don't think it's my brain Clark's attracted to, huh?' Flower laughed. 'Oh, well, I guess it's just the way the good Lord intended the world should work.'

'Wouldn't surprise me. Listen, Flower, if you speak to Clark, tell him I'll call him as soon as I have a chance. There's something going on here that needs to be taken care of first. Tell him I'm a big admirer of his.'

'Why lie?' asked Flower.

'Why not?' Phil said.

Long Gone

DuMont Dupre was fifty-two years old, five-nine and a nose tackle-thick two-thirty. The lower region of his jaw rolled over on itself twice whenever Du Du looked down. His wife, Lexa Ray, once commented to Commissioner Fange's wife, Floridanna, that nobody had seen the knot in her husband's tie for fifteen years. Du Du had preferred a four-in-hand during their courtship and early years of marriage, Lexa Ray said, but for all she or anyone else knew he could have switched to a half-Windsor by now. Du Du was at his desk in mid-morning, lighting up his second Macanudo of the day, when his secretary buzzed him on the intercom. Du Du made sure the entire circumference of his cigar tip was fired and drawing properly prior to responding.

'Yes, Miss Pulse,' he said, having depressed the TALK button on his unit.

'Mr Luneau, the principal at Saint Beverly Carothers High School, is holdin' for you.'

'I'll take it.'

Du Du punched up line one and said, '*Bonjour*, George, *ça va?*'

'Not very well, I'm afraid, DuMont,' said the principal.

'What's the problem?'

'It's your son, Larry Gene.'

'L.G.? What's the boy done now?'

'He brought a gun with him to school today, DuMont, pulled it out of his pocket durin' English class and shot himself in the mouth. Back of his head splattered all over Marcy Simmons, girl sittin' directly behind him, but the bullet went past her clean into the blackboard at the rear of the room.'

Du Du put the Macanudo into an ashtray and rubbed his free hand over his face a couple of times.

'He's dead, then.'

''Fraid so, DuMont. Don't understand it, myself. Larry Gene

281

been doin' excellent work this semester, I'm told. Had his grades up to about a C average and he just been named All-Conference tackle.'

'L.G. never did care for English. What type firearm he use?'

'Believe Sergeant Hoog mentioned it was a .357-caliber Magnum revolver. The students that seen him do it are pretty shook up, as you could imagine. I'm real stranged out myself. You don't believe how sorry I am to have had to tell you the news, Du Du, but I figured I ought to do it, me bein' the principal.'

'Lexa Ray know?'

'Don't believe so. I ain't called her. It's just damn unbelievable. Why on earth he'd do this thing, Du Du? We ain't had no evidence of drug use. You?'

'I suppose I ain't paid close enough attention to L.G. lately to know, George. I 'preciate it was you called.'

'Larry Gene was a right decent boy, DuMont. Boy with a future.'

'I'm goin' home now, be with Lexa Ray. Where's the body?'

'Police ambulance takin' him to the Orleans Parish morgue.'

Du Du hung up and stared at the framed photograph on his desk. In the picture, he and Lexa Ray were seated with Larry Gene and his sister, Taura Beth, standing behind them, each with a hand on one of their parents' shoulders. Du Du inspected the photograph more closely, noticing for the first time that Larry Gene's left ear stuck out almost perpendicular to his head, while the right one was more normally attached. Du Du wondered why this physical peculiarity of L.G.'s had never been apparent to him before.

The police captain slumped back and down in his chair. He unbuttoned his collar and loosened the four-in-hand knot in his tie.

The Unexpected

Pace heard the front door open and close and he jumped up from the kitchen table, where he'd been sitting with Phil drinking coffee, and hurried toward Sailor.

'Daddy, you OK?' Pace said, seeing his father set down a large canvas bag in the foyer.

'I'm all right, son. Just out collectin' the cash.'

'You got it, huh?'

Sailor nodded. 'Didn't even have to re-do the deal on the house. Bob Lee took the whole hundred K right out the Gator Gone main account.'

'I guess to hell he's your friend, Daddy.'

'Never have one better. You know how close your mama and Beany been all their lives. She and Bob Lee took us in when you was kidnapped, and it was him give me the opportunity to turn my own life around. Now here they come backin' us up again. They're rare folks, son.'

'Made some coffee, Daddy. You want some? Phil's in the kitchen.'

Sailor followed Pace back through the house and sat down at the table. Pace filled a cup and placed it in front of him.

'Mornin', Phil. Thanks, son.'

'Daddy got the money, Phil.'

'I have about ten thousand I can spare, Sailor, if you need it.'

'Thanks, Phil, but we're set.'

'What about Dupre, Daddy?'

'Called his office from Bob Lee's, but he was out. Apparently there was some family emergency. I'd decided to not bring the cops into it, anyway. Was just gonna check in again with Dupre, pretend I hadn't heard nothin', and ask if he had. Just as well he weren't in.'

'Sailor, I want to tell you how much I admire you,' said Phil.

'Also that I'm with you all the way on this. Just tell me what you'd like me to do.'

'That's great, Phil,' said Sailor. 'I'm workin' up a plan but I ain't got all the pieces in place yet. Think I'll take a nap and dope it out with you-all later. Bob Lee's comin' over this evenin'.'

Sailor stood up and walked out of the kitchen.

'Your daddy's a brave man, Pace,' said Phil. 'He's a cool one.'

Pace stared at Sailor's coffee cup, which his father had not touched.

'He been through a bunch, Phil, as you know. Time just don't seem to settle things down, though, the way you'd figure would happen.'

The doorbell rang and Pace got up to answer it. He opened the front door and there was Rhoda, his ex-wife, holding a garment bag over her left arm. A suitcase was on the ground next to her.

'Hello, Pace,' she said. 'I just had to come.'

Pace was stunned. He looked at Rhoda, ran his eyes over her dark brown curly hair, down the length of her slender five feet-seven inches and then stared directly into her big black eyes, which were shiny and wet.

'Hell, Rhoda, this prob'ly weren't your best idea.'

She lifted up her suitcase with her right hand.

'Pace, I'm a psychotherapist. If I didn't act on impulse every once in a while I'd be even more neurotic than I already am. The last unexpected move I made was when I married you. Are you going to invite me in?'

Pace took the suitcase from Rhoda's hand and stepped aside.

A Winter's Night in the Sub-Tropics

Lula thought about Sailor. She pictured him lying in their bed, smoking a Camel and staring at the ceiling. When she imagined him this way, Lula realized, Sailor always looked like he had forty years or so before, in the beginning of their time together. Sailor's hair and muscles had dropped away since then, as surely as Lula's looks had begun to fade, her own shiny black hair to turn gray and dull, her large breasts to shrink and sag. All of this was inevitable, Lula knew. No matter how dedicatedly she exercised and avoided bad foods, there was no way she could prevent her body from spreading, her skin from crinkling up like used Reynolds Wrap. Lula recalled the first time she noticed that the curve of her behind had flattened out. She had been trying on a knit skirt at Jaloux, a fancy dress shop in Covington owned by a former callgirl who had married a United States senator, and when Lula looked at her profile in the mirror she almost screamed. She felt like the former president did in that old movie when he woke up in a hospital bed after being run over by a train, discovered that his legs were sawed off at the knees and yelled, 'Where's the rest of me?!'

Lula felt the same way when she was separated from Sailor for very long. It was almost as if they had become one person named Sailula. She was afraid now, sitting by herself in a darkened room in a strange house somewhere in the swamp, wondering if the two demented creatures that were keeping her from being with Sailor really intended to release her once they had the ransom money. Most of the time, Lula knew, kidnappers killed their hostages whether or not a ransom was paid. Archie Chunk and Kitty Kat Cross had already committed at least one murder, Kitty Kat having gunned down a clerk at the Rinaldi Hotel during the robbery, so one more homicide certainly would not matter. If they were apprehended, the law would demand the death penalty. There was no good reason that they should keep their part of the bargain. The only chance Lula had to stay alive, she figured, would be to talk her way out of it, to somehow convince Archie and Kitty Kat to return her to Sailor.

Rain pelted the roof, leaking through the cracks in the ceiling. Lula refused to cry, keeping her face tight even though she knew the exercise would deepen the creases already established around her eyes.

'Oh, Sail,' Lula whispered to herself, 'this ain't where I want to be. Shit,' she said. 'Shit, shit, shit.'

Suddenly Lula felt a chill and her entire body shivered. She remembered herself forty years ago, lying pregnant and helpless in a crummy room in the Iguana Hotel in Big Tuna, Texas, just before Sailor Ripley, the only man of her dreams, made the single biggest mistake of his young life. A storm from the Gulf hurled itself desperately at Pointe à la Hache, rattling the walls. Lula watched through the window as a sliver of vertical lightning like in one of Archie Chunk's photos clove in two an oak that stood next to the house, leaving behind a black, electrical sizzle. In another room, Kitty Kat screamed and Lula laughed reflexively, then quickly covered her mouth with her hands. Lula was surprised at herself, unsure of what it meant, of what anything meant. The rain came down harder, blurring everything outside the window.

Sailor's Plan

Sailor, Pace, Rhoda, Phil and Bob Lee Boyle were seated around the diningroom table in the Ripley house.

'What about the car, Daddy?'

'They can keep it. Your mama's all I care about.'

'So how you figure on playin' this game, Sailor?' asked Bob Lee. 'Air strike? Ground assault? Seriously, you want to try somethin' or just leave the money and hope they turn Lula loose?'

'Thought about it real hard, Bob Lee, and I see it this way: Rhoda and I leave the duffel at the Judge Perez gate a half-hour early at one A.M., and drive away. I'll leave Rhoda in the car on Tupelo Street and walk back, keepin' out of sight, to a spot where I can conceal myself while keepin' an eye on the gate. Pace and Phil will already be there in place, one on each side of the road. Bob Lee, you'd be doin' us a real favor stickin' by the phone right here.'

'Whatever you say, Sailor.'

'If they make the pick-up, Pace and Phil will take after 'em in their car. Rhoda, you'll keep an eye out for my black Cad, which the kidnappers'll prob'ly be drivin'. If it comes by you headed for the park, creep after it with your lights off and pick me up right after they make the grab. If they come past you from the other direction, after they've made the pick-up, you wait until Phil's car comes by, then follow him. That happens, I'll go with Pace and Phil. If nobody comes to make the pick-up by two A.M., Rhoda, you come get me. If I'm gone, you go home. They might come from the other direction, make the pick-up and turn back the way they come. In that case, it'll just be Phil's car goin' after 'em.'

'You aren't going to call in the police, then,' said Phil.

'Think we're better off without 'em, Phil.'

'We gonna be packin', Daddy?'

287

'You bet, son. I got enough weapons to go around.'

Pace looked at his ex-wife.

'Rhoda,' he said, 'you don't need to be in on this.'

'That's right, sweetheart,' said Sailor, 'you don't. I can ride with Pace and Phil and you can stay here with Bob Lee, you'd rather.'

'Uh uh,' said Rhoda. 'I'll be glad to participate in any way you feel is best.'

'Bob Lee,' Sailor said, 'reason I need you here is you'll know what to do if one of us calls.'

'You got it.'

'Any other questions?' asked Sailor, looking directly at each person in turn around the table. Nobody spoke, so Sailor said, 'OK, then. We'll meet here tomorrow midnight.'

'Sailor?' said Phil.

'Uh huh?'

'What do you think of Clark Westphal?'

'You mean the actor? One who done them Filthy Al cop pictures, like "Ripoff" and "Ripoff II"?'

'Right. What would you think of his portraying you in a movie?'

Sailor laughed. 'Could do worse, I suppose. Know Lula'd like it.'

'I recently saw one of his early films on TV the other night,' said Rhoda, '"The Devil's Always Busy." He certainly was handsome.'

'So was Daddy,' Pace said. 'Mama always told me weren't no man handsomer in her eyes.'

'Gray with violet lakes in 'em,' said Sailor. 'Nobody in the world got eyes to match Lula's.'

Rhoda looked at Pace and smiled.

'We'll get her home, Daddy,' he said.

Snake Story

'My old man was sixty-one when I was born,' Archie Chunk told Lula, while he bound her hands and feet. 'Apparently he was pretty proud of the fact, too. We was livin' outside Bartlesville when he died. I was four. His name was Doc. Don't know why. Never heard anyone call him by another, and my ma was dead before I got old enough to ask her. Doc Chunk was a carny man most of his life, but by the time I was born he and my ma were operatin' a travelin' zoo. Had them a couple apes, a camel, black bear and a mess of snakes.

'One mornin' Doc looked in on this giant python that was his feature attraction and saw that he was sheddin' his hide. Way I heard it, my old man went in the cage to clean out the discarded skin and the snake got a whiff of paint thinner was on the old man's hands. Drove that reptile crazy and he locked his self hard around Doc's body. By the time Ma got out there, the python had clumb halfway up a utility pole and Doc Chunk was squoze to death.'

'That's a awful way to die, I'd guess,' said Lula.

'Yeah, my folks didn't have much luck in the death department,' Archie said, as he ran a line from Lula's ankles to her wrists. 'My ma was killed two and a half years later in a bar in Festus. Man she was drinkin' with was in a fight and she got inbetween him and the other guy, who stabbed her in the chest. She bled to death right there on the barroom floor before the ambulance arrived.'

'What was her name?'

'Havana Moon. Ain't it pretty? My grandma told me she named her after a song she liked, and named her other daughter, Juella, also after a song. Their unmarried name been Fike. Juella was eleven months younger than Ma, and she died a year to the day but one after her. Juella and her Osage husband, Charlie Chases Weasels, hanged their selfs after buryin' their infant son what perished in his sleep.'

'What are you gonna do with me?'

'Kitty Kat got a place in mind we put you, then go get the cash, I guess. With it and what we scored at the hotel, we might could have us a deluxe trailer home, set it down on a mountain out west somewhere, and never have to work a hard day the rest of our lives.'

'Don't sound half bad, Mr Chunk.'

'Archie, to you. Hush now while I tape your mouth. Be more comfort in the closed position.'

Tornado Weather

'Pace, I know what a difficult time this is for you,' Rhoda said, 'and I hope I'm not complicating things by coming here. I just couldn't help myself, though. The divorce was a terrible mistake, I know that now, and I need to talk to you about it.'

Pace and Rhoda were in Pace's boyhood room upstairs at the rear of the Ripley house. Pace was sitting on the edge of the bed and Rhoda was seated in an armchair next to the window overlooking the backyard. Rhoda pulled out a pack of Bel-Air Menthols and a gold lighter from her purse. She extracted a long, white cigarette and lit it. Pace recognized the lighter, with the initials RGR emblazoned on it in mother-of-pearl, that he'd given Rhoda as a gift for her birthday six years before.

'Thought you'd quit,' Pace said.

Rhoda took a quick puff and blew out a short cloud of smoke, shook her brown mop and said, 'Started up again the day our final decree arrived. I've been very unhappy.'

Pace looked out the window, hoping to see some birds. For some reason, the sight of birds in flight never failed to calm him.

'Don't tell me you was happy when I was around,' he said. 'Least not the last six or eight months.'

'I suppose I just didn't realize how difficult it was for you, working for Gombowicz and Sons, how dissatisfied you were. I still don't know why you didn't just quit earlier.'

'What was I gonna do in New York, Rhoda? You had your practice, you weren't about to abandon that. At first I didn't mind the diamond business. I mean, it was somethin' completely diff'rent from anythin' I'd ever known. And your fam'ly was great about takin' me in, 'specially your brother, Ethan. It weren't for him I might not of made it at all. Ethan's the one saved my bones on the Irish switch. It was a big change from livin' in Katmandu, sure, and workin' on Forty-seventh Street weren't like leadin' treks

291

in the Himalayas, but it was a new kinda challenge and I loved you and all, so I was willin' to take a shot. Lasted eight years, Rhoda, which ain't 'xactly punkin' out.'

'I'd leave New York now if you wanted me to.'

Pace shook his head and half-smiled. 'Rhoda, you'd really go crazy if you had to be anyplace else longer'n a month, three weeks. It's your place, your fam'ly's there, and like I said, so's your work. You do good up east, I don't.'

'I'd give LA a try. I could build up a practice there.'

'You might could, seein's how there's more sick puppies per square inch in Beverly Hills alone than there are in all five boroughs of New York City. But I don't know how long I'm even gonna stay there, Rhoda. I'm thinkin' 'bout movin' back down south somewhere. Here or Charlotte, maybe.'

'What about your work with Phil? Learning the film business and all?'

'We'll see how it goes. I like Phil OK, and he's serious now about makin' a movie based on Mama and Daddy's early life, but tell the truth, LA really ain't my kinda town. Besides, Rhoda, geography ain't our only problem.'

Rhoda looked around for an ashtray, found a glass one on the bedside table and stubbed out her Bel-Air over the words Stolen from the Hotel Ritz, Paris.

'We could adopt a child, Pace. I think I could handle that now.'

'This ain't really what I need to be talkin' about right now,' said Pace.

'Are you seeing anyone?' Rhoda asked.

'You mean a girlfriend?'

Rhoda nodded. She kept turning the lighter with the fingers of her right hand until she dropped it on the floor, then picked it up and replaced it in her purse.

'Nobody special. Plenty of good looks in LA, OK, but there ain't many women willin' to give very much. Never come across such a half-demented herd of vain, selfish folks, female or male.'

'Worse than I am, huh?'

'You ain't neither too vain nor the least selfish, Rhoda, not really. You just been brought up a certain way don't entirely mix with the way I am. It ain't your fault.'

292

'You wouldn't have left, Pace, had I been willing to have children. That's the truth, isn't it?'

'Prob'ly woulda been harder for me to go, we had. I'll admit that.'

Rhoda stood up. 'I'm sorry I came, Pace, I really am. I'm just adding to your problems.'

'Don't be sorry, Rhoda. Daddy's glad you're here, and so am I. We're glad to have your help. And Mama'll be happy to see you, too.'

Pace stood, put his arms around Rhoda and hugged her to him.

'We can talk some more soon's this mess is finished,' he said.

'The air outside felt strange today, Pace, as if nothing were happening. Do you know what I mean?'

'It's tornado weather, sweetheart. Been a while since you've been down here. You just forgot how it feels.'

'That's not the only thing I've forgotten how it feels,' Rhoda said, and hugged back.

Moviegoers

'Hey, Sailor, look at this,' said Phil, handing over the front section of the day's *Times-Picayune*, folded to page sixteen. 'There's an article about a kidnapping in Mobile.'

Sailor, Phil and Bob Lee had been picking at muffaletas and drinking coffee as they sat at the table in the Florida room.

'"Kidnapping Victim Back Home in Alabama,"' Sailor read aloud. '"A Mobile businessman was abducted from in front of his house Tuesday morning when he bent to pick up his morning newspaper. He was returned home safely by taxicab this afternoon after he had been dropped off at a shopping center, said a spokesperson for the Federal Bureau of Investigation. The authorities said they did not know the motive for his abduction or the reason why his kidnappers released him.

'"The 71-year-old victim, who was taken away by two men, was Alfred Thibodeaux, a soybean and cotton broker who is also a well-known thoroughbred horse breeder. Mr Thibodeaux assisted in the development of a port shipping terminal and is active in several charities.

'"Mr Thibodeaux suffered several cuts on the forehead and cheeks during the ordeal. He apparently engaged in active resistance to his abductors by attempting to beat them with a silver-plated cane he relies on to aid in walking due to his artificial left leg. A neighbor woman, Mrs Fabrica de Puro, who witnessed the kidnapping, was threatened by one abductor brandishing a handgun, the police reported.

'"At one P.M. today, however, Mr Thibodeaux contacted his wife, Antoinetta, from a pay phone next to a Big Gulp root beer stand at the Lureen Wallace Shoppers Planet. He told his wife he was coming home in a taxicab and that she should have his silver cane, which had been left behind during the initial scuffle, ready for him.

"'"He seems to be in decent shape, a little tired and stressed out,' said Doak Bullard, assistant chief of the FBI office in Mobile. Mr Bullard would not disclose whether a ransom demand had been made. He said the abductors were not in custody.'"

'Strange, huh, Sailor?' said Phil.

'Yeah,' Sailor said, 'maybe we'll get lucky with Lula, too.'

'Who you got in mind to play Lula in the movie, Phil?' asked Bob Lee.

'Flower Reynolds. She worked for me before.'

'Oh yeah, I remember her,' said Bob Lee. 'Shortina Fuse. She's a southern girl. That scene in "Sexual Re-education" where Señor Rafferty begs Shortina to use the tire tool on his anus is pretty damn unforgettable.'

'Didn't know you was such a moviegoer, Bob Lee,' said Sailor.

Bob Lee laughed. 'You be careful of this fella,' he said, pointing at Phil. 'He got a awful weird imagination.'

Fodder

While Sailor, Pace and Phil crouched in hiding around the entrance to Judge Perez Park, and Rhoda waited in Lula's Crown Victoria station wagon that was parked on Tupelo Street, Archie Chunk was at the wheel of Sailor's Sedan de Ville. Kitty Kat Cross sat in the front passenger seat with the visor down and the interior light on, applying her makeup.

'Man, I in love with this car, Arch,' she said. 'Got so many nifty convenience, must was design by women.'

'I'm glad we didn't kill that old lady,' said Archie. 'She reminds me of my grandma some.'

'Could I'd gone either way with it,' Kitty Kat said, as she wielded her blue eyeliner. 'Was kinda nice to seen again where my mama worked, though.'

'It was the right thing. Never pays to murder folks remind you of loved ones. Now we got fresh plates on the Cad here, and we gonna stop up in Slaughter, get the Barnwell boys to slap on a new paint job, be all set. What color you like it, Kat?'

'This kind classy car, oughta be some type red.'

'Sounds good to me.'

'You sure you can trust these Barnwells, huh?'

'Oh yeah. Jimmy Dean and Sal Mineo Barnwell been doin' this since they got out of prison, four, five years ago.'

'What beef they go down for?'

'Animal cruelty. They was sellin' videos of Rottweilers in leather armor rippin' apart a captured pig. Fish and Wildlife agents busted 'em at a warehouse out in East Feliciana Parish, confiscated four beauty Rotts.'

'Shit!' cried Kitty Kat, bending over and looking around the floor. 'Dropped my applicator.'

Kitty Kat crawled down and wedged her slender body between the seat and the dashboard.

'Hey, Kat, be careful.'

'There it is,' she said, reaching for the swab.

The car hit a pothole and Kitty Kat fell forward. She attempted to brace herself with her right hand and accidentally depressed Archie's right foot, which was on the accelerator pedal. The black Cadillac swerved out of control directly into the path of an oncoming Mack semi loaded with several hundred ten pound bags of Dr Fagin's Organic Fish Fodder.

Broken Blossoms

Two old men walked slowly together along the path connecting the main building to the greenhouse. Sparky Plombier and Buddy Rêveur, both of whom were octogenarians, had been friends for seventy years. Now they were residents of Naomi 'Hard Cash' Kamil's Just A Closer Walk With Thee Nursing Home in Belle Chasse, Louisiana, a few miles downriver from New Orleans.

The men had been partners in numerous business ventures, including ownership of a bar in Dallas, Texas, an exotic religious items mail order company in Waggaman, Louisiana, and, most recently, the S&B Organ Retrieval Service, based in Memphis, Tennessee. This last enterprise had proven their most lucrative, and they lived in pleasant circumstances at Closer Walk, as the residents called it, having invested a goodly share of their retirement funds with their old friend Naomi. Known as 'Hard Cash' Kamil both for the fact of her having been born in the Delta town of Hard Cash, Mississippi, and for her renown as an astute businessperson, Naomi made certain that Sparky and Buddy had everything they required to make them comfortable during their declining years. Their passion of late was for raising flowers, so Naomi had provided the greenhouse, which Sparky, an avid reader of mystery stories, had christened the Nero Wolfe Memorial Arboretum, in honor of Rex Stout's rotund detective whose own favorite hours were spent tending his Manhattan roof garden.

Buddy hummed the tune to 'Stardust' as he shuffled forward, finding himself unable to sustain a whistle of sufficient strength and timbre. He wore a black, hooded Los Angeles Raiders sweatshirt with the hood up, protecting his bald head against the morning chill. Sparky, who at eighty-three maintained a full head of brown hair remarkably absent of gray, went hatless but leaned heavily on a black walnut cane as he proceeded, carefully keeping

298

weight off of his swollen left leg, which limb had been bothersome to him in cold, damp weather ever since his best fighting dog, Meyer Lansky, a red-hued 110-pound pit bull Sparky had raised from a pup more than a quarter-century ago, had accidentally locked down on his left knee with almost one ton per square inch of pressure after Sparky's breaking stick, used to pry open a pit's engaged jaws, had cracked in two and turned the beast's head in the wrong direction during a training session. It broke Sparky's heart to have had to shoot Meyer Lansky through the right eye socket to get him off; he would have almost rather shot himself, but, as Buddy always said, almost is the twin brother of not quite, and even in his pain and near panic of the moment, Sparky knew how to cut his losses, figuring he would be able to acquire another fighting dog a whole lot easier than he could a new left leg.

'Meyer Lansky actin' up, hey, Spark?' asked Buddy.

'Some,' said Sparky. 'Be OK soon's we get snug in Nero Wolfe.'

Buddy held open the door for Sparky, who passed inside and immediately noticed that something was wrong.

'Buddy, either I'm sufferin' from some sudden kind of macabre brain damage or there's a body in the begonias.'

Buddy and Sparky moved as quickly as they could on the begonia bed and stared at the woman lying there, her hands and feet tightly bound by synthetic rope, a seven-inch strip of duct tape stretched across her mouth. The woman's big gray eyes glared at the two men, then blinked rapidly several times.

'Spark, either you ain't got no monopoly on geriatric mind disorder or this woman is Lula Ripley.'

Radiance

JETLINER CRASHES, BURNS
AFTER MID-AIR EXPLOSION

SAN ANTONIO, Jan. 18 (SNS) – A Pacific Continental Airways
K-711 commercial jetliner enroute from New Orleans to Los
Angeles crashed and burned yesterday approximately 250 miles
west of San Antonio. All 147 passengers aboard are believed to
have perished.

Witnesses in the nearby community of Big Tuna, Texas, said
that the plane appeared to have exploded in the air, raining metal
on the arid land below.

Among the passengers believed to have been aboard were US
Senator Rantoul 'Bingo' Blaine (D-La.) and Philip Reãl, the
internationally renowned film director ('Mumblemouth').

A spokesperson for PCA would neither confirm nor deny a
Southern News Service report that a note was delivered by an
unidentified man to the airline ticket counter at New Orleans
International Airport shortly after takeoff that read, 'They shall
drop from the sky like radiant cherry blossoms.'

Letter to Dal

Dalceda Delahoussaye
809 Ashmead Drive
Bay St Clement, NC 28352

Dearest Dal,

You are the only person in the world other than maybe Beany who ever really understood me so your the one I need to write this letter to. Thank the Lord Dal your still alive even though you been smoking since before I was born. Mama loved you more than anyone Dal including me probably. I know what a terrible loss it was for you when Mama died and so I feel its OK to tell you not only what has happened here but what Im thinking now about things.

The bad news is Sailor was killed in a wreck. I had to stop just now a minute to catch my breath sometimes it happens I lose control of my breathing and I kind of panic though not so much as I used to when I was a girl. This is Monday when Im writing so last Thursday Sailor was driving home from Bridge City where Gator Gone got there new storage facility and as he was headed on the Huey P. Long Bridge a dumb boy in a Apache pickup cut in front of Sailor from the shoulder and Sailor swerved his car to avoid him but couldnt straighten out in time before he hit the road divider. After smacking into it the car turned over and a transport truck carrying a dozen new Mitsubishi jeeps plowed him half way toward the Old Spanish Trail. Sail probably was already dead by then or knocked out for sure and didnt feel anything else at least its what I hope. The Cadillac with Sailor inside was crushed like it had been squeezed into a metal cube at the junk yard. There was no fire and believe it or not Sailors face was almost unmarked just his body was mashed in a 100 places.

There it is Dal I cant hardly believe it. Pace and me decided to cremate Sailor and we got his ashes here in a box we didnt want no funeral. I got to tell you Dal I feel kind of dead myself. I read once in Readers Digest I think about how often if two people been together a real long time and one of them dies the other dies soon after. Im only 62 and Mama lived into her 80s and youll most probably hit a 100 but I feel like how am I supposed to go on now? I know Mama would say look how she done after Daddy burned himself up so many years ago and didnt she have a long and useful life but you know me Dal and as much as Mama wanted me to be I am not really like her not in the way of strength. I am not exactly a serious religious person either I know that ever since I left the Church of Reason Redemption and Resistance to Gods Detractors. What do I have left Dal I mean it.

Pace is the greatest comfort of course. He and Rhoda tried there for a bit to tie the knot again but as Pace says once the string come unraveled you got to get you a new piece so its off for good. After his boss the movie director was killed in that plane crash Pace went to New York with Rhoda and then to LA to get his possessions and now he dont want to leave me alone so hes at the house. I told him hes 42 just about and I dont want him to end up like Sailors former hunting buddy Coot Veal what never left his mama and didnt make a real life. Pace is different from Coot of course since he been so many places around the world almost but itd be easy for him to stop his life on my account I can tell and I dont want that. He is a Ripley though as well as a Fortune and there aint too much good can be accomplished by arguing. I guess I should feel lucky in that regard to have such a good son and I do but you understand what Im saying.

Thats really about it I dont mean to go on you had plenty enough sorrows through your own life not to need mine. Just I felt you should know what happened to Sailor the way it did. I suppose Ill figure out what happens next for me Dal but if I dont it aint but the end of *my* world nobody elses. It aint either that Im feeling sorry for myself its different. I suppose since Sailor and me come back together thirty some years ago I never even give a thought to our being apart ever again and its the biggest kind of shock to face this knowing Sailor aint in prison this time hes dead and thats the end of that tune like hed say. I cant play no other tune Dal I wont. Remember how the Reverend Willie Thursday used to say a boy without a father is just a lost soul sailing on a

302

ghost ship through the sea of life? Well Im one now a lost soul that is without my man. Sailor Ripley was my man Dal he was the one and Im so glad we found each other the world being as big as it is it was a miracle Im certain. We was never out of love Dal all this time since I was 16 aint that something? I been a fortunate woman I know but I cant believe its over and truth is I guess I might never.

Love you,
Lula